Book One of Magick

# THE DARK WOLF

Derry Wadham

# PROLOGUE

Racing through the trees, Lucian had no idea where he was heading as long as it was away from those who hunted him. Glancing over his shoulder, he saw the first of them hit his magickal sphere of protection with a hiss of frustration.

'You cannot escape us, boy!' the man hissed, baring his fanged teeth in hate.

'Leave me alone!' Lucian cried, knowing him to be a vampire after listening in on his parents when he and his sister were believed to be asleep.

Picking up his pace, he darted from tree to tree like a frightened rabbit before seeing many of them race ahead to bar his way.

'Someone help me!' he screamed, trying desperately to remember how to perform offensive magick, but they were all around him now like a pack of hungry raptors.

'*Lightning!*' he quailed, the thought breaking through his mind-numbing terror.

Thrusting out his hands, he almost lost his life before his father's warning screamed through his mind.

'*Connect to the earth, or you'll die in the attempt!*'

Sending his awareness into the earth beneath his feet, he drew up the land's might to feed his shield before directing the flow into his hands.

A whipping whistle passed by his head, and he flinched instinctively as the sound became more insistent as a multitude of arrows flashed by.

The dark forms of vampires were cut down in droves, but there were still many more to take their place.

Trapped within the circle of converging vampires, Lucian fought to hold his attack at bay at the sight of silver armour and blurring steel that wreaked havoc upon the undead. Huge horses thundered all around him, scattering his pursuers before cutting them down with the single horns upon their heads.

Flinching back, he dropped to one knee as an arc of blue light crackled overhead. Looking about wildly, he saw his vicious attackers cast back either in flames or in ashes.

Not knowing which way to turn, he stayed rooted to the spot as more of the vampires swarmed towards him.

'*Be calm,*' a voice sounded within his mind, causing him to sob for the love in its tone, '*for you are not alone!*' it soothed, speaking in a soft feminine voice.

Energy suddenly gathered around him, and he knew intuitively that it was the power of the earth that had been summoned, but by far more practised hands than his.

Growing steadily brighter, his magickal spherical shield began to repair itself before another joined it from some unknown source.

'Help me!' he sobbed, seeing again the mass of vampires smash against it before something he could never have expected reacted in response.

Arcing golden light, like that of the blue, crackled across his shield's white surface before suddenly turning hostile.

There was no fire this time, for the vampires were there one moment and gone the next.

'*Draw upon the earth!*' the woman's voice stressed, sounding deeply concerned that he had not done so on instinct.

Doing as he was bidden, he felt his strength return almost immediately before she spoke again.

'*Now bring it into your fingers as your father has shown you, and kill these loathsome creatures!*' she roared, her voice so commanding that he could do nothing but comply.

# CHAPTER ONE

Sat staring with an expression of awe upon his face, Lucian looked down reverently at the flickering flame of the candle.

'*Yes!*' he thought excitedly, overwhelmed by his achievement.

Racing down the stairs, his sister Francesca entered before jolting to a stop, causing her blonde ringlets to bounce at her shoulders.

'You did it!' she gasped, clapping her hands together in quick succession. 'I knew you could!' she squealed, placing her hands upon her hips in a confident manner.

Having lit her first candle some time before, she had taken it upon herself to teach him the trick so that they could practice together.

As was always the case when there was something new for them to do, she would learn it before forcing him to learn it too… whether he wanted to or not.

In this case, however, after seeing her light the candle repeatedly by just staring at it, he had been only too eager to learn the trick for himself.

'How did you know I did it?' he asked after a moment, puzzled by how she had known of his success.

'I felt it!' she answered, staring at him with her wide blue eyes. 'It just popped into my head, and I knew!' she explained excitedly, clapping her hands in excitement. 'Can you do it again?' she asked, looking at him before narrowing them when he refused to answer, causing her to scowl and huff in frustration.

'You need to be able to do it at will,' she stressed, holding his chestnut brown eyes in her gaze. 'Please?' she coaxed, catching the moody expression darkening his features.

Scowling at her constant nagging, he glowered at her in annoyance before finally responding.

'Go back upstairs, then,' he grumbled, folding his arms stubbornly across his chest.

'Just do it, Lucian!' she sighed, bending low to blow out the light.

Reluctantly staring back at the candle and the wick in particular, he saw that it was still smoking and probably quite hot.

Breathing out slowly, he began to relax into the frame of mind needed for such a feat when the candle burst into life once again, shocking him with its sudden combustion.

'My bad!' Francesca apologised, smiling at him rather awkwardly. 'That was me, sorry,' she continued, looking quite embarrassed. 'I will look away this time so that I don't do it for you again,' she continued, smiling at him wickedly.

Frowning at her, he could not help but feel both incensed by her manner and envious of her skill.

'How do you do it so quickly?' he grumbled, staring sullenly at the flickering flame.

'I couldn't at first!' she confessed, spreading her arms a little. 'It takes practice in the beginning. Just try thinking it to light… picture it in your mind and then force it to happen,' she explained, blowing out the candle for the second time.

Widening her eyes in woeful response, she looked up at the ceiling in frustration when the candle immediately lit again like one of those joke candles that just won't blow out.

'Oh my god, I'm going upstairs!' she fumed, blowing out the persistent flame before marching from the room. 'Maybe you should pick a different one!' she cried as the candle ignited yet again.

Blowing out the flame irritably, Lucian picked up another candle from the kitchen drawer before slamming it closed behind him.

'I can do this!' he whispered, glaring at the object in his hand.

Placing it on the table, he saw the first candle flicker into life again and snatched it up before screaming up at his sister.

'Cesca!' he roared, casting it into the sink to send cold dishwater splashing against the windowpane behind.

'Shut up, Lucian!' her muffled moan replied, sounding more distant now from up in her room. 'And hurry up!' she added, slamming her door with a shuddering thud.

Stalking back to the kitchen table, he took a deep breath in an attempt to clear his mind — a difficult thing to do as minds are known to chatter.

Closing his eyes, he sought solitude in the darkness of his mind and the silence that accompanied it, striving to drive away all his needless thoughts and concerns.

Finally opening his eyes to look at the candle, he pictured it getting hotter and poured his desire into the fibres of the wick.

'*Light!*' he commanded silently, driving his intention as hard as he could. '*Burn!*' he stressed, holding his breath in the failing attempt.

A minute passed, followed by another, causing his frustration to mount at the stubbornly unlit braid of cotton.

'Burn!' he roared, his anger erupting in time with the wick.

Staring at the brightly dancing flame with wide eyes that reflected its light, he knew instantly that something was wrong.

'Oh, no!' he moaned, seeing the candlestick begin to melt across the kitchen table. 'Cesca!' he cried, standing back from his handiwork as she came racing down the stairs.

'What?' she panted, drawing up short at the sight before her.

Turning to the half-melted candlestick, she held out her hand and closed her eyes to focus more clearly. There was a hissing sound as the flame extinguished, and the liquid wax began solidifying as it cooled across the wooden surface.

'Wow!' she approved, nodding her head sincerely.

Tearing his gaze from her, he looked at the smoking wax before turning back to her with a look of uncertainty.

'Why did it do that?' he moaned, saddened by the fact that he had not her talent.

'No, Luc, this is good… better than good! Your flame burned so hot that it… well…' she replied, looking pointedly back to the table. 'You're powerful! Now, keep practising until you can control it, and then we'll move on to something really cool,' she continued, looking at him with a mysterious twinkle in her eyes.

Rolling his shoulders, he eased the built-up tension from himself and ran both hands through his short brown hair in an attempt to compose himself.

'*Powerful,*' he thought, liking the sound of that very much. Smiling to himself, he walked to the sink to retrieve his sister's candlestick.

\*\*\*

Francesca's bedroom was large and spacious, with princess dolls lined up along the windowsill as though bearing witness to the activities within.

Upon the far wall, a mural had been painted, depicting a fairytale scene that spread from one side of the room to the other, with a beautiful crystalline palace sketched at its centre, standing out in stark contrast against the dark lake that surrounded it.

'Next, we learn to move things!' Francesca whispered covertly, nodding her head enthusiastically.

Staring at her with a vacant expression, Lucian clearly had no idea what she was talking about.

'Move... things,' she repeated slowly, speaking the words as though he was hard of hearing. 'Like without touching them... with our minds?' she prompted, staring at him expectantly for him to acknowledge her with at least a little understanding.

Ever so slowly, her mouth quirked down before she huffed out a tired sigh.

'Like using the force?' she asked before closing her eyes as the look of understanding dawned in his own.

'Really?' he asked, moving his hand slowly before her face.

'Stop it!' she stormed, annoyed by his daydreaming and determined to keep his mind on track. 'This is for real, so if you go pretending, then it's just not going to work!' she stressed, placing her hands on her hips sternly.

Shaking her head, she felt annoyed that she had to act like this to keep him focussed.

Glaring back, his dark eyes flashed at her condescending tone.

'Okay!' he snapped, his brow lowering in anger.

She really annoyed him sometimes, almost all the time actually, and too often, he had to bite back his angry retorts.

Lucian was considered a rather handsome boy, as Francesca was thought to be pretty, but they were almost the exact opposite in appearance. His dark hair and matching eyes were a total contrast to her blonde curls and deep blue eyes, but both had their father's quick temper, which caused them to row with each other more often than not.

His mind wandered back to his father suddenly, picturing his dark, almost black hair and deep scowling eyes that made most people feel unnerved in his presence.

*'But not us!'* he thought, for to them, he was everything.

Remembering a time when they had been separated after one of their many fights, Lucian recalled being taken aside when it had nearly come to blows.

Seeing the image of his father towering over him, he had felt ashamed as the frown of disapproval glared down upon him.

'My little wolf,' his father had begun, looking so disappointed in that moment, 'you are not to fight your sister... no matter what! You must protect each other and always be on the same side,' he admonished, his stern manner dissolving into a sadness that had impacted upon the boy more than he knew.

On seeing his son's lip start to quiver, Lucian's father had closed his eyes and pulled him into his embrace.

'I love you with all of my might, my tough little wolf, and it breaks my heart to see you two fight all the time. Will you please stop, for me?' he asked, kissing him gently on the top of his head.

This was one of Lucian's clearest memories of his father, of his strong arms wrapping around him and holding him close. Safe.

Shaking off the memory, he looked at his sister and instantly forgave her.

'Okay, let's do it,' he said softly, the words sounding thick in his throat.

Seeing the unexpected change come upon him, Francesca narrowed her eyes and tilted her head to one side.

'You were thinking of Daddy then, weren't you?' she asked, her own eyes taking on a glassy aspect.

Nodding as a solitary tear fell to his cheek, he reached up absently to wipe it away.

'I miss him too, Luc,' she whispered, stepping forward to hug him tightly. 'I'm sorry,' she apologised, then breathed in deeply to push the emotion down. 'Now, come on! Let's use the force, Luc.'

***

The living room was large and very long, for what was once two rooms had been converted into one open liveable area. To the front, a large, rounded bay window looked out over the valley below, while at the rear stood a set of wide patio doors that looked out over an impressively sized garden and onto the forest that lay beyond.

A dark-stained wooden floor stretched from one end of the room to the other, with two large, patterned rugs placed where the two rooms had once been divided.

Seemingly fixed at the centre of the long external wall was what could only be described as a hearth, for the size of the fire could easily have been more suited to a medieval castle than the house it was actually in.

To either side of this large open fireplace, two long grey sofas sat facing each other, with an impressively carved coffee table positioned between them, giving the room a rather homely feel despite the openness of the area.

Sitting on one such sofa, Kristina lounged with a book on her lap, absorbing the knowledge within. Though in her late thirties, she did not look it, for her curvaceous body and lush brown hair gave her a youthful complexion that could easily have belonged to a much younger woman.

Dressed in an old-fashioned summer dress, she had an air of 'Mary Poppins' about her. Even the way she spoke was proper and very precise.

Loving her single life, just her and her children, she felt that life was so much easier without their troublesome father.

There had been no real arguments to traumatise her children, but it was definitely heading that way after they had steadily grown apart, and though she knew that her children missed their father, she just could not help thinking that it was just so nice – for her – without him.

Having been lulled into her daydreaming by the rare silence around her, she thought for a moment about what it was that had caused them to finally part.

It had been his unbending will in almost all things for her, and though she knew that it had been unintentional on his part, she simply felt free without him.

Sighing to herself, she sometimes missed the sense of security he had provided, but the freedom she had felt when he left more than made up for her nervousness at night.

*'And I am not without power,'* she thought, smiling to herself confidently.

Of course, she had known nothing of magick before he had shown her, for it had always been his interest and never hers.

She had let him have his little pastime for much of their relationship, believing him to be a little deluded, if truth be known. She thought him to be living in a dream world, indulging himself in fantasy or something equally absurd.

He had let her believe that way for a very long time, keeping his secrets even from her, and would have continued to do so if she had not twisted the knife.

Claiming the attic space for himself, he had converted it into a liveable area with his occult books littering the shelves.

*'Such a waste of time,'* she had thought, secretly scoffing at his fanciful beliefs, *'but there are worse things he could be doing,'* she had supposed, letting him have his childish obsession.

And then one day, near the end of their relationship and during one of the many disagreements they seemed to have had, she had belittled his interest to his face.

'You need to grow up, Daire!' she had said, igniting his anger as she knew it would.

Always one to overreact, he had held out his hands with his palms facing each other and showed her then what real magick was.

Standing speechless when the electrical currents had arced between his hands, she was instantly reminded of a 'Tesla coil' she had seen in her youth.

That had been when her world had really changed, for there was no going back after witnessing such a feat.

He had regretted it, of course, but what was done could not be undone, and her fascination with the subject had grown exponentially over the following weeks.

Pestering him constantly after his show of power, he had finally relented and agreed to show her the fundamentals of the art, hoping that she would stop after failing to replicate what he had shown her.

'This is true magick, not "magic" but *magick*, with a "K". Magic is for the illusionists you see on the television, but magick is the reality that they pretend at,' he began, looking at her with a deadpan expression. 'You don't need to be born with it, though it does need to be in your blood,' he continued, frowning as he always seemed to do in those days.

'So, you were born with it?' she asked and was surprised by the honesty of his answer.

'I came into my power later in life,' he confessed, speaking with a sadness she had not seen in him before. 'You have to understand that there is a definite probability that you just won't get the gist of it. You'll either get it or you won't,' he continued, staring at her with his brooding dark eyes.

Sitting down on one of the sofas, she watched as several candlesticks were placed on the coffee table and looked up grumpily at what she knew he wanted her to do yet again.

Ignoring her moody expression, Daire stood back and snapped his fingers before winking at her wickedly, causing the first of the candles to flicker into life.

'You wanted to learn this stuff, so learn it! I won't leave again until I'm certain that it is beyond your capability,' he said, seating himself opposite her.

After reading the first of his books, she could not so much as get the candle to flicker, let alone go out, and after another hour of trying, she threw up her hands again in frustration.

'Impossible!' she growled, shocking him out of his thoughts and annoying him in the process.

'Is it?' he snapped, just as the flame snuffed out, and she stared in open-mouthed awe as all seven candles burst into sudden spontaneous life. 'What one man can do... another can do!' he growled, still annoyed by her outburst. 'If you can't "will" the flame to go out with your mind, then try to trigger it another way,' he advised, narrowing his eyes at her doubtful expression.

Sighing tiredly, he sat up a little straighter to explain in more detail.

'At the point where you want it to light, instead of *thinking* it, try *speaking* it. Unleash your desire verbally,' he advised, with a hint of resignation in his tone. 'It would be better if you could do it without your tongue, but I suppose that is your most dangerous weapon,' he continued, chuckling to himself.

And so it was that by verbalising her final command, she had yielded far better results than with her will alone.

The flame had not gone out at her command, but it had dwindled a little, and she had looked up immediately to see his reaction.

'It's a relationship,' he whispered, calling the flame to his outstretched hand. 'You will not rule the fire. You have to coax it at first… but I think you will now get the hang of it,' he continued, giving her a double thumbs up.

Feeling ecstatic that she had actually caused the flame to move – with magick – she could not help but clap her hands excitedly.

He studied her for a moment as though chewing something over in his mind, and she could almost hear the cogs turning as he pursed his lips in thought.

'Out with it,' she demanded, knowing only too well that he had something to say.

Arching an eyebrow in response, he sighed again before finally answering.

'I didn't expect you to do it,' he admitted, still turning the problem over in his mind. 'I suppose I should tell you about the world into which you have just stepped,' he began seriously, still pursing his lips.

Her eyes flashed with excitement as she leant forward in her eagerness to learn more.

'Should I be afraid?' she asked dramatically, widening her eyes to simulate fear before his nod of response caused her joviality to falter, and she looked at him as though he must surely be joking.

Searching his face for the smile she was sure would come, she swallowed nervously when no such amusement was forthcoming.

'Okay…' she said at last, drawing out the word slowly before waiting for him to continue.

'There are a couple of things you should know,' he began,

chewing on the inside of his cheek. 'Firstly, we are not alone in our use of magick, but before I go into all of that, I must give you a brief lesson on the true history of this world,' he said quietly, closing his eyes as he rested his head back on the sofa.

'Shouldn't you have told me beforehand?' she asked, seeing him grimace and wave the question away.

'Would it have made a difference?' he countered, shaking his head for her. 'You would still have tried to copy what you saw, and who could blame you?' he conceded, feeling annoyed with himself for showing her magick in the first place.

Shrugging and then nodding her agreement, she knew only too well that she would have done exactly that.

'Go on then,' she sighed, getting more comfortable herself.

Clearing his throat, he closed his eyes again and began the telling.

'There has been a time like this before, long ago. A world very much as it is now, in which science held sway. It was a great time to be alive, at least for a while,' he remarked, picturing a world a little more advanced than it was at present.

Pausing, he appeared lost in what *was* and what would never be again.

Watching him in silence for a time, she was about to speak when he continued.

'Mankind was on the brink of war, a conflict that would have destroyed everyone and everything,' he whispered, pausing again to gather his thoughts. 'It was a frightening time,' he added, causing her to look at him quizzically.

Listening to the way he was telling the story, she thought it sounded more like he was remembering it rather than simply re-telling her what he had read.

Oblivious to her expression, he continued with his eyes still closed.

'One night, the world erupted, and the feared war was thought to have begun. The land shook, and the technology of mankind fell, swallowed now, deep within the earth. Great tsunamis washed across the land, and there was fire… *everywhere!*' he whispered, feeling the horror of it anew in his mind.

With a look of realisation dawning on her face, she waited for him to continue.

'Mankind was brought to its knees on that first night. There was so much death and destruction that few were lucky enough to survive, and for three days, it seemed that the earth had turned against us… even the wind ravaged the land terribly as it sought out those still breathing,' he whispered and then sobbed unexpectedly.

Not wanting to interrupt what was clearly painful for him, she waited patiently until he was ready to continue.

'Those that survived were changed by the ordeal, seemingly to no longer age or even grow ill. But most fantastic of all was that some of them had what we now call magick,' he continued, opening his eyes again. 'Maybe it was caused by all the pain and suffering they had endured, or maybe it was something else entirely. I honestly don't know. Anyway, we were changed, and mankind stumbled on. Many centuries passed, and we miraculously began to recover from our near extinction, though now we were changed and unequivocally enhanced. Not all had the same level of power, however, or even the same kind, for that matter. Some were only physically enhanced, developing great strength and speed over the years, while others had something more, in varying degrees. These others appeared godlike in this new magickal age and took it upon themselves to take control of mankind's future direction,' he said, leaning forward to stretch his aching back.

Sighing as though the weight of the world was upon him, Daire smiled at her sadly before continuing.

'As time moved on, these magickal people became the wizards of our myths and legends,' he announced, leaning back to look at her again. 'Questions?' he asked, knowing she would have many by now.

'So, there are wizards living today?' she asked, blurting the words out in excitement.

Raising his eyebrows, he nodded in answer with a sad smile as she clapped her hands in excitement.

'Let me ask you a question,' he asked in a tired voice. 'If you had all that power and had everything you ever wanted, what is the one thing you would want above all else and would even kill to get?' he asked, narrowing his eyes as he awaited her response.

Shaking her head, Kristina tried to think of something that would be so elusive to these magnificent people that they would resort to murder to get it.

'Love?' she asked, shrugging her shoulders.

Throwing back his head, Daire burst out laughing before finally looking back with tears in his eyes.

'Love?' he asked, laughing again with genuine amusement. 'Love,' he chuckled, wiping away the tears. 'Immortality!' he answered soberly after reading from her expression that she was fast becoming annoyed. 'They wanted what they already had to last forever,' he explained, his expression hardening once again.

Nodding her understanding, Kristina tried to keep the touch of colour from entering her cheeks.

'Time passed, and the weaker ancients began to die off before a way was eventually found. So desperate were some to live on, they sought immortality in the most horrific way possible,' he said, failing to keep the note of loathing from his voice.

Leaning forward in her excitement, Kristina could not contain herself any longer.

'Did they succeed?' she asked, daring him to laugh again with her widened eyes. But he merely nodded, ignoring her challenging stare.

'Some believed that to gain life, you had to take it, and so used their power to drain the life from others, feeding on them like a leech,' he answered, grimacing at the thought.

With hands to her mouth, Kristina felt disgusted at the mere thought of it.

'Oh my god, that's so vile… did they succeed?' she asked, disgustedly intrigued that such a creature could exist.

'Yes, but not in the way they had intended, for the act itself corrupted them far beyond anything they could have foreseen. They were irrevocably changed, losing much of their humanity and almost all of their magick in the process. They consider themselves sexless now, neither male nor female, believing themselves demons with the rest of us their food source… but it did work,' he answered, clenching his teeth as he pictured what he was speaking of. 'Vile, loathsome creatures they are now, and exceptionally dangerous!' he warned, raising his eyebrows at her expectantly and waiting for her to guess what he was describing.

'Oh my god!' she exclaimed again, widening her eyes in disbelief. 'You actually mean vampires, don't you?' she asked, doubting that she could be right.

'Vampires,' he confirmed, nodding his head. 'One of the most dangerous beings to walk the earth. Deadly, vicious, and devoid of emotion, save maybe hate or lust. They are the closest to true evil I have ever encountered,' he explained, running his fingers through his dark hair before massaging the scalp beneath. 'There are actually two vampire factions now – "Bloods" and the Energy Vampires, who call themselves the "Egni," which means "energy" in the modern tongue.'

Pausing for a moment, he reached down and began massaging one of his knees, relieving the ache he felt there.

'The Egni are not really vampires, to be fair, not in the way the Bloods are anyway, but they do come from the same stock. They were wizards once too, who, in their desperation, made peace with the Bloods in exchange for the secret to their existence and swore an oath to never war with one another after the pact was made. And so it was that they used their knowledge to perfect what the Bloods had intended, becoming similar but also something different. The Egni can drain the life force from almost anything at will – anything with life to give, that is – and are therefore as much a blight upon this world as the Bloods!' he continued, shaking his head before glaring at her with a look of warning. 'If you ever come across a Blood, put up a shield and attack it with fire! Don't engage it in conversation or stare into its eyes. They do have some willpower and can unhinge the untrained. Very few can go head-to-head with a Blood and live to tell the tale!' he warned, worry flickering briefly in his eyes.

Paling at the thought of one of these creatures entering the house, she guessed that he had imagined a similar scenario.

'Why would I ever meet one?' she asked, rationalising that she had never met one before.

'There was a war many centuries ago. I have books on it upstairs. Basically, long story short, a truce was made between the wizards and the vampires, and a law passed that any new power...' he stopped, indicating her, '... has to choose a discipline or, rather, a side. All factions have the right to talk to or seduce these "newbies" into their fold, and failure to join one or the other would ultimately result in their death. The problem is that the Bloods nearly always turn up first and kill said "newbies" before the other factions arrive,' he said, looking at her seriously.

'They'll come for me?' she whimpered in a small voice, looking scared out of her mind until he shook his head.

'Obviously not! I have hidden this place and you along with it. Newbies, like yourself, project an aura or signature that is sensed by those who know how to look. Your power at this very moment is wild and, for the most part, uncontrolled. When you learn to hone your craft, you will harmonise with the world around you and therefore blend in. Right now though, you stand out like a sore thumb... or would have, had I not intervened on your behalf,' he replied, smiling reassuringly at her deadpan expression. 'I simply added your "signature" to my shielding and hid you before you could be sensed. It is why I did not leave until I was certain about you,' he continued, smiling at her confidently.

Looking unconvinced, she glared at him accusingly.

'You should have told me all this beforehand!' she hissed, looking at him as though he had tricked her somehow.

'Yes, yes! We've covered this!' he growled, irritated by her words. 'There are books in the attic that will teach you all you need to know. Read them and learn for yourself. Master their contents and keep them from everyone else. Don't share my books with another soul, Kris! If someone else reads from them and manages to achieve something, anything, without me there to prevent it, they will be seen and hunted until found. I mean it!' he said forcefully, holding her eyes with his own.

'Okay, okay. I promise! Jeez, Louise,' she sighed, rolling her eyes. 'Why do these Bloods kill us?' she asked, moving past his overbearing rules but still feeling fascinated and grossed out enough to continue on the topic of vampires.

'Because they can!' he snapped, annoyed by her lack of empathy for his concerns. 'Vampires rule this world and flaunt their dominance over mankind constantly. To them, there is no greater threat than newbies strengthening their enemies' ranks or the rare occasion that one might be too strong in their own right and challenge them directly,' he answered, shrugging his shoulders. 'Sometimes, some who ascend into magick have tremendous power, even more than the ancients themselves, but they never seem to live very long,' he said and then paused, leaning forward for effect. 'These, if they live long enough, the Bloods force to become like them!' he whispered, knowing that this would scare her.

Looking positively ill, she swallowed hard against the dryness in her throat.

'*Good!*' he thought, thinking that if she would not take his concerns seriously for her own sake, then he would frighten her into it.

Taking a deep breath, she composed herself as best she could.

'How did the war between the vampires and the wizards start? Or end, for that matter?' she asked, causing him to look down again.

'It started and ended with me,' he confessed, pointing back at himself with both thumbs in turn. 'I have a knack for killing vampires and very much like to do so. Seeing me as something like the wizards, they did what any race would do when under threat… they retaliated,' he answered, raising his eyes to meet hers.

Seeing her mouth open after his confession, he held up a hand to stop her interrogation.

'Yes, I'm one of the ancients, and the one that started the war. It ended when they thought to have killed me and when the Egni were finally created,' he continued, gesturing for her to ask what she wanted.

Looking at him thoughtfully, she wondered what else he could be keeping from her.

'I don't know you at all, do I?' she asked, but then shook her head and waved the question away. 'Why would the remaining wizards not fight on?' she asked, deciding against arguing for the time being.

Grimacing at her first question, he sighed, too tired to have another argument with her.

'Because of the wizards that made the pact with the Bloods. They were the most powerful of the remaining ancients, and their leader was the High Wizard himself,' he explained, nodding his head at her reaction.

'What a betrayal!' she gasped, shaking her head in disbelief.

'Life, you will find, is full of them,' he replied, sounding as though he had tasted enough of it himself. 'Afterwards, what was left of the wizards splintered off into many different factions, splitting themselves into separate disciplines. Wizards, witches, druids and many more now have their own ideas for the future of mankind. That is why the Bloods go unchallenged, for there are none now to oppose the might of both vampire factions,' he replied, shaking his head sadly.

Snapping her head up suddenly, a frown creased her brow after a thought popped into her mind.

'Why would wizards try to recruit me… aren't they all men?' she asked, causing him to look at her blankly, and she knew then that she had done it again.

'Wizard means "wise one". So, I guess that most are actually men,' he replied, smiling to himself. 'There are, however, female wizards, as there are male witches. Look, Kris, read it up. You have the time,' he added, yawning and readying himself to rise.

Still looking uneasy, Kristina looked at him with a dubious expression.

'So… what are you exactly? I'm guessing that since you're able to hide us, you don't belong to one of these factions?' she asked, looking at him as though for the first time.

Intrigued by her inquisitiveness, he nodded mysteriously and smiled his knowing little smile.

'Very astute of you, young lady. I am indeed something else entirely,' he replied, settling himself once more on the sofa.

Rolling her eyes at him, she indicated with an impatient wave of her hand that he should explain.

'A druid is basically a wizard, but with one vital difference. They focus on the elements, and though they don't worship them per se, they do have a deep respect for them,' he continued casually, keeping his tone light and carefree.

'You speak as though the elements are alive,' she scoffed,

making a face to suggest that the very thought of it was ludicrous.

Seeing him smile with a narrowing of his dark eyes, she knew from experience that he knew more than he was letting on.

'It's a belief system,' he replied, dismissing the question for another time.

Looking fearful again, the knowledge of what he was saying slowly sank in.

'What if they come when you've gone?' she asked in a hushed tone, clearly thinking of the vampires again.

'Worst case scenario?' he asked, pursing his lips as he stared at her seriously.

Nodding, she said nothing as she held her breath for the answer.

'I will make this place safe before I leave. Have no doubt... you will be safe!' he assured, getting up from the sofa before stretching dramatically. 'I'm off to bed then. Goodnight,' he announced abruptly, and almost made it out before her last question stopped him at the door.

'How old are you?' she asked, her voice now barely a whisper.

'Older than this world,' he replied without turning back, deciding he had said enough for one night.

Shooting out of her seat as he continued to leave, she followed after him haughtily.

'You can't leave it on a cliffhanger like that!' she whispered hoarsely, trying not to wake the children.

'Read it in the books! It's too long a story to tell tonight, and I'm knackered,' he replied, beginning to climb the stairs.

'At least tell me what you were called back then?' she pleaded, making him stop yet again.

Looking back impassively, he wondered what she would think if she truly knew the answer.

'Read the histories, and then you tell me,' he replied, looking at her with an expression of finality.

She let him leave then, albeit reluctantly, and turned to the candles with a sigh. Willing with all her strength for the flames to go out, she finally uttered her chosen word of command.

# CHAPTER TWO

Storming across the landing and into her son's bedroom, Kristina brandished a large, leather-bound book that could have been a family bible for the age and thickness of it.

'Where the hell did you get this book from, Cesca!' she demanded, slamming the offending tome down hard upon a chest of drawers. 'Daddy's attic has been locked and... how did you get in?' she shrilled, picking the book back up and waving it in the air like a maniac.

Looking up in fright, both children were startled by her rampaging outburst.

'It was open, and I just walked in!' Francesca whined, shrinking back from her mother's wrath.

Glaring at her with a look that spoke volumes, Kristina slammed the book down again before placing her hands on her hips.

'Tell me the truth!' she screamed, daring her daughter to lie with the widening of her eyes.

'I was walking past, and the door just creaked open a bit,' Francesca stammered, clearly caught off guard by the incriminating tome.

Scowling with a look that said she was not buying a word of it, Kristina leant forward as she pressed on with her attack.

'Why were you up there... walking past? What were you doing?' she demanded, feeling her anger slowly subside into fear as the possible consequences began to sink in.

Turning to her brother for support, Francesca sighed woefully at his wide-eyed spectator's expression, and knew that he was of no help to her whatsoever.

'I'll tell you what happened!' Kristina stormed, stepping in closer as she spoke, 'You went snooping to see what you could find. How did you get past Daddy's... locks?' she asked, struggling to find the right words to explain the door's magickal enchantment. 'What other books have you read?' she asked furiously, placing her free hand on her waist in annoyance. 'Well?' she shrilled when Francesca did not answer fast enough.

'I haven't taken any more books out, I promise! Just that one, but it's only tricks, like moving stuff and lighting candles.' she confessed, trying to get back into her mother's good graces.

Frozen with inaction, Kristina's stomach churned at those fatefully chosen words.

'Have you actually tried any of the tricks?' she asked nervously, the colour draining from her face.

'Yes!' Lucian answered innocently, happy at last to be involved now that the shouting had died down. 'They are quite hard at first, but the more you do them...' he began before Francesca cut him off by screaming at the top of her voice.

'Shut up, Lucian!' she cried, clearly expecting more wrath from her mother.

However, all Kristina could do at that moment was to stand still, her eyes wide and teary as she stared at her son.

'You've been practising...' she whispered hollowly, speaking the words softly as her tears fell to her cheeks.

Walking swiftly to the window, she peered out nervously before scanning the road that led down to the village.

'You are both grounded,' she murmured, searching for anything that seemed out of the ordinary. 'Do you hear me?' she screeched, still looking outside. 'You are not allowed to leave this house until I say otherwise. Cross me on this, I dare you!' she growled, rounding on them both. 'Do you understand? You do not leave this house! Do you understand?' she shrieked, causing both children to flinch in response.

'Yes!' they cried in unison, shrinking back from her terrible tone.

***

Within the hour, Kristina could hear a car tearing through the forest lanes up towards the house. Taking a nervous breath, she went to the front door to greet the one who came.

His face was livid, just as she had expected it would be, as she watched him stalk up the path.

'Three months!' Daire growled, his anger peaking and ready to explode. 'Three bloody months you've had access to my books, and you have ruined everything!' he seethed, shaking in his fury.

Placing her hands on her hips, Kristina went immediately into defence mode.

'You can't blame me, Daire! Francesca broke in somehow and...' but his fierce glare cut her off before he shook his head slowly.

'That's absolute rubbish!' he growled, rounding on her angrily, 'Cesca wouldn't be able to get into *that* room, not when the door was closed... only you!' he replied, stabbing a finger in her direction. 'You alone could unlock that door. Even if you had simply closed the damned thing, she wouldn't have been able to get in. You left it open!' he accused, grabbing at his hair in exasperation.

Breathing out in defeat, her eyes filled with tears as she accepted that this must have been the way of it.

'What can we do?' she asked, fear etched into her features.

'We?' he asked, shaking his head in anger. '*We* will do nothing!' he stormed, snarling as he spoke through his teeth.

'I alone will hide their signatures, and it will be me who protects them when *they* come,' he growled, nodding in acknowledgement of her fearful reaction.

With hands flying to her mouth, she began to tremble as her fear threatened to overwhelm her.

'Vampires?' she whimpered, shaking her head in denial.

'Bloods!' he hissed, running his fingers frantically through his grey-flecked hair. 'Useless, negligent woman!' he stormed, pacing the floor like a caged animal and glaring at her all the while.

Stopping suddenly to just stare at her, he shook his head with defeat in his eyes.

'Even though you think you know what you've done, you don't! It's too late to hide them completely... the damned things will be coming already!' he whispered, shaking his head.

Knowing how to treat his anger, she just stood there and waited for it to burn itself out.

'Where are they?' he demanded, his fearful expression causing her to sob, having never before seen this emotion in him.

Motioning her head upwards, she hugged herself tightly as fresh tears began to fall.

'I've told them not to come down. Not until we've talked,' she sobbed, covering her face with her hands.

Immediately, his fire cooled, and she could see tears glistening in his eyes.

'How long have they been practising?' he asked, looking scared for the first time she could remember.

Crying silently, she shook her head and shrugged.

'They can light candles and move things, Cesca a little more, maybe. I don't know,' she sobbed, crying louder suddenly when he dropped to his knees in defeat.

'You've undone us, Kris,' he moaned, staring up at her woefully. 'I can't hide them!' he whispered, slumping his shoulders as though a great weight was pressing down upon them. 'I can obscure and deflect their presence, but they know where they are now!' he cried, bending low to cover his face.

'Can't we just run away?' she asked weakly, but he shook his head and looked up to the ceiling.

'The Bloods will track them wherever they go and will get to them quicker that way. They would be here already if not for what I have already done. I need to see the attack coming so that I can fight it on my terms. Here, I can protect them better than anywhere else, but it's just a matter of time before they finally get through,' he explained, putting his face into his hands whilst rocking himself in misery. 'What to do?' he stressed, shaking his head.

\*\*\*

Hearing footsteps upon the stairs and then the sound of the bedroom door opening, Francesca hid herself under the covers whilst Lucian tried desperately to squirm his way under her.

They both knew why he had come and knew, too, the reason they were in trouble.

As the quilt was pulled from her slowly, Daire took in the golden curls and fearful blue eyes with a look of sadness.

'Oh, my baby girl,' he whispered, his expression instantly

creasing into pain. 'You don't ever need to be afraid of me! No matter what!' he promised, tears welling in his eyes.

Seeing his anguish, Francesca burst into tears and sat up to wrap her arms around his neck, leaving a wide-eyed Lucian totally exposed.

Popping his head up, he peered over his sister's shoulder, causing his father to laugh through his tears.

'And you, my little wolf,' he whispered, pulling him into his embrace.

'Daddy?' Francesca whispered, keeping her voice low as they lay cuddling on the bed.

'Whaty?' he asked, making his reply rhyme with her question.

'Am I still allowed to do the tricks?' she asked, holding her breath nervously for his answer.

Closing his eyes, the question forced him back into the horrific situation with a gut-wrenching twist.

'You weren't allowed to do them in the first place!' he admonished, scowling down at the top of her head. 'But to answer your question… yes, just so long as you're careful. It really doesn't matter anymore,' he sighed, taking a deep breath before letting it out slowly.

Knowing now that it was best for them to learn all they could, he pursed his lips as he pondered his next move.

'In the book is a trick to put a shield around yourself to stop things from hurting you,' he began, closing his eyes at the thought of such a thing. 'Will you learn that one for me first?' he asked, kissing her head tenderly. 'I need you to learn everything in that book now, and as fast as you can. Can you do that for me?' he asked, feeling her nod sleepily against his chest.

After some time, he slowly disentangled himself from the sleeping children and stood to look down upon them in quiet contemplation.

'I will burn this world to keep you safe,' he whispered, chewing on the inside of his cheek as he considered his options. 'I will die before you do,' he swore aloud before reaching out to touch the wall.

\*\*\*

Jumping in surprise when she became aware of him studying her from the doorway, Kristina noticed that he looked somehow weaker than he had, more fragile than when he had first arrived.

'Can I trust you to keep them safe from now on?' he asked emotionlessly, an unreadable deadpan expression set upon his face.

Holding his stare with guilt in her eyes, she felt a flush of embarrassment turn her face red.

'Yes,' she replied, a little annoyed by his subtle rebuke. 'I will die before they do,' she swore, knowing nothing less would suffice for him.

Widening his eyes at her choice of words, he studied her for a moment before narrowing them cynically.

'Well put,' he replied dryly, still staring at her with his unreadable expression.

After a moment, he nodded and entered the room to sit opposite her.

'We have much to discuss before I leave,' he informed, still struggling to hide his displeasure.

'What?' she gasped, but a held-up hand silenced anything else she might have said.

'Only for the night. I know what I have to do now. The only option left open to me,' he said, unconsciously turning the rings he wore on each little finger with the thumbs of the same hand. 'But first, we talk,' he said, sitting back a little to stare at her again with that stony expression of his. 'Have you read the histories?' he asked, the question catching her off guard and causing her to falter.

'Um, yes, I've read quite a bit actually,' she answered, lifting the book suggestively from her lap.

'And have you figured out who I am yet?' he asked, his face still impassive, showing not one ounce of emotion.

Smiling sadly at the look on his face, she nodded her head in answer.

'I think you were or are, Pwl or Paul? The pronunciation is unclear,' she answered, raising her eyebrows to see if she was right.

Seeing him smile for the first time since his arrival, she noticed with sadness that it did not reach his eyes as he nodded for her to continue.

'Either will do… why him?' he asked in a lighter tone, noting her reaction.

Taking a deep breath, she cleared her throat before giving her analysis.

'Well, he was a great warrior, was there at the beginning, and I picture you when I read of him. He was a major player back in the day until he was nearly killed by some nightmarish creature and then kinda faded from history,' she replied, smiling at him triumphantly.

Nodding whilst quirking his mouth down at the sides, Daire looked pleased by her reasoning.

'Very good… what nearly killed him?' he asked, causing her to pull a sour face.

'A rather unsavoury creature known as The Dark Wolf. Pretty much feared by everyone back then because it killed everything it came into contact with. It said that you would have died if not for your father's intervention,' she answered, sighing contentedly at her knowledgeable answer.

With his poker face still intact, he indicated for her to continue.

'I didn't read much more about it, only that it was as scary as hell and that even the vampires avoided it. During the Great War, it killed more wizards than the Bloods did but was finally put down when "the first rose up against the last." Whatever that means. This was towards the end of the war,' she finished, placing the book back upon her lap.

Nodding his approval, Daire looked impressed by the speed at which she could retain the information.

'Good. You understand enough of it, I think. The Dark Wolf did appear to kill indiscriminately in the end. Feared more than all the vampires put together, it was in his downfall that the end of the war was finally achieved. His death allowed the vampires to ultimately win,' he replied, causing Kristina to frown.

'I thought a truce was made?' she asked but immediately regretted it as Daire shook his head in annoyance.

'The wizards joined the vampires, remember? The vampire lords of today are the very same creatures that fought all those ages ago. Today's wizards and witches are almost all descendants of those who survived. Vampires won the war, that is why they break the laws so frequently and kill "noobs" like yourself,' he replied angrily, annoyed that he had to explain this to her yet again.

Flushing at his words, Kristina looked about to retort before shrugging off the comment.

'What happened to you and your brothers after the war?' she asked, having found nothing of this in any of the books she had read.

Shaking his head, he smiled humourlessly at her unseeing mind.

'They became vampires,' he replied flatly, causing her to frown again in confusion.

Saying nothing more, he raised his eyebrows and waited for her to connect the dots.

'You are not Paul,' she realised slowly, searching his face for the answer.

'No,' he confirmed, his features remaining like that of stone. 'I am the monster that beat him,' he said quietly, watching her reaction intently.

Shaking her head, Kristina was unable to understand how this could be.

'But it was referred to as a demon of the old world! It was the bloody bogeyman, for god's sake! I only remembered the name because of what you call Luc…'

Looking at him with wide, incredulous eyes, she shook her head in horror.

'Oh my god! You call Lucian…' she faltered again and just stared at him, unable to say the final words.

'My little wolf,' he finished for her, a cold smile playing at the corners of his mouth. 'I always secretly liked that name,' he added, smiling wider at the look in her eyes. 'More so because it was the Bloods themselves who named me, fearing me more than any other! For it was them I sought! Them whom I hunted! Who would you rather fight for you? Paul, the Blade Master, or the dreaded Dark Wolf?' he growled, incensed by her repulsed reaction.

Nodding his head for her, he replied to his own question.

'Me!' he snapped, jabbing his thumb into his chest. 'Every damned time!' he hissed, rising to his feet in anger. 'History,' he announced, indicating the book on her lap, 'is nearly always written by the victors. There is and always shall be two sides to any given story,' he continued, rubbing at his aching knee with the same thumb. 'I will be happy to see the end of you,' he remarked, still massaging the joint.

Narrowing her eyes, she looked him up and down before shaking her head.

'Why have you grown older if you have been alive for so long?' she asked, wondering what his reasons could be behind it.

Looking at her for some time, he pursed his lips again as though deciding upon something.

'I was happy to grow old with you, Kris. To have a normal life and watch our children grow,' he replied, his face full of regret. 'It just didn't work out that way. So tonight, I will become the legend once again. I will become the thing they all fear. The thing they will think twice about before crossing paths with. They will rue the day they awoke me again and would hate you too if they knew that it was all because you left that bloody door open!' he growled, getting angrier by the moment. 'This is the last time you will see me as I am,' he announced, striding to the door. 'The Daire you know dies tonight!' he said dramatically, his eyes growing colder as he looked down at her.

Shaking his head sadly, he could not truly believe that this was what it had come to.

'You have left me with no other choice. Your negligence has forced my hand, and I will do what is necessary to protect my children. No matter the cost!' he growled, shaking his head again at her failings.

Seeing that she had no words of reply, he shook his head once more.

'Time to leave,' he whispered, bidding her stand also, and without warning, he hugged her tenderly. 'Goodbye,' he whispered, turning on his heel to stalk from the house.

# Chapter Three

The air was colder than he had anticipated, causing his breath to fog as he walked through the trees. With every step, he drew up the earth's energy, feeding the change that was already taking place.

Looking within himself, he focussed his attention upon the very core of his biological makeup, seeking the image he knew would come.

Having learned long ago that contrary to popular belief, the human race was not made of the clay that religion would have him believe but instead, of the very water that made up the majority of this world, he had reasoned that if he was indeed mostly water and that if he could influence it, he could ultimately change himself.

It had taken him some time to finally recognise what it was within himself – the search made more difficult by not knowing what he was looking for – and he had felt a flush of excitement at finally finding the white glow within.

He had been awed at first, seeing the little snowflakes in his mind, and knew immediately that his search was over. Seeing a rotten-looking snowflake within his mind, he had instinctively made it brighter with an almost ethereal glow and, in so doing, had taken a great many years off his slowly ageing body.

Throwing his research into the element, he had learned more than he could have imagined upon experimentation, finding that the purer the water, the more perfect the snowflake appeared and deduced that by perfecting said 'snowflake', he ultimately perfected himself.

Walking now through the dense foliage of the forest, he focused on perfecting every detail of it and made it as bright as he possibly could within his mind.

On first looking within himself after leaving the house, he had barely even recognised the thing, having aged it in time with Kristina's. All he could sense was a goopy, decaying and formless sludge that appeared far removed from what he knew it should have been, but within moments of renewing it, he felt stronger than he had in many years.

His knee was the first to heal. The cold, dull ache fading almost immediately as he set out on his quest. Smiling with renewed confidence, his stride lengthened as his old strength returned.

Walking from the trees, he came upon a glade that spread out before him, appearing like an overgrown football pitch at the far edge of the forest. Looking to his left, he saw the foothills of the mountain that stretched up gradually to the rolling hills beyond before his eyes drifted higher.

The moon shone down with an enchanting ease, seemingly there to witness what he was about to do.

He had waited in the attic for the appropriate hour before finally setting out, knowing that he had to be where he was now, at this precise moment, for a time when it was neither night nor day but the mystical crossover in between. The time between times, it was called, where gateways open, and the gods themselves lend an ear to those that would speak. Only then could he commune with the one he sought, as he had done so very long ago.

He had summoned the element of earth before, calling it up in a time of great need, and such a time was upon him again, he knew, for there was no other option left open to him.

His heart was beating faster than he would have liked, for the spirit of the land was colossal and had only helped him that last time on a whim rather than out of any true desire. The element had been caught off guard by his summoning, and he remembered thinking that it had only agreed to help so it could stay a while longer in this previously forbidden dimension.

Not knowing the reason for its exclusion in the first place, Daire had sensed that it somehow just did not belong, and now felt great trepidation at calling upon it again.

Guilt had racked him at the end of his last summoning, upon his realisation that the spirit could not stay without him there to bind it, and he had imagined its futile attempts to remain after he was gone.

Stopping at the tree line, he surveyed the open area before

him and waited a moment within the shadow of the trees.

The moonlight seemed cold to him, casting an eerie light on the open expanse of grass and edging the leaves above in its mystical silvery brilliance.

Breathing out nervously, his hot exhale billowed out to dissipate upon the cold night air.

'Here we go,' he whispered, breathing out the words with a tightening of his stomach.

Walking to where he deemed the centre of the clearing to be, he lowered himself to sit upon the cold, hard ground. Looking skyward, he noted the shade of blue creeping across the horizon and knew that the 'time between times' was almost upon him.

Clearing his mind, he drove his awareness down into the earth beneath his feet and uttered the words of summoning.

*'Elfen o bridd i awl i chi,'* he whispered, invoking the ancient summoning in the oldest of tongues.

The response came immediately, far quicker than he had anticipated, which only added to the growing uncertainty he felt.

*'Why have you called upon me?'* a deafening voice rumbled, causing him to wince from the sheer magnitude of it.

Bowing his head, Daire showed the entity its deserved respect and spoke his reply in a soft, humbled whisper.

'You have slept for too long, and it is my need that you rise once again,' he answered, keeping his tone low and respectful.

A deep rumble of displeasure shook the land, causing him to look about warily.

*'Why?'* the thunderous voice demanded, speaking with a note of anger in its mind-numbing tone. *'You do this for nought but yourself, and we are not to be used thus,'* the element continued, cutting off Daire's link to the energy beneath his feet.

Feeling the magick of the land sever, Daire felt fear gnaw at him and desperately fought for control over it.

*'Why cut my connection to the earth?'* he wondered, believing it to be an aggressive move.

Feeling unprepared for such an eventuality, he shook his head in regret for calling upon this colossal entity a second time.

'All acts are self-serving in one way or another. I am in need of you as you are in need of me!' he stressed, shifting his weight a little as he spoke.

The silence that followed was deafening, and he thought for a moment that the element might have withdrawn before the ground shook once again, forcing him to put his arms out to steady himself.

'*We remember you!*' the element thundered, sounding far angrier than it had the moment before. '*You seek to use us as once you did, before casting us aside when your need is met!*' it thundered, speaking now in an accusatory tone.

Straightening up, Daire put power into his voice to make it boom like the element before him.

'I had to leave! Is it not enough that I have awakened you at all?' he thundered, his voice echoing deeply across the clearing.

Like the sensation of static before a storm, Daire felt the energy building around him and felt a shiver of fear running up his spine.

'You said, "*we*",' he whispered, feeling the hand of fate weighing down upon him as the realisation sank in.

A peel of rumbling laughter came down from the hills as though the mountain itself was amused by his observation.

'*We,*' the land confirmed as the forest came alive around him, issuing forth the same mocking amusement.

Without warning, the wind lifted to howl around him, bringing with it the rain that should never have been on a cloudless night.

Hitting him with tremendous force, he leant against the deluge before lowering himself against the torrential assault.

Summoning his shield, he saw it expand from him in a sphere of white light that drove the attack back several paces. The wind increased, blowing harder at him in its attempt to tip him over, but his protection held as it began whitening at the edges, appearing then like a crescent moon.

The onslaught turned away suddenly and then gathered speed as it swirled into something different. Darting away with a life of its own, the newly formed tornado began to twist precariously at the edge of the forest, swaying this way and that before abruptly turning back. Stopping a short distance away, the rotating column of air blew itself out, leaving an unsteady pyre of wood in its wake.

A deafening boom of thunder overhead heralded the flash of intense light that struck the shaky structure with an explosion of sound, sending small chunks of burning wood out in all directions. A loud hiss issued forth, like that of a snake, as the fourth and final element presented itself before him.

Thinking that to show weakness at this time would surely seal his fate, Daire stood tall and masked his fear with anger.

'Enough!' he roared, the magick in his voice making him sound like an enraged god.

The wind instantly dropped, taking with it the rain, and even the fire froze in that singular moment, leaving the glade in a deathly silence.

A mist began to rise, blanketing the earth in a luminous white that appeared to glow under the light of the moon.

Glancing at the lightening sky, Daire knew that he needed to act before the time had come and gone again all too quickly. In silence, he waited for the land to speak again, but it was the fire that broke the dreadful silence.

*'You think that you awoke just one of us that first time, child?'* it asked, its tone hissing from all the nearby fires.

Taken aback, Daire took time to organise his thoughts before replying.

'I thought that was what I had done, yes,' he confessed, shrugging in the firelight that began to flicker once again.

Hissing low, the fire blazed more fiercely, causing him to feel its intense heat against his skin.

*'You bid one to come, and we all hear the call!'* came the fire's roaring response, the flames from the scattered chunks of wood flaring dangerously around him. *'Only you have the spirit to call us, and only you have the will to keep us here. You will not abandon us again as you did that first time,'* it continued, the threat against refusal evident in its tone.

A branch within the fire split suddenly, sounding more like the crack of a whip than any splintering of wood that Daire had ever heard.

'Do not lay the fault of your exclusion at my feet! You must appreciate the time I give you. It is not my doing when you fade back into the night,' he argued, desperately trying to draw up the earth's power but still finding his attempts blocked.

All four elements cried out at his words, igniting the sky with a sheet of lightning, but Daire stood his ground and would not be intimidated by their show of aggression.

Looking up once again to the fading night sky, he spread his arms in exasperation.

'What do you want from me?' he asked, his voice rising in desperation.

The mist began thickening into a dense fog that swirled about his knees and then up around his thighs. In a soft and tender tone, it was the water that answered him next, and he could feel the vibration of it against his legs.

*You have put your will upon us, mortal man, and opened our eyes in this forbidden realm for the second time. Here, we are not allowed and are not meant to experience the things that we did the first time. You did this for us and shall now reap the rewards of your labour,'* the soft voice answered, making him feel languid and in desperate need of sleep.

The fog thickened to the point where he could no longer see his feet, and he felt himself drifting within the swirling vapour.

'What do you want?' he breathed dreamily but then shook his head as though to clear it.

Anger ignited within him as he realised what was happening, and with a grunt of effort, he cast the element from within his protective circle.

Wind caressed the back of his neck, causing goosebumps to rise on his skin and a shiver to ripple up his back.

*'What is the fifth element?'* it asked seductively, speaking like a lover's whisper in his ear, causing him to shiver and feel the hairs on his neck stand on end.

'Spirit,' he answered, looking involuntarily to one of the rings on his fingers before a sinking sensation began in the pit of his stomach.

*'Yes!'* came the collective reply, causing him to wince before appreciating the strength of his shield that had dulled the sensation. *'You are our spirit and our only link to this world. Only you have been able to summon us since the fall of the first world, and we would bind ourselves to you to remain when your need of us is met,'* they continued, the force of their conviction driving him back a

step.

'I will not be dominated in this way. If you desire something of me, speak it plainly!' he growled, seeing both day and night in the sky above him.

*'You are our spirit, for only you can awaken us. The spirit in you is strong, and we would bind you to us so that we, too, can live,'* they said again, causing his lips to purse in thought.

It did not take long before the wind came again, breathing against him enchantingly.

*'You will become Spirit,'* it whispered, but said nothing more of what this might mean.

Closing his eyes, he tried to see past their words to the heart of what they were saying and their true intent.

'Damn!' he cursed, shaking his head in frustration. 'How can I become Spirit?' he asked, spreading his arms in exasperation. 'Spirit is everywhere and nowhere. It is the ethereal and surely not a single entity, certainly not a physical being!' he replied, shaking his head at his lack of understanding.

*'We will put ourselves in you, and, in turn, you shall be placed within us. You will be born again to this world, but from us, and in so doing, anchor us to this realm. You will dwell in spirit and walk all the roads of the worlds. All this we give to you in recompense for the gift you shall give unto us,'* came their insistent response, as if they, too, sensed the passing of time.

Dread flushed through him, and he shook his head in refusal, leaving no more room for debate.

'No! I must remain as I am and stay here to protect my children,' he replied, turning to seek an escape route.

The pyre erupted, blasting more chunks of wood up into the air, the wrathful element of fire venting its anger at his refusal.

*'We will not go back to the darkness!'* it hissed, the flames suddenly burning white and turning much of the remaining wood to ash. *'In creating you anew, we bind ourselves to this realm and shall be forbidden no more,'* it hissed, all pretence at wooing him gone from its tone.

'What of my children?' he roared, fearing that he would not be himself if he allowed their intent to come to fruition.

Kneeling upon the grass, he put his head into his hands and pleaded desperately.

'If you do this, my children will be lost! I need them to be protected,' he cried, frantically trying to think of a satisfactory compromise.

Closing his eyes, he split his mind and boxed off his personality as it was now.

*'Remember!'* he willed, splintering his mind and locking it away deep within his subconscious.

*'We will protect them if that is your wish, for your desires will then be ours,'* came their combined response, gentler now, as though sensing his distress.

'And what of me?' he cried, backing away defensively before connecting his life force to his shield in desperation. 'I will protect them myself, but to do that, I must be me!' he stressed, desperately backing away and wishing futilely for the sun to rise.

Lightning suddenly struck him, the force driving him to his knees, buckling him under its immense attack. At the contact, his shield crackled with electrical currents forking over its surface as though trying to find purchase on the whitened exterior.

Straightening himself, Daire stood once again within his white orb of power and cleared his mind of all negativity.

'I refuse!' he growled, deciding to fight and die before losing himself forever.

The howling wind hit him next, blasting at him from all sides to pin him to the spot. Thunder boomed overhead, a prelude to the lightning he knew would follow.

Throwing out his power, he caught the expected strike and dragged the bolt down, grounding it with a shocked wail from the earth that now housed the element he had summoned. The combined attack was neutralised, and the area around him convulsed from the contact.

Realising that he was free of the air's brutal hold, he bolted for the trees but was stopped by a wall of intense heat as the element of fire reared up before him.

With his shield glowing ever whiter, he felt an immediate drain upon his energy after his protection took what it needed from the only thing it could.

With a wave of his arm, he threw the element aside and saw

it wash from him like lava, causing the fog to evaporate from the intensity of its heat.

All he could do was deflect the attacks, and with a cold, dreadful realisation, he knew that he could not win this fight. A calm settled over him, the knowledge that this was indeed his end shining in his dark eyes.

'*You bloody arrogant fool!*' he berated, knowing that he had now left his children totally defenceless and alone against those who hunted them.

He cried then, not for himself, though the thought of dying after so long terrified him beyond words. He wept for his children and the level of protection they would now be denied.

'You fool!' he admonished himself again, cursing his egotistical belief that he could control these fathomless beings.

A stone the size of a bus landed on top of him, shattering his shield and draining him further. Spider-web cracks spread across its white surface, growing thicker by the second as it held the incredible weight aloft.

Falling back in agony, Daire felt his life leach from him, the strain of maintaining the shield too much for his body to bear. Feeling weaker than he ever had, he feebly fought to get to his knees and then, with even greater effort, cast the giant stone aside with a deep, ground-shaking thump.

On shaky legs, he began to rise, but another blinding strike from above blasted his protection into leafy fragments that faded into the wind.

Standing there, old and bent, his white hair blew gently in the wind as he peered up at the moon before closing his eyes in defeat.

'Protect them!' he rasped as the sodden earth began to climb up his length like quicksilver.

Attempting to scream as it entered him, all he could do was gag as it surged down his throat.

\*\*\*

He was dead, he knew, sensing nothing of the physical world around him and feeling bereft of the emotions that had once defined him.

'I think, therefore I am,' he reasoned, trying to make sense of what he now was.

Sightless and without feeling, he sent out his thoughts into the darkness of the void.

'Where am I?' he asked, finally sensing something other than himself.

'The grave,' came the earth's rumbling reply, although with a softer tone than it had before.

'Explain this to me?' he asked, mildly curious as to what this meant.

'You are in spirit, though still tied to your mortal shell, and for three days would you remain thus,' came the reply, sounding compassionate as it wrapped itself around him.

'Why am I not to remain?' he asked, feeling compelled to do so for some reason.

'You are... to ascend,' came the answer, the words appearing to be carefully chosen.

Time passed, an age or a second, and the spirit felt a pull towards the darkness.

'I will sleep,' he said, invoking alarm in the presence around him.

'Do you not wish to save them?' the voice asked, igniting emotion where none should be and causing images to flash through his mind.

His daughter... his son... and an overwhelming need to protect them.

'I do wish it,' he replied, quelling the sudden fear before thinking the problem through.

Calm once again, he scanned his consciousness but could find nothing that would aid him and again had to suppress the feeling of panic.

Desperately, he searched for the other's mind and found it waiting, seemingly ready to help.

Remembering what had occurred that had caused him to be here, he knew what he had to do to move on.

'We are one,' he said, accepting the elements into himself.

'We are one,' they rumbled together as he was lifted high into the sky.

'What are you?' another voice asked, continuing the creation in a more whispered tone.

'I am the earth, the land, and life itself,' he rumbled thunderously, feeling the power of the land within him now.

'You are Spirit,' came the caressing reply, wrapping itself about him as the earth had done. 'You are Air,' it continued, lifting him higher into a spinning vacuum.

Understanding flooded through him, knowledge that he was indeed more, or could be.

Next came the pain, unequivocal agony as his whole being was engulfed in flame. He burned then like nothing before and screamed in his agony, for there is no worse pain than to be burned in spirit, having every fibre of your being set alight by the purifying flames of ascension. Fire meant change, burning away the old to make way for the new.

'What are you?' hissed yet another voice, the words barely understood from within his torment.

Burning, he was unable to think and incapable of answering as the hissing element spoke again.

'What are you?' it asked, though now with a sense of urgency in his mind.

Instead of resisting the pain, Spirit tried to accept it, to become one with the element and the pain it represented. He attempted to live within the fire, to become the living flame that was intended. Without answering, for he could not, he found that he was thrust into the final element as though he were a sword being quenched within water, hardening him into what he was to become.

Aimless and without control, he welcomed the release from the pain and began to drift without direction in its aftermath. Not intended to undergo such change, the flickering light seemed about to go out, its glow diminishing rapidly before the final step could be made.

The elements quailed at his signs of departure and shouted aloud in their dire desperation.

'Do you not wish to save them?' they cried, causing the light to flash with renewed strength and to finally become what they had intended.

'I am Spirit,' he intoned before instinctively looking inward for what was no longer there. 'Have I always been so?' he asked, still searching for the elusive snowflake that he somehow knew had once been there.

Sensing the elements' happiness at what they had created, Spirit knew the reason for its creation and what it was they had done to him.

Taken from his mortal body, they had reshaped his spirit into something more. They had recreated him in their own image and in so doing, made him greater than he had previously been. The pain he had endured had been that of spirit burned into purity and then cooled within the quenching embrace of life.

No longer would the ages pass for the elements in darkness, for now, they would be able to appreciate every single moment of it and interact without fear of ever having to leave. That is what it had taken to be accepted by this world, the creation of this new life, physical or not, within this mortal realm.

The elements rejoiced at their accomplishment, ecstatic for the gift that they had bestowed upon him.

Yet this new being was troubled and felt that something was amiss, something not quite right.

'Be not vexed, brother,' came the soothing speech of water, concern emanating from its aura.

'Something is wrong,' Spirit replied, feeling somewhat incomplete in his current state of being and a desperate need to be something more.

'Be not troubled, for we are with you,' they spoke together, gathering to him in support.

Irritation stirred in him, and the feeling of being bound caused him to rebel.

'I feel trapped!' he cried, mentally shrugging them away before searching for a way out.

'You are Spirit and are free to do as you please,' they soothed, backing away so that he could see for himself.

'My memory lingers, reminded as I have been by you all!' Spirit replied, knowing that he had at one time been a man and had been cheated out of something precious by these seemingly caring elements.

Casting his senses out beyond the ethereal beings, he could feel the world of the living once again, sensing, too, the elements that these entities controlled. He knew that these physical elements were the embodiment of the beings around him and desperately wished the same for himself.

'Where then, is my body?' he asked, sensing immediately their reluctance to respond to this line of questioning.

'You are Spirit and are beyond such things. Send yourself out into the world and appreciate all there is to know,' they coaxed, backing away further to let him pass.

Sending out his awareness, he searched for what he knew was there, the memory of the battle and the death of his body still bright in his mind.

'This was me,' Spirit thought, studying the lifeless form with a feeling of loss.

The body was burned beyond recognition, and the light that had been within it appeared to have departed, the thread that had connected them forever broken.

The elements did not respond to his thoughts at first and seemed agitated by the lack of spiritual presence within their new creation.

'This is no longer you!' they replied finally, moving forward once more to drive him away from his previous body.

Anger flared in Spirit, and in rebellion, he forced himself into the broken shell, sending his vast intention into the decimated corpse, renewing its strength and healing its horrific wounds.

Crying out in anguish at being unable to link with the replenished body, he reluctantly withdrew, realising that he was now too vast for it to contain him.

'It is mortal flesh and can no longer house a being such as you,' the elements confirmed, saddened by the knowledge that these words would hurt him.

'No!' Spirit cried, enraged by what they had done to him.

Pausing as an idea formed in his mind, he gathered his newfound might and poured his power into his desire.

Gathering the essence from the healed body and that of the world around it, Spirit bound them by sheer force of will, merging them with the same fire that had enhanced him in spirit.

Sensing a trace of something unknown within the makeup of his old flesh, Spirit drew the quality forth and, on a whim, poured his might into it to make it stronger.

'Stop! You corrupt yourself!' the elements cried, but were ignored as he had been before his untimely death.

With a popping sensation, the great Spirit joined with his creation and opened his eyes with a start. Panting hard, he sat up to stare around the clearing with a look of wonder.

'I live!' he announced, feeling the breeze against his skin and loving the sensation of it.

Rising to his feet, he threw back his head and roared, the sound as alien to his ears as it was to the world around him.

The sun was on the rise, and he took the time to stare dreamily at the lightening sky above him.

'What?' he asked suddenly, frowning and shaking his head in confusion. *'What was I just thinking?'* he wondered, the memory of what had occurred having faded like a forgotten dream.

Closing his eyes, he let the dream go and rested his head back to enjoy the sun's warmth.

*'So strong!'* he thought, feeling more powerful than he had ever felt before. *'But more powerful than whom?'* he wondered, flexing his powerfully muscled arms experimentally.

A thought nagged at him, a memory forgotten, trying to break free from somewhere deep inside.

'Who am I?' he asked aloud, shaking his head before leaning forward to place his head within his hands. 'Remember!' he pleaded, but there was, of course, no reply, and so he looked inward, searching for anything that could help him find his way.

Thunder crashed above him, and he found that he could not think through its constant grumblings.

'Stop!' he growled, rocking himself back and forth. Silence descended on the glade immediately, and he felt his mind beginning to clear. 'Thank you,' he whispered, settling himself into his meditation.

'You have been corrupted,' the element of earth informed, breaking his concentration yet again.

'I live!' he snarled back, angered by the constant interruptions. 'A state of being that you would deny me?' he asked, feeling anger for the first time, or so he believed. 'Leave me,' he pleaded, speaking in a much softer tone this time before sensing the element respond.

Seeking his inner peace once again, he concentrated and searched the memories of his spirit.

Images flashed before his eyes, and he saw a sweet-faced little blonde girl and a dark-haired boy who looked a little younger. The images faded into a sinister-looking man with swept-back black hair, who stood over a castle's ramparts hurling lightning from his hands like some Greek god of war.

The scene shifted again into that of a fair-haired man, who crouched low in defence before him. The man's long hair was tied in a topknot, and he was clad entirely in black leather. Many knives of various lengths were strapped about his body, and he had a sense that this man had been a danger to him. Without warning, the man attacked, and their blades clashed with a flash of light, the warrior's black blade colliding against his own sword of red.

The vision rippled again into a tall, lithe young man with curly brown hair who stood smiling back, resembling a marble statue of some ancient king of old.

Sheathed at his hip was a large silver sword that seemed to glow mysteriously with a light of its own before he was joined by a jovial-looking man with the same dark brown hair, though cut a little shorter and without the curls. Stockily built, this other carried a similar sword, but instead of silver, it glowed with the colour of gold as he, too, smiled genuinely before making a goofy face that made the first man laugh.

Looking past the many images, he searched for something more and thought that maybe his emotions might unlock what he knew was within.

'Unlock,' he thought, suddenly seeing what he had stored away within his mind. 'Has this been locked away for good reason, or could I be opening Pandora's Box?' he mused, pursing his lips in thought.

Securely bound though it was, he could tell that it had been done so by his own hand and that the binding upon it was as much a part of him as anything could be.

'Touch it not,' the voices warned, voices that had seemed to be his own until recently.

Ignoring them, he focused on the box and gently probed at it with his mind.

'Remember!' it echoed back to him, and he felt an

overwhelming compulsion to unravel the mystery within.

He had put it there, he knew this, and could feel that it was a part of who he was, or rather who he was meant to be. A memory came thundering to the fore, and he reeled back from the force of it.

'Do you not wish to save them?' they had asked of him, these same voices that now warned him to stop.

'I do want to save them,' he whispered, seeing the children again in his mind.

Taking a deep breath, he closed his eyes in readiness before opening the box in his mind.

The instant enlightenment took his breath away, causing him to sit back before laying down in the grass. He was himself again, back from the dead, but as different as black was to white.

'Okay,' he finally whispered, feeling mightier than he remembered, invulnerable but with a feeling of completeness that he could not put into words.

The elements were close, he could sense them, but they made no further attempts to converse with him.

Raising his hand, he was about to give them a gesture they would not understand before freezing with inaction.

'Oh, balls!' he moaned, resting his head back in misery.

They were black now, not deeply tanned or painted but black, like a depthless void that swallowed the light.

Seemingly without definition of any kind, he held his hands over his face before shaking his head slowly.

*'Not even the sun can touch them!'* he realised, feeling the cold flush of dread drain his face of warmth.

Closing his eyes, he looked inward and quailed at what was missing and what had replaced it.

'No more snowflake,' he whispered, seeing instead a sphere of bright white light with arcs of energy crackling through it.

Opening his eyes again, he looked down the length of his body to see that the depthless black was not restricted to his hands alone.

Running his fingers through his hair which was as black as the rest of him, it felt somewhat thicker than it should have been as he swept it back to fall past his shoulders.

*'How long have I been here?'* he suddenly wondered, believing that it would take more than a year to grow his hair to this length before remembering with a jolt that this was not his old body but the new one he had created from it.

Sitting upon the damp, scorched earth, he visualised himself floating free and pictured how the clearing would look from that vantage point.

Seeing mostly energy from within the astral plane, he noted, as he always had, that everything looked subtly different from that of the physical world.

The trees had the same shape but were somehow different, glowing slightly from the energy within. The imperfections of the leaves caused by insects or the discolouration of the passing seasons were gone here, leaving only that which mattered, the energy of life itself. He saw that the dead leaves were barely visible here, showing only as faint shadows amid the light of life.

The familiar bluish hue appeared over everything, and he saw again that this world was crisp and clear, without the complications of mortality.

Turning to his new body, he saw immediately that it did not belong, looking like a black and white photograph superimposed over a colour one.

The blackness of what he was now stood out in stark contrast against the beauty of the living world, and his thick mane of hair hung wildly past his shoulders to give him a sinister and somewhat evil countenance.

Two luminous white eyes stared out from the blackness of what he was now, adding to the overall look of evil and making him look even more terrifying.

*'Except that I am not evil,'* he thought, at least not by his reckonings.

The definition of muscle in his arms and shoulders could be clearly seen, and there was a depth to his facial features that gave him some sort of description, though not lit by any light that he could see.

It was as though his features were outlined by something other than the light around him, as though the sun's rays were forbidden to him.

He felt its heat, of course, but the light either avoided him altogether or was absorbed upon contact.

The thought suddenly struck him that he looked like a man standing in the dead of night, draped in the light of some foreign moon.

*'Except that it's bloody daytime!'* he stressed, wondering at the reason behind it.

Upon seeing the thread of silver light connecting his astral form to the creature before him, he knew that, for better or worse, he was now bound to his new creation.

Relaxing his mind, he clicked back into his body and gave a little start as he breathed in deeply once again.

Turning to leave, he froze mid-motion as his unnaturally sharp eyes fixed upon the crumpled remains of his old body.

Moving to squat down beside it, he tentatively turned it over and moaned at seeing himself in death.

Studying the face, his face, he saw that it was young and full of character even after life had left it. Stroking the hair away from the ashen face, he flinched at the contact, and without knowing why, he wept for the loss of it.

Never again would he be the man he had been, for he could only move forward as he was, and the realisation brought him to his knees.

Standing up, he thought on what was best to do with his remains. Seeing it lay there naked filled him with remorse, and somewhere in the back of his mind, he realised that the clothes had been burned away during his fight with the elements.

Silently staring down at his old self, he noticed the twin silver rings that he had crafted so long ago.

Adorning each little finger, they glinted softly in the early morning light and looked identical but for the symbols set within them. Looking at each design in turn, he traced the intricate lines with his new eyes.

The first he had created was the pentagram, which signified the four elements with Spirit at its peak and, looking upon it now, he smiled tightly with a shake of his head.

*'How apt,'* he thought, thinking again of the elements and the question they had asked him.

*'What is the fifth element?'* he heard them ask.

'I am,' he answered aloud, believing that this is what he was now.

Removing the ring for himself, he placed it on the little finger of his left hand. It was too tight at first, but the enchantment upon it reshaped the metal quickly so that it slid on after only a momentary pause.

Lowering his gaze to the second ring, he could see the snowflake design clearly, a symbol that signified the purity within, bringing together a person's mind and body into seamless harmony, perfecting the one who wore it.

Infusing the rings with the same magickal protection, he had designed each to react to all manner of threats against its wearer and work independently once triggered into action, giving them both a little of himself to that end.

The finesse had been in binding the rings to the power of the earth so that they became a conduit between the wielder and the land itself. The result was an inexhaustible supply of power that continuously fed both the offensive and defensive magicking of its wearer with a mirror of his mind placed within to govern it.

*'Unless you are fighting the elements themselves!'* he thought darkly, looking back to the pentagram design before placing it against his lips.

He had created this ring first to unlock his full potential and allow his subconscious mind to come to the fore, resulting in lightning-fast reflexes and a razor-sharp mind. Sighing softly, he frowned at seeing the silver ring shine from the blackness of his hand – the gold pentagram insert almost glowing as it caught the light of the sun.

Leaving the snowflake ring where it was, he placed his large black hand upon the chest of his old body and visualised it turning to a more natural colour, bringing the essence of his old flesh into the pentagram ring before binding it there.

Standing once more, he looked down and felt a pang of guilt at what he had done, staring now at the blackened husk that lay shrivelled at his feet.

'Forgive me,' he whispered, feeling that his old body deserved better somehow.

Binding the ring to himself, he willed the essence of humanity into his flesh and, in silence, watched the depthless black gave way to more natural tones as the colour spread up his arm.

Letting out a slow breath of relief, he saw his hand appear human again and chuckled to himself nervously.

'Dark indeed,' he whispered, shaking his head and wondering at what had caused this taint in him.

Walking a short distance through the trees, he came upon a river that twisted through a deep ravine. Jumping down, he stood at the water's edge and peered at his reflection.

Knowing that to pass as human, he would need to look with his physical eyes, he had sought out the river to do just that.

'Thank you!' he gasped in relief, taking in the fleshy tones and dark brown hair that now looked as it used to.

The face that stared back at him was indeed his own, though looked much younger and somehow harder than it had.

Having always had a 'cheeky' face, especially when smiling, he found his reflection had no such character and looked to be far more unyielding.

Smiling humourlessly at the shimmering image, he shrugged in a way that looked recognisable to him.

'It's still my face, though,' he reassured himself before rising to scan his surroundings.

Marvelling at the strength of his new vision, he stared at objects and seemed to draw them nearer the harder he focused, making him feel like he was moving through the trees.

Relaxing once again, he turned in the direction of his house and, without much effort, made his way home.

# CHAPTER FOUR

The building was one of many that sat in the heart of London and outwardly blended in with the corporate businesses surrounding it. However, this structure was not what it seemed, for hidden away on the uppermost levels was the most secretive branch of the human establishment.

The one function of this agency was to protect against any threat of a magickal origin, but more specifically to monitor the vampire factions. Here, mankind made a stand against those who would threaten them. Here, was the head office of the wizard faction.

Only the very highest levels of the human government ever knew of its existence, with those few knowing only that those inside were the single defence against total annihilation by the true power in the world... the vampires themselves.

Realising that neither one could truly survive without the other, magickal factions and humans worked together to hold back the dark tide that would swiftly wipe them from existence given the opportunity.

Stepping from the lift, the man's footsteps could be heard echoing down the marble corridor that led to the restricted section of the building until he came upon a set of wide frosted glass doors that stood tall before him, giving the man an impression of great wealth and unequivocal power.

To either side of these impressive-looking doors, two impossibly large men stood with a predatory look in their fiercely bright eyes.

The guards were massively built, as you would expect from those in their profession, and had a presence about them that screamed of danger, unnerving all who came into contact with them.

Clearly not there for decoration, these men were the protectors of those beyond and took to the role as though their very lives depended on it.

On closer inspection, the guards looked rather peculiar with their longer-than-normal bodies and shorter, more powerfully built legs. Above their long flat stomachs, each had huge, oddly shaped chests that protruded sharply, giving them a somewhat top-heavy appearance.

The man thought that they could have been brothers but for the colour of their eyes, for each was distinctive in their own way, setting them apart as fire was to ice.

The tallest of the two had dazzling light blue eyes that seemed a little too bright as they locked onto the visitor and reflected the light like those of a cat.

The second guard, however, had eyes of what looked like gold, marking him the more unusual despite the hulking mass beside him. Both had dark brown hair, shaved short at the back and sides, giving them the look of fighters, as if their other attributes were not proof enough.

As the heavy-footed man came into sight of them, he unconsciously held his breath under their scrutiny before coming to an abrupt halt when they made no move to let him pass.

Smiling nervously up at the pair, the heavy-footed man stated his business, as was customary when visiting those inside.

'I am here to see the High Wizard,' he announced cockily, his voice sharp, his pronunciation perfect.

Regarding him in silence, the guards narrowed their eyes at him as the smaller of the two sniffed at the air with a look of disdain.

*'Why do I always feel like I'm about to get eaten?'* the visitor thought, just as the golden-eyed guard took a step towards him.

Stopping a little too close for comfort, the shorter guard towered over the visitor by more than a foot.

Feeling a fearful shiver run up his spine at the close proximity, the man decided not to speak as the guard walked around him, sniffing continuously as he did so.

Letting out his breath slowly when the inspection ceased, he waited expectantly for the doors to open.

Stepping back to the door, the guard smiled wide, causing the visitor's eyes to widen in alarm.

'Good god!' he baulked, seeing that the expression was altogether too wide, stretching literally from one ear to the other and showing large, pointed fangs that had no right to be in the mouth of a man at all.

'What do you think, Gav? Should we let him in?' the shorter guard asked, his golden eyes never leaving those of the visitor.

'I don't know, Vince,' Gavin replied, looking down at the visitor without expression. 'I just don't know,' he sighed, shaking his head as though pondering the matter.

Stepping forward again, Vince stood even closer than he had before and would have been nose to nose with the man but for the height difference between them.

Looking down his nose, Vince glared at the man, his fierce golden eyes widening threateningly.

'Name?' he barked, the violence in his voice making the man jump.

'I beg your pardon?' he replied, shocked by the question and at the way it was delivered.

'Your name?' Vince growled, making the man visibly jump again and take a step back.

'You already know my name! It's Anthony!' the man squeaked, his voice high and full of terror.

'Anthony,' Vince repeated slowly, shaking his head with a sigh of what sounded like disappointment.

Flushing red, Anthony remained silent, fearing to provoke these animals further and turn the situation into a far worse one.

'Ask him why he wants to see the High Wizard, Vince,' Gavin sighed, sounding rather bored from behind.

Anthony's eyes flickered to the giant briefly before returning to Vince.

'Why do you want to see the High Wizard, *Ant?*' Vince asked, sounding like he was calling him an insect rather than by name.

Anthony quaked and looked at Gavin again with pleading eyes before slowly returning his gaze to Vince.

'Don't ignore me, *Ant,*' Vince advised softly, tutting and shaking his head in warning. 'That would make me angry, and you wouldn't like me when I'm angry, *Ant,*' he continued, a whisper of a smile tugging at his lips.

At that, Gavin threw back his head and burst out laughing.

'You absolute tool,' he bellowed, holding his stomach as he

creased into hysterics.

Unimpressed, Anthony once again looked from one to the other and back again in astonishment.

*'They're playing with me!'* he thought haughtily, feeling his heart pounding in his chest.

Stepping back to his post, Vince made a grand gesture with his arm and bade him enter with a jerk of his head, smiling that wide 'raptor smile' of his as the door opened before him.

Walking briskly through the entrance, Anthony caught a shared look of amusement between the two alien-looking guards and felt his blood begin to boil.

*'Animals!'* he thought darkly, though kept the thought from influencing his face.

Entering the secure area, he observed once again that the entire area looked to be at odds with itself, appearing to be a cross between a twelfth-century castle and a multi-million-pound corporation boardroom.

Slim-line computer monitors lined up along the outer walls, while at the centre of the large area stood an ancient-looking wooden table with strange magickal symbols carved all along its sides.

Sat around it, hooded men of various sizes sat one man per symbol, all with heads bowed in quiet contemplation.

Seeing that the men's robes were of different colours, Anthony had assumed on his previous visits that it must have something to do with discipline or status among them.

At the rear of this large, chamber-like office stood an impressive hearth with a roaring fire blazing from within, casting unsettling shadows past those who knelt before it.

Looking at the three lightly-robed figures, he thought them to be in a trance of some kind, noting the way they stared as though hypnotised by the dancing flames.

Coming to a stop just inside the doors, he brushed himself down and used the time to compose himself after his ordeal in the hallway. Smoothing down his blazer with his hands, he mentally cast the memory of the sadistic guards from himself.

After completing the ritual, he looked down upon his expensive suit and smiled. He put a lot of stock in how a person dressed, believing that a man's attire was what made him something more than what he was.

His suit was an expensive pale blue modern brand with a bright white shirt underneath, the cut away collar carefully chosen, as was the trend with these highflying officials. His necktie was of the same shade of blue as the suit, matched also to that of his shoelaces, completing his attire with careful consideration.

'My lord,' he called out nasally, causing many hooded heads to jerk in his direction.

At the centre of the table sat a black-robed figure, hooded like the rest and one of the few to ignore his loud interruption.

Very much used to such treatment from these high and mighty wizards, Anthony cleared his throat loudly and clapped his hands in the pretence of warming them.

The black-hooded head snapped up angrily at this, and Anthony was sure that he saw a twinkle of light from the wizard's eyes as he studied the source of the disturbance.

Glaring from under his hood at the rude intruder, the High Wizard straightened and shook his head after recognising the white hair spiked up rather peculiarly on one side of the man who stood before him.

'Anthony,' he finally acknowledged, sounding rather lazy as his deep voice echoed around the large open area. 'What is it?' he asked, speaking in the same bored manner.

Patience in regard to these government officials was not his strong suit, and he did little to disguise this fact when conversing with them.

Stiffening at the tone, Anthony spoke quickly and a little too loud, which caused many more wizards to glare in his direction.

'I have come to inform you that the Bloods are on the move and are gathering in force towards the southern region of Wales,' he announced in his clipped tone of voice, for the dislike the wizard felt towards him was more than mutual. 'What draws them to this particular area is unclear at this time, but there have been more than fifty tracked so far in groups of three. We believe…'

Shooting him a withering glare that was now clearly seen from within the shadows of his cowl, the High Wizard silenced his report abruptly.

'Three means a choosing. They send that many to complete the task should things get... complicated,' he cut in, looking back at the fire briefly or, rather, at the wizards who knelt there. 'We have sensed a rising power in the west, but its location has since been hidden from us. It seems the vampires have felt this disturbance too and have chosen to go in blindly, as is their way,' he continued, rising suddenly from his seat. 'Why have they sent so many?' he mused before glaring back at the man. 'Have you intelligence on this?' he asked, hating that he had to rely on the humans in this way.

Smiling to himself, Anthony knew that the vampires could not be sensed by the 'all-powerful' wizards, for they were unnatural to the world and therefore, unseen. So it was left to science and technology to track these deadly creatures, relying on pitiful humans like himself to get the job done.

'They were seen entering a forest in the southwest of the country but have yet to come out again, as far as we can tell,' he replied, waiting for the wizard's reaction.

'And?' the High Wizard snapped, causing his antagonist to smile a little.

'We have scanned the area, and they are gone. We sent in scouts, but they somehow got turned around in there and came out empty-handed,' he replied, pausing again, but not long enough to anger the wizard further. For he was not so stupid as to incur the wrath of a wizard, let alone the head of their order. 'There is a house that backs onto the other side of the forest, and it is the only dwelling for miles around,' he continued, smoothing his hair rather awkwardly with the palm of his hand. 'We can't seem to get to it, though. A most peculiar thing to be sure. We seem to get lost whenever we attempt to approach the area. All the roads we take seem to miss the turning, and it's the same when we try by air. We know it's there because it shows up on... Google,' he finished sheepishly, feeling even more embarrassed than he had before and shrugging his helplessness on the matter.

Shaking his head, the wizard sighed before looking up to the heavens.

'So you've been subtle, is that what you mean to say?' he asked, his tone portraying his boredom again. 'We have significant power in Wales,' he continued before suddenly barking an order. 'Contact Richard!' his deep voice boomed, causing the official to jump in fright. 'Thank you, Anthony,' he added, looking back at the table.

Ignoring the dismissive tone, Anthony had one more piece of information that would agitate the wizard.

'There is one vampire from the other faction also in the area, but he has yet to make a move on the property,' he announced, a curl of dislike creasing the corner of his mouth.

Ignoring him completely, the High Wizard turned to those who sat at the table, and they all stood at once, causing the official to take an involuntary step back.

Watching them standing there with their hands touching those strange symbols, he shivered and felt goosebumps rise on his flesh. They creeped him out, these wizards, standing there, looking at each other in silence.

With a shake of his head, he slowly backed from the room, retrieving a handkerchief from his suit pocket as he did so.

'Bloody arrogant...' he began, dabbing at his brow, but immediately regretted it as two sets of predatory eyes turn slowly in his direction.

Without further ado, he turned and began power walking back the way he had come, the sound of his footsteps echoing once again upon the smooth surface of the marble corridor.

*\*\**

Walking to the sofa, Kristina sipped at her steaming mug of tea before seating herself to stare into the flames of the fire.

Always the early riser, she liked the solitude and peacefulness in these predawn hours before the children woke up. Cupping her hands around the hot brew, she enjoyed its warmth as it seeped into her hands.

'Mmm,' she breathed, taking a sip as the hot liquid steamed past her eyes.

Yawning, she felt exhausted and silently berated herself for staying up so late after getting carried away reading the histories of a world she knew not to have existed.

*Dark,'* she thought again, still unable to accept that the man she had known was this legendary monster.

She had believed, in her fanciful way, that he would have been a hero figure and not this ancient devil he was portrayed to be. All references to him were warnings, describing him as a creature and not as a man at all. She found it fascinating that the Bloods had feared him more than any other and that when he had eventually fallen in battle, there had been much rejoicing by all. He had been depicted as a thing apart from all others and killed without discrimination – wizards, vampires, all of them! He was chaos, deadly and unstoppable.

*The Dark Wolf* the books called him – the hunter of souls – and there was not one mention of him being anything else.

She had sought hard to find something redeeming about the man she believed she had known, but the stories of his exploits only got darker in the telling until she had put the book down in depression.

Glancing at the candles on the table, she waved her hand before them with a whispered word of command.

*'Ignium,'* she said, causing all seven candles to flicker into life. *'Suffocatur,'* she continued, causing the flames to die with an acrid smell of melted wax that touched her nose as a whiff of smoke curled up to the ceiling.

Taking a deep breath, she craned her neck towards the doorway to call her children from their sleep before stopping mid-motion.

For standing there was a wild-eyed young man that just did not look right to her somehow.

Scowling at her, he put a finger to his lips to keep the scream in her throat before entering the room.

'Very Harry Potter,' he whispered, indicating the candles with a sideways tilt of his head.

'Daire?' she gasped, her breath rushing from her in surprise.

Staring at him in open-mouthed shock, she could barely believe her eyes as he moved up alongside her. Gone was the middle-aged man with the grey at his temples, for the man who stood before her now was barely recognisable. All she could do was blink at him slowly, shaking her head at how this could be.

This was a man in his mid to late twenties, broad-shouldered and narrow-hipped in a way only youth could provide.

*'Where the hell has his stomach gone?'* she wondered frantically, looking up at him in bewilderment.

Corded muscles like that of a gymnast flexed powerfully when he moved to the opposite sofa, and she noticed with increasing alarm that he appeared to glide rather than walk in his usual way.

Looking beyond her initial shock, she saw that he looked out of place somehow, as though he did not belong, and as if to prove the point, she could feel the hairs on her neck rising at his close proximity.

Caught by his movements again, she saw him almost float to the sofa, and it occurred to her then that he was holding himself back as though he were far quicker than he was letting on. He was struggling, she could see, struggling to perform the simple act of moving in a way that looked normal to her.

Seeing him smile as he settled into place, she saw that it, too, was a pretence as he raised a hand to forestall the expected outburst.

'Please?' he asked, not wishing to answer the many questions she no doubt had.

So she just stared at him, shaking her head with a mixture of concern and horror written on her face.

*'His voice is deeper,'* she observed, unable to take her eyes from him. 'What have you done to yourself, Daire?' she asked, ignoring his request completely.

'I told you I would be changed,' he sighed, seeing that he would have to explain at least a part of what had happened during the night. 'I have set things in motion that should guarantee your safety,' he continued, trying to smile again.

Tears suddenly welled in her eyes, the knowledge that it was she who had forced this change upon him weighing heavily upon her mind.

'Oh, Daire, what have you done to yourself?' she cried, seeing that he was struggling with some inner turmoil.

'It is more... what was done to me,' he confessed, trying to sound reassuring but failing in the attempt.

Rising from her seat to sit beside him, she reached out to comfort him before something inside warned against it.

'Are you still... you?' she asked in a petrified whisper, looking fearfully up at his face.

Turning to the fire, he remembered what it was to burn before flinching away.

Seeing him turn back to her, she backed away from the reflected flames that still danced in his eyes as though trapped there.

Staring at her silently, the flames began to fade as he shook his head slowly.

'I died out there, Kris,' he whispered, gesturing back towards the forest with his head.

'Oh my god!' she wept, hearing a deep rumble in his voice that sounded more like distant thunder than anything living.

'But my priorities have not changed,' he announced, his face set in determination.

Fighting for control over the instinct to flee, she forced herself to look back into his eyes which were dark once again.

'You're scaring me,' she whispered, forcing herself to hold his unnatural gaze.

'That is not my intent,' he rumbled, sounding even deeper than it had before.

'Daire, you can't let the children see you like this!' she stressed before grimacing, clearly expecting some backlash from her hurtful but needed words.

'I've changed myself already!' he defended, looking at her doubtfully before raising his hands out for her to inspect. 'See?' he asked, looking at her with concern.

Regaining her confidence, she grimaced again and shook her head before shrugging in apology.

'You look like no one I have ever seen!' she whispered, still shaking her head to enforce her statement. 'You look... creepy,' she added and shrugged again, unable to find a better word of description.

Raising his eyebrows at the insult, he stared at her for a moment before frowning at the implication.

'Creepy,' he repeated, his mouth forming a pout that caused her to smile despite herself.

'Okay, not creepy, but you do look frightening, Daire!' she amended, squinting her eyes in further apology.

Sitting back, he closed his eyes and frowned in frustration.

'Find me a mirror will you, please?' he asked, becoming statue-like in an instant with all signs of life leaving him.

'Jesus!' she whispered, thinking now that he looked like a corpse, just sitting there, unmoving as he was.

Getting up quickly, she walked to her bag on the kitchen table and returned with a makeup mirror in hand.

'You haven't got a smaller one, have you?' he asked sarcastically, eyeing the compact mirror with a grimace.

Her raised eyebrows caused him to sigh, and he took the mirror before leaning forward to inspect himself. Scowling, he saw that his human appearance had held and that it was his eyes that she must be referring to. Looking at them now, he saw that they shone with an unearthly light that hinted at what was hidden underneath.

Closing his eyes, he snarled suddenly in frustration before her startled cry caused him to open them again.

'Are those bloody fangs?' she gasped, causing him to instantly bite down upon his lips.

'No,' he replied gummily, looking at her incredulously for a moment before he sighed and turned back to the mirror. 'Balls!' he whispered, seeing that his canines were twice the size they should have been. 'Now, why and for what purpose would they need to be that length?' he asked, looking back at her in alarm.

'You said that you've changed yourself already… from what exactly?' she asked, staring at him nervously.

'Trust me when I tell you that you don't want to know,' he replied, avoiding her eyes.

Rising quickly to her feet, she stared down at him sternly.

'You look like something that is trying to look human,' she accused, still struggling to find the right words of description. 'What have you done to yourself, Daire?' she demanded again, putting her hands on her hips in her usual manner.

Looking at him for the longest of moments as he, in turn, studied her, she patiently waited for his answer before he shook his head in exasperation.

'It is more *what* was done to me, as I have already said,' he finally answered, avoiding the question as he rose to his feet.

Yelping in surprise, she jumped at the suddenness of movements.

'What?' he snapped, startled himself by her reaction, but she just stood there with eyes widened in fear.

'You moved too fast, Daire, like… vampire fast,' she answered, a look of comprehension dawning upon her face.

Screwing up his face, Daire rolled his eyes at the suggestion before looking up to the heavens to give him strength.

'I'm not a bloody vampire!' he stressed, his mouth setting into an exaggerated look of disgust. 'I may not know what I am, but I'm definitely no bloody *vampire!*' he continued, shaking his head at the ridiculous idea.

'Then what are you, Daire?' she demanded in a hoarse whisper, involuntarily looking up in fear of waking the children.

'I have no clue, but I intend to find out,' he assured, pursing his lips as he pondered the problem.

Noting her hands placed back upon her hips, he sighed expectantly at what was to come.

'Away from here?' she asked, raising her eyebrows.

Looking back coldly, he shook his head with a look of disgust.

'Yes, Kris, away from here,' he answered, walking away still shaking his head.

Entering the kitchen, he called back, determined to leave things on a positive note.

'Seeing that you have some "Granger" skills now, I have some homework for you!' he said, turning back as she followed on his heels. 'What do you know of water?' he asked, catching her completely by surprise.

Thinking for a moment, she finally shrugged her ignorance on the matter.

'You drink it?' she replied sarcastically, shrugging again at the ridiculous question.

Ignoring her tone, he stared out through the kitchen window and sounded lost in thought as he dreamily replied, *'Clear I am, but white at my core. Pure I must be, for you to endure. New you will be, if you find a way to fix me,'* he paused then, feeling the weight of having to leave again so soon.

Though having moved out a month or so before, he had

returned often and rarely stayed away for long. The longest he had stayed away was for a week. He had not intended to, but it had taken time to weave his protection around the house.

Francesca had roasted him on his return, making him promise never to leave her for that length of time again. But this new body worried him, and so did the anger he felt bubbling just beneath the surface. So he would leave again until he could get a handle on it. He had to leave, and he had to do it soon.

'Solve this while I'm gone, and you'll *really* impress me. Study everything you can about water and, more importantly, how you can manipulate it,' he challenged, staring out of the window but seeing only his children in his mind.

Looking at him as though he were mad, she spread her arms irritably.

'Did you just make that up on the spot?' she asked, clearly wanting him to leave before the children woke up. 'Why should I bother?' she asked, placing her hands at her hips again.

Rounding on her with a scowl, he read the desire in her eyes and felt anger bubble up within him.

'Don't, then!' he snarled, but turned his back on her just as quickly to stare into the forest.

Heavy footsteps came thumping down the stairs and he looked back at her sharply before closing his eyes.

Drawing again from his essence within the ring, he enhanced it with his will and a spoken word of power.

'*Cuddliw,*' he whispered, casting an illusion upon himself that would add to the lie.

Speaking the binding in the ancient tongue, he knew he could take no chances in regard to his children.

Opening his eyes at the sound of Kristina's gasp, he looked at her with an arched eyebrow before smiling wickedly.

'Oh my god!' she exclaimed, seeing him appear as he had the night before.

Bringing his middle and index fingers to his temple, he whispered to her mysteriously.

'*Unagi,*' he announced in a wizened tone before turning to his children as they came running into view.

Lowering himself to his knees, he wrapped his arms around them and growled like a lion, causing them to squeal in hysterics.

Finally letting them go, he saw a frown cross Francesca's face and knew she could sense something.

'You're going again, aren't you?' she asked, looking up at him sadly.

Pulling her back into his embrace, he held her tightly before kissing the top of her head.

'I have to work away for a while, but I will be back as soon as I can,' he answered, trying to keep his emotions under control. 'I will always come back to you. To both of you!' he stressed, looking at his son fondly. 'Nothing will keep me from you for long,' he promised, but being younger, Lucian did not understand or feel the way his sister did and seemed fine with him leaving again so soon.

Standing up, he looked at Kristina and smiled with little warmth.

'Okay, well, I guess I'd better be off,' he sighed, causing an awkward silence between them.

'Okay, bye then, Dair… Dark,' she amended, folding her arms crossly over her chest.

Scowling at her, he felt his anger rise again and took a deep breath to control it.

'Daire is my name, my true name. I did not lie to you, not ever! Dark Wolf was merely a name I acquired from those who feared me,' he replied, his eyes flashing as her ungratefulness ate into him. 'A name that I must be known by again,' he added, feeling the bile inside threaten to consume him.

'Dark?' Lucian echoed, looking at him quizzically.

'I am Daddy to you!' he growled, causing the boy to laugh before skipping out of reach.

Latching onto the name, he began bidding him farewell with a mischievous look in his eyes.

'Bye, Dark. Goodbye, Dark,' he chimed with a bow and curtsy as though in the presence of royalty.

Forcing a smile, Daire stepped away to bow theatrically with a flourishing sweep of his arm.

'Goodbye, Daddy,' Francesca murmured, only now seemingly to notice the change in him as she cocked her head to the side. 'You look different,' she noted, squinting at him as though seeing past his illusion.

Smiling at her nervously, he shook his head proudly at the gift she must possess.

'Good different?' he asked, giving a little twirl in front of her.

Looking concerned suddenly, she ignored his attempt at joviality.

'Are you okay, Daddy?' she asked, looking up at him with those deep blue eyes.

*'How much do you see?'* he wondered, his forced smile beginning to falter at the corners of his mouth. 'I'm fine, baby girl,' he assured, stroking her cheek tenderly with his thumb.

Looking unconvinced, she moved in to hug him again.

After opening the back door, he walked towards the waiting forest, turning often to wave his goodbyes. At the tree line, he stopped one last time, but the window stood empty, and he saw that his children had been distracted by something their mother was doing.

*'Bitch!'* he seethed, hating her for not allowing him this one simple pleasure.

Checking himself, he knew that something had changed in him and began to fear that it was not only his body that had changed but also his mind.

'Corrupted,' he whispered, knowing that he had to fix himself or be lost forever.

Though feeling worried for him, Kristina knew that the days of him fully opening up to her were a long way in the past. Sighing to herself, she started to prepare breakfast, feeling a little lightheaded and more than a little giddy.

*'It's finally happening! Just me and the kids,'* she thought as her excitement began to build.

Though she knew that he would eventually get to grips with what was happening to him, she had the distinct feeling that it was going to be some time before he would see her again.

Thinking of how much he was changed, she felt more than a little concerned about what he had hidden from her, believing that he was acting like himself instead of just being who he truly was.

*'Why did he leave the back way?'* she wondered, but a moment

later, she shrugged, telling herself that it would all be okay in the end. 'Everything will be fine,' she whispered, smiling to herself as she continued with her chores.

# CHAPTER FIVE

The dreary weather was enough to dampen the spirits of all who lived in the mountainous regions of Wales, for it always seemed overcast once the summer sun had set. It felt like the clouds had come the moment autumn had arrived, and it had only got colder when winter settled in, hanging over the region like a cold, wet sheet.

Almost lost within a low-hanging cloud, a farmhouse stood alone upon the mountainside, tall and white against the lush green that surrounded it.

Though not to everyone's taste, the location was perfectly suited to the one who lived here, a place of much-needed peace and meditation.

Staring out of the large front window, David had felt them coming for quite some time before finally seeing a car driving up the winding country lanes.

Sensing immediately that something was amiss, he had the feeling that the vehicle itself heralded some future doom for him.

'Are you going to tell me what's going on?' Gail asked from the sofa, clearly fed up with him glowering out of the large front window for most of the morning.

'They're coming,' he answered, frustration putting an edge to his voice.

'Oh, good god, Dave! Just tell them that you're done with them!' she moaned, never once looking away from the wall-mounted flat-screen.

He had been approached by the faction many times to consult on certain matters, for he was considered one of if not the most powerful wizards in the Western world but this time, he knew that something was different.

Huffing out an exaggerated sigh of annoyance, he walked to the cloakroom to put on his blue 'wizard's coat', as he called it. Long and flowing, it gave him a more wizened look, or so he liked to think.

Eyeing himself in the full-length mirror, he pulled up the deep hood, covering his short, dark hair to leave a stern face staring back at him.

'That'll do, Pig,' he approved, putting on his best Hoggett impersonation before stepping outside.

The black Bentley entered the courtyard at a speed before turning in a wide arc so that it could set off again without reversing.

Noting the blacked-out windows, David knew instantly what manner of creature was driving the vehicle and immediately felt his heart begin to race.

The back door opened suddenly, and a slightly-built man stepped out, his hand adjusting his thick-lensed glasses as he did so.

'David,' the man greeted, speaking in a soft, almost hushed tone of voice.

'Richard!' David gasped, clearly not expecting this welcome stranger. 'This must be good if they've sent you to me,' he reasoned, shaking his friend's outstretched hand.

'You could say that, mate. Can we talk?' he asked, blowing hot air into his hands to warm them against the chill.

Studying his friend momentarily, David gauged the seriousness of his expression and finally realised that this was going to be *very good* indeed.

'Yeah, come on in... alone if you don't mind. Gail is in the house, and I don't want them frightening her,' he said, eyeing the tinted front windows of the car dubiously.

'Of course, David. Of course,' Richard replied smoothly, gesturing for him to lead the way. 'In your office, if you don't mind? This is not for her ears,' he said, following his friend.

Taking his guest straight through to the rear of the house, they sat themselves down in his back office. The room was large, with the outer wall comprised entirely of glass which gave an astonishing view of the valley below, causing Richard to take a moment to appreciate it.

'I do miss this,' he sighed, his eyes wide as he drank in the scenery. 'You never know how much until you see it like this. It's the one thing about the city I hate,' he continued after a momentary pause.

Looking at him patiently, David was forced to observe the niceties before delving into the business at hand.

'It's why I came home,' he replied indulgently, giving just a hint of his reluctance to return to the faction after his retirement. 'Why are you here, Richard?' he asked, considering that he had adhered to the rules of hospitality for long enough.

Letting out a 'whoosh' of exhaustion, Richard took the seat opposite his old friend and leant back into it before speaking.

'We need you to look into something,' he began softly, raising his hands in defence before he was automatically refused outright. 'Hear me out, please?' he asked, seeing the wizard's mouth opening in protest. 'You don't have to leave the country, or even travel very far, for that matter,' he continued, smiling as the other's eyebrows rose in interest.

Staring at his friend, Richard gauged his reaction as he spoke.

'You see, there's a house about an hour's drive from here and, putting it bluntly, we can't seem to get to it, and we do need to get to it, Dave!' he stressed, finishing with a serious scowl.

Grimacing with disbelief, David gave a look that suggested he needed a little more to go on.

'What do you mean, you can't seem to get to it?' he asked, interested at last.

Smiling with a little embarrassment, Richard lowered his tone conspiringly.

'Exactly that! We can't get to it. We can't drive to it, fly to it or even walk to it,' he shrugged, spreading his arms in bewilderment. 'All we know for sure is it's there and that great power resides in it. Bit ridiculous really, if you ask me,' he continued, eyeing his friend suspiciously.

Pondering the problem for a long moment, David looked lost in thought as he threw the idea around in his mind.

'Why would you want to go there? What put you onto the house in the first place?' he asked, noticing at last that he was being read by his friend.

Shrugging again, Richard relaxed his features into a more friendly expression.

'The Scries have sensed a new power there, two to be exact, and the power they project is mind-blowing, apparently,' he replied, unable to keep his eyes from narrowing.

Leaning back in his leather-bound chair, David looked deep in thought before bolting upright.

'Where is this house?' he demanded, his voice high and shrill.

Taken aback, Richard leant back in surprise and adjusted his glasses self-consciously.

'Why, David? What's there?' he asked, recomposing himself immediately.

Glowering at him, the muscles of David's face began twitching nervously as he leant further forward.

'Answer me, damn you!' he growled, clenching his fists to stop them from shaking.

Slowly leaning forward to meet him, Richard studied his old friend intensely.

'I think you know exactly where it is, my friend!' he replied, causing David to check himself.

Forcing a smile but knowing that it looked false upon his face, David took a moment to collect himself.

'How would I know that?' he replied, opening his top drawer as he did so. 'I'm just excited to be off looking for it,' he continued, focusing now on the contents within as he shoved things aside with impatience.

Being a field agent, for want of a better term, and a wizard himself of no small standing, Richard knew absolutely that his friend was lying. He was an enforcer of the faction laws and 'remover' of those that broke them, for despite his frail appearance, Richard was one of the most dangerous wizards that David had ever met, and that was saying something.

Sitting forward, Richard placed his thumb and forefinger at either side of his chin as he studied his friend with a cold, calculative expression.

'I have known you for far too long to believe that crap!' he replied evenly, staring deep into his friend's eyes.

The silence between them grew, and Richard slowly shook his head with a look of betrayal.

'Is this your magick at work, your power that stops us from finding it? If so, I would very much like to know how it was done,' he said, raising an eyebrow in begrudged admiration.

'This is beyond me, I'm afraid,' David replied robotically, in total control of his emotions at last. 'I'll check it out though, if you want,' he continued in a lighter and more carefree manner.

Arching an eyebrow, Richard breathed in deeply before smiling in apology.

'Don't worry about it, mate. I should not have bothered you with this nonsense. I will go there directly with my friends out there,' he said, nodding his head in the direction of the car.

Staring blankly as his guest began to rise, David knew he was being manipulated but still felt he could not take the chance.

'Sit down!' he commanded, causing Richard to blanch from the power behind the words.

'Why?' he gasped, seemingly forced back into his chair by the will of the other.

As if growing in stature, the power within David radiated forth in waves of impossible might, and Richard felt every bone-jarring ounce of it.

'Because you will die if you do,' David answered, towering over the other with terrifying menace.

Opening his mouth to speak, Richard found that he had not the words, so closed it again. With his eyes unfocused, he masterfully masked his alarm at seeing the awesome power leaking from his friend and wondered what it would have taken to hide such a thing from him for all these years.

'The house... is Dark's,' David announced, causing his friend's eyes to widen.

'*The* Dark?' Richard blurted, his owlish expression fixed upon David's face. '*The...* Dark?' he asked again, causing David to respond irritably.

'Yes! *The* Dark!' he snapped before they simply stared at one another, both knowing that neither would lie about such a thing.

'The *actual* Dark?' Richard began again, causing David to lean back in his chair and put his fingers to his temples.

'Gilga's balls!' he exclaimed, rolling his eyes in frustration. 'This reaction of yours is why I haven't told you before now,' he stressed tiredly and began digging around in the drawer again.

At last, he pulled out what he had been looking for and opened up the packet. With a flick of his thumb, he inhaled a lungful of smoke and held it there for a moment before blowing it back out with a satisfied sigh.

Seeing his friend rise to pace the room, David rolled his eyes again and shook his head even more tiredly.

'How long have you known about all this?' Richard asked, wringing his hands together anxiously.

Closing his eyes, David took another long drag on the cigarette before responding.

'Does it matter?' he countered, breathing out the smoke through his nose, feeling tired suddenly from the weight of so many secrets.

'Answer the damned question! How long?' Richard demanded, still pacing before the wall of glass.

Sighing in resignation, David opened his eyes again and looked at his friend sombrely.

'Since the beginning, Richard. Since the very beginning,' he answered, smiling at the reaction.

Richard's mouth flew open, the owlish expression back upon his face.

'The beginning? I assume you mean that literally? How old are you, Dave? If that even is your real name?' he asked, staring unblinkingly at the seated wizard.

David smiled ruefully at that but was not willing to give up all his secrets just yet.

'It's one of them,' he replied dismissively, then looked at his friend with a more serious expression. 'Look, mate, I like you, I really do, and I only tell you this so you don't go off getting yourself killed. Some of us were here at the start of this world, or this version of it. I am such a one. Dark is another. There are many more, as you probably know. You've read the histories and should know who and what he is. Dark will not hesitate, not for a second, and absolutely will not stop until you are dead if he perceives you a threat,' he continued, remembering the legendary figure. 'He tends to overreact and will kill you like *that!*' he said, snapping his fingers for emphasis.

Looking at his friend in a new light, Richard wondered if he had ever truly known the man at all.

'How could you be friends with him? I can't believe this!' he stressed, his voice rising uncharacteristically high. 'The Wolf, for Christ's sake!' he blurted, taking off his glasses to wipe them.

Stifling a laugh, David was amused at his friend's choice of words.

'Christ?' he repeated, finding humour in the religious outburst.

Richard, however, would not be deterred.

'It's a turn of phrase, David, and there might actually be something to it anyway. Not the last Christ! I refer to the one before,' he replied, and then waved off the distraction for what it was. 'How is he alive? Is he planning to attack? Are we safe?'

Holding up his hands for peace, David tried to calm his friend's clear show of hysteria.

'Stop with the frantic chatter!' he growled, annoyed by the multitude of questions. 'Whom I choose to befriend is my concern and mine alone. I am not in his circle, nor he in mine, but when needed, we are there for each other,' he continued, looking at the man sternly.

Richard's face flushed, his normally controlled manner now lost to the winds.

'You just described friendship!' he blurted, his eyes now as wide as they could go.

'I haven't seen him in more than a year. Now, shut up!' David snapped as his friend sat back down haughtily, mouthing the words, 'A year!'

Ignoring him, David lit another cigarette before breathing in more of its contents.

'I'll contact him and see what's what. I suggest you put "the powers that be" off his scent or, I'm sure you'll agree, they will regret it.'

Richard's face paled at that, knowing well the reputation of the legend long thought dead.

The silence grew between them until Richard finally broke it.

'How is it that you have lived for so long? I am in my three hundredth year and probably won't see much of my fourth. How, David?' he pleaded quietly, seeking the knowledge as all others did.

Regarding his friend with a sad expression, David sighed regrettably.

'It was Dark's knowledge that allowed me to live on. Apart

from that, I cannot say,' he replied, feeling a pang of guilt for withholding the secret. 'I have sworn a life-oath to him, Richard. I'm truly sorry,' he continued, smiling apologetically.

Deflated by the knowledge forbidden him, Richard understood that life-oaths were not to be taken lightly.

'I thought I knew all there was to know about this world,' he admitted, shaking his head in disbelief.

'This is just the tip of the iceberg, mate. The very tip. Now, leave it to me. I don't want this getting any bigger than it already is,' he replied, taking another long drag of his cigarette.

Nodding his head, Richard collected himself at last.

'What shall I say to the High Wizard?' he asked, causing David's eyes to grow a little colder.

'Tell Kreig that I'll check it out,' he answered, knowing only too well that his friend would report every sordid detail.

***

The weeks that followed were wonderful for Kristina, the threat from the vampires fading with the passing of time.

She had slotted into their new routine with blissful ease, for she loved it being just her and the children and wished dreamily that it had always been so.

The only thing to spoil it, however, was her daughter's continuous line of questioning as to when her father would return and the reason he had left in the first place.

'*She'll get used to it,*' she told herself, having become quite proficient at putting the problem from her mind. '*If he stays away!*' she thought drearily, knowing that it was only a matter of time before he came back into their lives.

Reading up on water, she was intent on discovering its secret before his eventual return, but there was just so very little to read on the subject, and what she had read was clearly of no use to her. Water, it seemed, had no discernible power of its own, at least, not that she could determine.

'*What the hell does he want me to find?*' she stressed, feeling a little out of her depth if truth be known.

Having exhausted the internet, she had only learned of its physical makeup and that it was in all living things, but she had known that already.

Switching tact, she had watched a documentary explaining that water contained memory blocks, and was intrigued to find that positive or negative thoughts could influence it. She learned that the cells of the purest water appeared remarkably like snowflakes whereas dirty water looked more like faeces.

Stopping dead in her tracks at this line of thinking, she rethought the problem, and it was not long before an idea began to form in her mind.

'Dirty water looks like a turd,' she whispered excitedly, her mind racing at the prospect.

Changing tact yet again, she experimented with how to manipulate the element, finding that she could boil, freeze and move it with her magick but could think of nothing else to do with it.

'*Bugger,*' she thought, frustrated beyond belief at missing what he wanted her to find. 'What is so special about water?' she asked aloud, closing her eyes before starting again from the beginning. '*Back to basics,*' she decided, pondering the puzzle anew. '*What is made of water? What is water in?*' she wondered, throwing the question around. 'Cucumbers!' she whispered, her eyes widening fiercely as the thought expanded. '*A cucumber is mostly water!*' she thought, smiling triumphantly. 'Humans are mostly made of water!' she said, her mind exploding with excitement. 'So, we need to manipulate the water in ourselves somehow?' she mused, standing up abruptly and walking to the bottom of the stairs. 'Cesca! Lucian! Come on, we are going shopping!' she called, smiling at the sound of stampeding feet.

'Can we buy sweets?' Francesca asked, eyes wide with hope.

*** 

Staring at the cucumbers that she had bought, Kristina had picked the two before her for very different reasons. The first was soft, blackened and looked well out of date. The second one, however, was fresh, firm, and glistening a luscious dark green as though picked that very morning.

Closing her eyes, she focused her mind on the fresh-looking fruit and sought the image of its general makeup in her mind.

'Snowflakes!' she breathed, finding them easily enough after knowing what to look for.

Turning to the rotting one, she closed her eyes to concentrate again, finding gloopy, brown and nearly lifeless particles that caused her excitement to build to fever pitch.

Opening her eyes, she smiled grudgingly with a shake of her head.

*'How did he even think to do this?'* she thought, impressed despite herself.

Returning her attention to the rotting cucumber, she closed her eyes and sought out the gloop again. Seeing it within her mind, she pictured it changing back into what it had been, but every time she felt like she was succeeding, another 'gloopy turd' took its place.

Opening her eyes again, she felt disheartened by her failure and leant back in defeat.

*'Bugger!'* she pouted, frowning down at the still-rotting cucumber. 'One cell at a time isn't going to do it,' she realised, and on closing her eyes again, she summoned the image to her mind, picturing it as a whole this time.

Snowflake after snowflake, she cast at it, picturing a snowstorm in her mind that drove into the rot, turning it white as much as she could.

'Mammy?'

Kristina's eyes flickered open before looking down at her son.

'Yes, what is it?' she snapped, instantly regretting it. 'What is it?' she amended in a softer tone before smiling rather sheepishly.

'Can I have one of those, please?' he asked, pointing at the two fresh cucumbers.

Frowning back at the fruit, she smiled and clapped her hands excitedly. Though not as fresh as the first, the cucumber appeared much healthier than it had just a moment ago.

'So that's how it's done,' she thought, feeling very pleased with herself.

Walking to the sink, she pulled a knife from the drawer underneath and sliced up the fresher cucumber before giving him the plate, narrowing her eyes at him as she did so.

'Share them with Cesca,' she ordered, smiling at the

expression on his face.

Ignoring her completely, he walked back with his eyes firmly fixed on the prize.

Turning back to her experiment, she sent out her awareness to find that though it no longer looked gloopy, it was still no snowflake.

Standing back, she leant over the kitchen worktop and frowned at it in concentration.

*'I'm trying to do this like he would!'* she thought, feeling a desire to do it her own way.

Having read many of the books of magick, she had discovered that not all were written in his hand. His library was extensive, and though his own books appeared to be the more powerful, she had felt more of an affinity within the books of witchcraft. They seemed more romantic to her somehow, and she secretly longed to be a part of something greater than herself.

Closing her eyes, she threw words around in her head in the way she had read that witches do.

*'Snowflake, snowflake, alight in my head, renew this cucumber that once was dead,'* she whispered, casting the spell.

Feeling it building in strength, she pictured every facet of the snowflake in her mind, bringing the image to life out of the decay.

After she felt the spell fade, she tentatively sent her awareness out again and immediately sensed what she had been waiting for. Breathing out nervously, she opened her eyes to be greeted by a perfectly fresh cucumber.

Reaching out, she picked it up and smiled, feeling its hardness between her fingers.

'Yes!' she cried, bringing her hands to her mouth and sighing happily.

\*\*\*

After putting the children to bed, it had become a routine of Kristina's to secure the house at night, feeling more paranoid and somewhat less safe now that it was just the three of them. And so it was with some surprise that when she looked up from her book, she felt the chill of goosebumps and a sensation of dread washing up through her.

Shrinking back into the sofa, she froze and held her breath as a wraithlike figure materialised in the darkened hallway. Unable to move, all she could do was watch as the image shifted into something more real.

'Good god, Daire, you frightened the hell out of me!' she admonished, her heart hammering fearfully in her chest.

Looking as though he was about to reply, he seemed to pause to correct what he was on the cusp of saying.

'Indeed,' he finally replied, keeping himself draped in the shadows.

*'How did he get in undetected?'* she wondered, having cast several protective spells about the house.

'I know what you've been doing,' he accused, still concealed within the darkness. 'You think I wouldn't smell a witch in my own house?' he asked, his voice rumbling low from his chest. 'I gave you the knowledge to exceed them, and yet you still choose to become one,' he growled, staring at her with eyes that reflected the light.

Shrinking back from him with her eyes filled with terror, she fumbled at the book in her lap as it tumbled to the floor.

Seeing her reaction, the reflective eyes narrowed, and she felt the power in them like a slap to her face.

'Why do you look at me like that?' he asked, stepping finally into the light with a disapproving shake of his head. 'You do what you want,' he sighed, looking at her as though she were mad. 'You're limiting yourself, you know that, right?' he asked before his expression turned darker. 'Have I ever hurt you?' he demanded, the question catching her off guard.

'No, of course not!' she answered, colour flushing into her cheeks.

'Then stop looking at me as though I have!' he roared, stalking to the opposite sofa before seating himself there.

Relieved to see that he now looked more human, though he had definitely not the moment before, she still desperately fought the urge to run.

As if reading her mind, he continued in his accusatory tone.

'I can't help how I look or how I make you feel!' he growled, looking so alone in that moment.

Guilt flushed through her, and she rose to put her hands on his shoulders but felt her fear spike before she could do so. Flinching, she tried to steel herself against the urge to back away, but it felt like she was about to stroke a rabid dog or something far worse.

Sensing her reaction, he pulled away, and she hated herself for it.

'I'm sorry, Daire. I just wasn't expecting you to feel so... wrong,' she confessed, looking at him sadly. 'Just tell me what's wrong, and maybe I can help?' she asked, feeling ashamed by her reaction.

Watching as he shook his head, she was surprised to see tears in his eyes.

'You can't help me, and I'm running out of time! I don't know what to do,' he whispered, sounding so lost as he sat there cloaked in defeat.

Seeing the previously hidden panic emanating from him, she felt helpless, not knowing what to do or say.

*'What could frighten him like this?'* she thought, wondering for the first time if he could indeed recover from whatever it was that ailed him. *'Please, just leave!'* her mind screamed, silently wishing that he would leave them to their tranquillity.

'I will leave soon enough,' he growled, speaking as though he had heard her thoughts aloud. 'I feel that there are two of me, but that the real me is fading away... and you had best hope that doesn't happen!' he hissed before putting his face into his hands.

The spike of fear she felt then almost made her cry out, for she had caught a glimpse of what he was speaking of when he had watched her from the hallway.

'What happened to you?' she asked, feeling the need to know more than anything else. But he shook his head and rose to his feet. 'Tell me!' she cried, reaching out to hold him back. 'I know it has something to do with the land,' she said, nodding her understanding. 'I've seen the change in it,' she whispered, taking his hand in hers and squeezing it pleadingly. 'I can't help if you don't let me,' she stressed, desperately trying to mask her fear.

'I've told you already!' he growled, his human facade slipping again. 'I died! I went there, and I died!' he hissed, the whites of his eyes beginning to brighten far beyond what was deemed normal.

Instinctively stepping away, she stood aghast as he fought for control over himself.

With her eyes unfocused, she sought his aura and instantly regretted it, for what had initially been a vibrant light blue was rapidly darkening into something far more sinister. Involuntarily putting a hand to her mouth, she backed away in horror.

Seeing the fire once again mirror in his eyes, she watched in dread as the flesh of his face began to have a darker cast like that of his aura.

Something changed in him then, like a switch being pulled, and the feeling of danger receded as the darkness was somehow locked away. He was himself again, the old Daire, confident and definitely human.

*'It's like he's just turned the bloody light on!'* she thought, feeling her dread switch off at the same instant.

'We must prepare them for the inevitable,' he said, his deep, thunderous voice still present. But after checking himself again, he continued in a more normal tone. 'Okay, Kris?' he asked, arching an eyebrow at her.

Staring at him for a long moment, she knew that she had only glimpsed a fraction of what he was now.

'Will you be back?' she whispered, secretly wishing that he would not.

'I don't think so,' he answered, shaking his head.

Staring at each other, they let the ramifications of that sink in before he continued once again.

'I have protected them as best I can and will continue to do so until...' he paused, letting the rest go unsaid.

After lifting his head as though listening to something, he rose abruptly to walk into the kitchen.

Looking at the cucumber, which still sat on the counter, he nodded in satisfaction before glancing over his shoulder as she followed from behind.

'Impressive, most impressive, but you're not a Jedi yet,' he commented wryly, speaking as though without a care in the world.

Rolling her eyes without humour, she ignored his casual attempt at levity.

'Please, talk to me! What's happening to you? You're like Jekyll and bloody Hyde, for god's sake!' she cried, spreading her arms in exasperation.

Staring back at the worktop and the magick she had achieved, he ignored her plea completely.

'You've worked it out, I see. I really am quite impressed,' he remarked, speaking as though she had not spoken at all.

Looking at him blankly, she finally shrugged dejectedly before resigning herself to the fact that he was now closed off to her.

'Okay,' she conceded, shaking her head and following his gaze.

Narrowing his eyes in thought, he stared at it for a moment longer before turning back to face her.

'Why haven't you tried doing it on yourself?' he asked offhandedly, as though he were discussing the weather or something equally as trivial.

'I'm not sure how, or even if I want to,' she admitted, shrugging noncommittally.

Turning to her seriously, he stared at her for a moment before nodding knowingly.

'And you didn't want to cock it up?' he asked, arching an eyebrow at her.

Shrugging again, she smiled half-heartedly for him to continue.

Lifting one hand to tap his temple with his index finger, Daire placed his other hand upon his chest.

'Turn your mind inward and look at yourself as you did the fruit,' he advised, seeking to give her one last gift of knowledge.

Pulling a face at his word of description, she rolled her eyes again before setting him straight.

'It's a vegetable,' she corrected, looking pointedly at the cucumber.

Frowning at her, he shook his head slowly.

'It hangs from a plant and has seeds. It's a fruit!' he argued, sounding a little irritated by her interruption. 'The point is you look at yourself in the same way. Don't be afraid of what you see because it will not be too different from the *vegetable*,' he continued sarcastically, grimacing at the same time. 'Then change what you see to the snowflake. Simple enough? You won't get it perfect, but the closer you get it, the younger you'll be,' he continued, narrowing his eyes at her.

Looking thoughtful for a moment, her attention finally slipped from what was happening to him.

'So if I overdo it, I could...'

Smiling at the suggestion, he finally saw the reason she was reluctant to experiment.

'You will shrink into a baby,' he answered before chuckling at her wide-eyed expression. 'You dope! You will just bring your body into its peak condition and then some. You will never get the snowflake perfect because you are continually ageing, but you can get it damn close,' he continued, smiling in amusement.

Nodding with a determined expression on her face, she made herself a promise there and then.

*'I'll prove you wrong on this one. I'll get my perfect snowflake,'* she thought, and as if reading her mind again, he answered.

'We shall see,' he said, smiling again at her reaction.

A frown suddenly crossed her features, and her hands moved unconsciously to her hips.

'How did you know?' she asked, squinting at him suspiciously. 'How did you know that I did it with a cucumber?' she clarified before blushing profusely at his look of disgust.

'The things that come out of your mouth, woman!' he chastised, shaking his head in mock disapproval.

'You know what I mean!' she laughed in embarrassment and found that she had missed his banter.

Seeing his smile again, she found that one expression conveyed more to her that he was the man he had always been than countless promises to the contrary.

'I need to get some rest,' he said after a moment, letting the humour die between them. 'I've missed my bed,' he continued, heading out into the hallway.

'Oh, goodnight,' she replied, taken completely off guard by his sudden departure.

'Goodnight, Kris,' he whispered back, and it was only after

he had gone that she realised her question had gone unanswered.

\*\*\*

Being in the children's presence forestalled the change in Daire, keeping him calm and more himself than not. They centred him somehow, and he began to fear ever leaving them again but knew that it was only a matter of time before he would succumb to the darkness within him.

Never leaving the children's side, he took to instructing them on how to defend themselves with the use of magick.

Various toys littered the grass, causing him to scowl at the children after having told them repeatedly to tidy up after themselves. With a grand sweep of his arm, all the toys gathered up and organised themselves into orderly lines off to the side.

Not one to normally use magick in such a way, his intention was to get them excited and eager to master the art.

'Wow,' Francesca whispered, having never before witnessed her father performing magick.

Smiling at her mischievously, he winked before becoming more serious.

'Have you learned how to create a shield?' he asked, looking at his daughter, but her flushed face told him before her tongue ever could.

Shaking his head when she was about to speak, he raised his hand to cut off her excuses.

'Visualise a sphere of energy all around you, a ball of light that will stop anything that might hurt you. Can you do that?' he asked, folding his arms across his chest. *Just like her mother!'* he thought, annoyed that she had not followed his instruction.

Frowning, Lucian looked doubtfully up at his father.

'What is a sveer, Daddy?' he asked, his eyes wide and innocent.

About to answer, Daire was cut off by his daughter as she tried to make up for not learning the shield trick first.

'Pretend that you are inside a ball, Luc. Like you're inside a bubble,' she amended, smiling encouragingly.

Nodding his understanding, Lucian acted as though he had known all along.

'A really tough bubble,' he replied sagely with a purse of his lips, drawing a chuckle from his father in the process.

'Yes, Luc, really tough. Now you have to visualise it. The key to the best magick is how good you are at visualisation,' he paused, seeing once again the vacant expression and quickly correcting himself. 'You have to *pretend* it's there, really strongly, so you can see it. Can you do that? Pretend you can see it?' he asked, winking at his son confidently.

Both children nodded, and he was pleased to see that their eyes had that familiar unfocused look to them.

'Now pretend that under the grass there is a network of energy that you can pull up into your feet, through your legs and into your body,' he continued and then paused, his own vision unfocused to see the energy of the land flowing into them.

The bright light of the land infused their bodies, giving them a glow of their own.

'Good,' he approved, impressed with how much of the earth's might they could summon. 'Now, send the energy into your bubble and make it harder than anything. Nothing can break it, nothing can get past it,' he continued, seeing that their shields had now turned a bright white. 'Okay, excellent!' he congratulated, sighing in relief.

Seeing his daughter literally bask in the praise, he had to stifle another chuckle before he lost his focus.

'Now, let the bubble be and leave it at the back of your mind, like a memory. You will feel if it gets weaker, and if it does?' he asked, arching an eyebrow questioningly.

'Feed it more earth-power?' Francesca asked, hoping desperately that she was right.

'Correct!' Daire replied, clapping his hands together in time with a deafening peal of thunder overhead.

Staring at him in open-mouthed awe, they both knew without a doubt that he had caused the amazing feat.

'How did you do that?' Francesca gasped in amazement, looking from him to the sky again.

'Magick!' he whispered, smiling mysteriously.

Drilling them late into the evening, he focused them on the art of defence until they could both raise their shields in an instant, summoning greater defences than the most powerful of today's wizards.

Seeing how tired they were getting, he considered calling it a day before Francesca changed his mind with one simple question.

'Daddy?' she asked, waiting until he looked at her before continuing. 'What if someone breaks through my shield?' she asked innocently, little knowing that the question awakened his greatest fear.

'Then you shoot lightning at them,' he answered, deciding there and then to show them one of the most dangerous methods of attack.

Widening his eyes at the mere mention of offensive magick, Lucian began jumping up and down in excitement.

Frowning at him, Daire had many reservations about the dangers involved, but the need to protect them came first and foremost.

'If I find out that you have used this magick on each other, I will go absolutely berserk on you. Do you understand?' he asked, looking from one to the other as they nodded in excitement, which did nothing to alleviate his concerns.

'Do you understand? You never, *ever* use magick on each other! It's only for bad people. Do you understand?' he stressed, looking at each in turn.

Seeing the smiles fade, Daire saw them turn to each other and nod their agreement.

'Yes, Daddy,' they answered in unison, shaking hands to cement the promise.

Satisfied that his first point had been made, he continued onto another.

'Secondly, unlike the shield, you must first draw power from the earth before unleashing your attack. You must channel the earth's energy through you and never do otherwise. To do so will kill you because you will use your own life's energy in the attack and kill yourself in the attempt. Do you understand?' he shouted, sounding like a drill instructor to make his point felt.

'Yes, Daddy,' they echoed immediately, their faces set seriously.

'Okay,' he replied, pursing his lips as he stared at them.

Sighing sadly that it had come to this, he took a deep, composing breath and prayed silently that what he was about to show them was the right thing to do.

The darkness in him was growing just beneath the surface, and the time to leave was now upon him. Believing that he would be gone for some time, if not indefinitely, he knew that they would need to know this kind of magick if they were to survive.

'Okay, connect with the earth,' he ordered, sensing the immediate pull on the land.

With his sight unfocused again, he nodded, satisfied that both had done as he had asked.

'Now, it's visualisation time again,' he said, raising his eyebrows at his son, who nodded back seriously before awaiting the next set of instructions.

*'I will not get this wrong,'* Lucian thought, determination masking his features and keeping his young mind sharp.

Closing his eyes to better sense the magick at work, Daire shifted his awareness more towards his daughter.

'One at a time,' he said, focusing on Francesca. 'Cesca, visualise the power rising into you as before,' he advised and scowled, sensing Lucian also reacting to his words.

Opening his eyes, Daire glared at his son and folded his arms in irritation.

'Not you, Lucian! Only Francesca!' he growled, feeling the draw from the land extinguish immediately. 'Listen to what I say!' he said sternly, frowning at his son in disappointment.

'Sorry, Daddy,' Lucian replied, looking at the floor and shuffling his feet.

Walking over to him, Daire leant down and kissed the top of his head. 'I want you to be able to protect yourself when I'm gone,' he whispered, roughing up the boy's hair.

'I'll listen, Daddy,' Lucian promised, nodding his head to see the words home.

Nodding back after winking at his son, Daire walked back to where he had been and motioned for them to keep some distance between them.

'A little more,' he advised, shooing them apart with his hands. 'Actually, come and stand by me, Luc,' he added, feeling a little overprotective.

About to start again, he saw that Francesca had maintained her link with the earth and nodded his approval, pleased with her strength of will.

'*Good control,*' he thought, feeling a little more positive about the lesson. 'Okay, Cesca,' he said, looking meaningfully at his son, who folded his arms and raised his chin in response.

Fighting the urge to laugh, Daire had to force himself to look away.

'Hold up your hand, Cesca, and spread your fingers a little,' he began, pausing to take a nervous breath.

Doing as she was bid, Francesca frowned in concentration and held onto his every word.

'Now, visualise the magick leaving you a little and picture it just between your fingers,' he coaxed, his voice soft and gentle.

Francesca's eyes widened as the energy began crackling between her fingers, and she had to bite her lip to stop from screaming with joy.

The magick leaked from her like electrical currents that arced between her outstretched fingers and crackled loudly with unspent energy. As her confidence grew, so too did the power in her hands, and they began to glow ever brighter.

Flashes sparked here and there as the magick begged for release, causing her to look up expectantly.

Looking around the garden, Daire searched for a target to aim at, but after seeing nothing that wouldn't give him grief later on, he cast a shield around the woodshed before pointing at it quickly.

'Visualise!' he commanded, indicating the structure with his pointed finger. 'See the lightning strike the shed and keep it flowing,' he instructed, nodding for her to try.

Thrusting her arms out, she released the magick in a blinding arc of light that flashed across the garden. The lightning left her hands in a steady stream of unyielding light and clashed violently against his protective shield, causing it to turn white immediately.

'Control the flow,' he coached, sensing the magick weakening a little. 'The magick comes from the land. The more you can summon, the more powerful your attack,' he said, raising his voice above the crackling din.

Summoning all she could from the land, she caused the magick to intensify suddenly and the white shield split, issuing a loud cracking noise that caused her brother to jump in fright.

Surprised, Daire began talking her down, clearly not expecting the barrier to falter so quickly.

'Okay, ease off and bring it back to your fingers,' he advised, seeing her react immediately to his words.

The magickal attack reversed instantly to crackle once again between her fingers and, without further need of guidance, retreated from whence it came.

'Did you see that?' she screamed, looking from one to the other. 'Did you see that?' she repeated, her excitement taking over.

'Awesome, baby girl,' Daire replied, laughing at her show of emotion before sweeping his arm forward for his son to take the stage. 'Your turn, Little Wolf,' he said, winking at him reassuringly.

Standing to face the woodshed, Lucian spread his legs wide in readiness and breathed in slowly before letting it out slower still.

Reminded of a young 'Mr Miyagi', Daire smiled and almost laughed out loud at his comical little boy.

'I need you to listen to my every word. Okay, Luc?' he said, more nervously this time.

Nodding but saying nothing, Lucian's focus remained fixed upon his target.

'Summon up the magick, just a little now, and then let it ease out to your fingers. Like Cesca did,' he coaxed, anticipating something different this time around.

A few seconds passed, and Lucian's brow furrowed in frustration.

'Pretend the magick is rising from the ground into your feet, travelling up into your body and into your arms,' Daire coached, sensing the flow of energy travelling as he said so. 'Now it's in your fingers. Keep it there for a moment and then let it out slowly,' he continued, reaching out to his side and positioning his daughter behind him.

There was a crackling sound, louder than before, and then the magick could be seen lighting up between his fingers before travelling back up towards his forearms. Looking less attractive than that of his sister's, this magick also looked more dangerous as it flashed up towards his elbows.

Taken aback by the sheer might of it, Daire knew instantly that it was more powerful than what any of the ancients could summon, and definitely greater than his own.

Eyes wide with exhilaration, the bright sparks of unleashed magick reflected brightly in the boy's unwavering stare.

'Keep drawing from the earth and then pretend that it leaves your hands to hit the shed,' Daire coached, narrowing his eyes at the expected result.

The lightning that struck the shield was unnerving, and though it lacked the grace of his sister's strike, this lightning was far more destructive.

Looking more like a beam of raw energy, the lightning hit the newly formed shield with an explosion of light and sound. Within seconds the first crack appeared, splintering right up the middle, and a moment later, it failed completely, breaking apart as though in slow motion.

Before his father could react, one side of the woodshed was ripped away, sending shards of wood blasting into the forest.

'Whoa! Whoa! Whoa! Nice shootin', Tex!' Daire shouted, catching Lucian's eye. 'Okay, bring it under control,' he called, nodding at him confidently.

With a slight grimace at having to stop so soon, Lucian cut the power and the lightning blinked out, seemingly without the need to draw it back slowly, simply turning off the magick as though from many years of experience.

Unable to speak, Lucian simply stood with his trademark open-mouthed smile upon his face.

'Wow!' Francesca whispered in an awed tone of voice, peeping out from behind her father.

Daire was flabbergasted, staring at his son with barely concealed elation.

'Bloody hell!' he gasped, shaking his head in wonder. 'That

was pure bloody brilliance!' he erupted, before rushing forward to hug his son.

Glancing at Francesca, he smiled and shook his head.

'Both of you did brilliantly,' he said, knowing how competitive his daughter was.

Rising to his feet, he placed his hands upon their shoulders.

'Now listen to me, both of you! If you use this on each other in temper, you will kill one another. You know that, right?' he asked, looking at them both worriedly.

The children looked at each other and then back to him before the first of them responded.

'I would never do that to Cesca!' Lucian replied, looking briefly back at the shed.

'Nor me! We do love each other, you know?' Francesca admonished, frowning up in disapproval.

'Only for bad people,' her father replied sternly, looking from one to the other. 'Okay?'

Smiling, the children nodded before Lucian suddenly looked ready to drop from exhaustion.

'I'm tired,' he mumbled, stumbling into his father, who picked him up immediately.

'Come on then, let's go inside, I'll fix the shed later,' he replied, scooping up his daughter before a pout could begin. 'Didn't think I would forget about you, did you?' he roared, pulling them into a fierce hug. 'I love you,' he whispered, holding them as close as he could.

'I love you too, Daddy,' they replied together, cuddling him a little tighter.

'I have to go away tonight,' he whispered, feeling Francesca stiffen in response. 'I have to go, baby, but I'll be back, I promise,' he swore, kissing her on the temple.

Pushing herself back from his chest so that she could see his face more clearly, she looked him right in the eye.

'Why, though?' she whined, her face looking desperate.

'Because I need to fix myself,' he replied, and then pleaded with her in his mind, *Please understand!* Her eyes were wide as they searched his own, but there was an understanding there that he had not expected. *You see it, don't you?* he thought, wondering what else she could see.

'When will you be back?' she asked with a pained expression on her face.

Swallowing hard and fighting back tears, Daire looked at her and fought down the emotion.

'I don't know, baby, but I will come back, and when I do, I will never leave you again!' he promised, nodding his head to cement his oath.

Finally, she settled her head against his chest once more. She had already known there was something wrong with her father and had known it for quite some time. She did not know what it was exactly, just knew that there was something different about him and that he was trying hard to hide it from her.

'Can I help you, Daddy?' Lucian asked sleepily, causing tears to finally brim in his father's eyes.

'I think you will help me, Little Wolf. I think you both will,' he replied, crying silently as he carried his sleeping children back into the house.

*\*\*\**

With the sun's descent and the gathering of night, Daire could feel his own darkness rising, as it had every night since his corruption.

It was past eleven when Kristina finally returned home from visiting her friend, creeping silently into the house like some wayward teenager.

Holding the door's latch so that it didn't give the normally loud 'click', she eased it back slowly and walked as softly as she could, heel first, into the living room.

Stopping abruptly in the doorway, she spied him sitting there in the darkness, watching her failed attempts at stealth.

'You have a rare gift indeed,' he remarked sarcastically, shaking his head at her noisy approach. 'I've told you a million times to walk on the balls of your feet if you wish to move silently. They call it *tiptoeing* for a reason,' he added, laughing darkly to himself.

'Oh, shut up!' she replied, taking off her coat and settling down with a glass of wine in her hand.

Gesturing towards the unlit fire, she pictured it roaring to life an instant before it did so, illuminating the room with its warm light.

Smiling confidently at having done so without the need for speech, she looked at him with her elation fading after seeing that the change was upon him again.

'*Vampire!*' her mind screamed, but she forced the panic down, not wishing to provoke him again.

'Maybe you should do that thing you do,' she remarked, speaking in a tight voice. 'You've got that look in your eye again,' she added, taking a large gulp of wine.

'I have tried,' he replied, his voice sounding deep and thunderous as it always did when he was like this.

Forcing herself to look at him, uncertainty masked her features for what this might mean.

'So, what now?' she asked nervously, taking another mouthful of wine.

Looking back to the fire, he took a slow, deep breath and let it out with a rumble.

'It means that my time is up,' he answered, sensing her relief as it washed through her.

'*Thank god!*' she thought, wishing to be rid of him at last.

Seeing her reaction, his head snapped up, and the reflective eyes grew round in anger.

'You think that you are safe now, after my sacrifice?' he asked, causing her to flinch at his tone. 'You think that because none have come, none will?' he asked, hissing the words through his teeth. 'Many have come, more than you know! The forest is teeming with them!' he seethed, struggling to control the anger inside, 'And if not for me, they would be here already,' he hissed, hating her in that dreadful moment.

He saw her there, self-centred and thinking only of herself.

'*Ungrateful witch!*' he thought, his eyes burning with the reflected flames of the fire.

Seeing her petrified expression, he grew silent again, though still looked at her dispassionately.

'The protection holds,' he said awkwardly, trying to sound reassuring but failing in the attempt.

A silence lingered between them for a moment, each caught up in their own private thoughts until Daire sighed and shook his head.

'Keep out of the forest,' he warned after a time, waiting for her to acknowledge his concern before continuing.

Nodding but saying nothing, she kept her eyes on the burning logs so as not to look upon his face.

'How's Jan?' he asked, causing the colour to drain from her face. 'Do you think for one second that I don't know what's going on?' he asked, shaking his head in disappointment. 'Haven't you learned anything, Kris? Have you no respect?' he hissed.

Sensing the illusion of humanity slipping from him, she saw the shadows gather when she finally glanced his way.

The light of the fire seemed not to touch him now, and only his reflective eyes could be seen within the darkness. She was glad that the lights were off and that she could not see the nightmare that began to take form just a couple of feet away from her.

Swallowing hard against her fear, she felt a sudden flush of anger at his condescending tone.

'What I do with my time, with my life for that matter, is my business and no longer yours. Don't judge me, Daire!' she replied, throwing the words at him challengingly and glaring into the darkness where he had been.

He regarded her silently, and it was some time before he finally replied.

'You are right, of course,' he whispered, speaking the words in a measured tone, the thunder in his voice sounding a little farther away. 'You can do whatever you like,' he answered with an unseen dismissive gesture of his hand. 'But I warn you now,' he continued, his voice straining against the growl that threatened to erupt. 'Keep my children out of it,' he stressed, the threat in his tone unmistakable. 'The protection is for you all, not just the children,' he said, his sudden admission surprising her. 'You will be safe here, I think, when they eventually break through my protection. When that day comes, you must stay within these walls, for I have charged the house to protect you,' he said, looking at her from within the shadows. 'Things will hopefully be different if I return,' he continued, seeing her eyes flash at that.

'What do you mean, different?' she asked, peering unseeingly in his direction.

Narrowing his eyes with intolerance, he wondered what more this woman could want from him.

'You must know that they will come at some point. They will all come, and if you think differently then you're deluding yourself. They will come, and you have to be ready,' he warned, looking at her incredulously, realising that she had shrugged off the threat as she had with all his concerns. 'You honestly haven't thought about this, have you?' he asked, shaking his head in frustration. 'They are in the forest at this very moment, and would be here already if not for my protection!' The thunder in his voice caused the fire to splutter.

Jumping to her feet, she put her hands on her hips.

'I'm thinking of bringing them into a witches' coven,' she confessed haughtily, trying to be upfront with her intentions.

'Absolutely not,' he thundered, the very walls beginning to shake in his anger. 'My children will not be bound to a bloody cult and limited to one line of thought. They will be free of all such things and will never be ruled or used by another. They will be free, as I am free. Not one of the factions will have them,' he promised, his voice growling out the words with a glint of fanged teeth flashing in the darkness.

The house groaned around them as though straining against something unseen, causing Kristina to look about wildly.

'I will die before I allow you to do this and will kill to prevent it,' he warned, hissing the threat in a dreadful whisper.

Cowering from the violence in his voice, Kristina knew absolutely that he meant every word of what he was saying and began to see what all the history books spoke of.

Taking a deep, calming breath, Daire fought the urge to smite her on the spot but knew the act would leave the children all alone.

'Let's not part like this,' he said finally, putting his head into his hands.

She looked at where he had been, seeing nothing of him now, not even his eyes.

'Please don't take them away from me,' she pleaded in a weak voice that shook heavily with emotion.

His features softened at that, though she could not see it as he shook his head in the darkness.

'Don't you know me, woman?' he asked, closing his eyes in pain.

When he rose from the shadows, she was relieved to see human arms pull her to him in one final embrace.

'That will never happen, Kris. You will all be leaving together,' he promised, sounding like himself again. 'Believe me, when the time comes, and the wolves are at the door, you will be only too glad to leave this place,' he intoned, speaking the words in a prophetic tone of voice. 'I need to leave now,' he whispered, his eyes starting to glint reflectively again.

Striding to the doorway, he turned suddenly to look at her. 'Goodbye, Kris. And please...' he begged, waiting for her to look at him, 'Keep them safe!' he stressed, opening the double doors that led to the garden and the forest beyond.

She stood there, unable to respond, and silently watched him dissolve into the night.

*'Is this really happening?'* she thought, and after reseating herself slowly, she wept.

# CHAPTER SIX

The wind came howling through the trees, bending the branches and nearly snapping them. Sheet lightning lit up the dark sky with a soundless flash that illuminated everything in an instant.

*'Wake up!'* a voice screamed, causing David to start awake and look around wildly.

Cold sweat lathered his slender frame, and the hairs on the back of his neck stood on end at the rising panic he felt. Sitting there in the darkness, an increasing sense of foreboding fell upon him. Feeling unsure whether he had heard the scream aloud or not, his eyes darted from corner to dark corner in search of the threat.

With his heart racing, he scrambled out of bed and ran flat-out for his office to stand breathlessly before the wall of glass, searching the woods beyond.

The night was black, the turbulent, dense clouds preventing all light from reaching the land below. Something was coming – he could feel it as surely as if he could see its approach with his own eyes. It was out there and coming fast.

Seeing nothing after enhancing his vision so that he could see in the dark, he raised his hand, placing his palm to the glass to send his awareness out into the night.

Passing straight through the glass, his senses swept out into the darkness and on into the trees before him. After a time, he lowered his hand and shook his head in relief.

'Just a dream!' he sighed, tutting and rolling his eyes at his foolishness.

Letting out a calming breath, he moved behind his desk and slumped down in his chair, sighing heavily as he leant his head back against its high back.

'Just a dream,' he repeated, closing his eyes.

Taking several more deep breaths, he composed himself and finally began to chuckle at his reaction.

*'But why do I still feel scared?'* he wondered, glancing nervously

back towards the window before shaking the feeling away.

Reaching for a pack of cigarettes, he tapped them on the desk a few times before retrieving one and placing it between his lips.

'Someone change my shorts!' he chuckled, shaking his head whilst scoffing at himself.

Leaning back again, he breathed out a huge plume of smoke that hung in the air as though suspended in time for a moment. Chuckling again in nervousness, he shook his head once more and took another deep drag on the smouldering weed before breathing it out through his nose.

He had set many magickal defences around his home, employing magick that few, if any, could ever get past undetected. His magick was strong, and he felt confident knowing that it would stop any who came too close and kill those who were able to enter uninvited.

Squashing the finished cigarette into the glass ashtray, he put the half-empty pack into it before placing them both back into the desk's top drawer. Sighing tiredly, he stood up and stretched in exhaustion.

Standing there for some time, like some lifelike crucifixion, he remained still for far longer than was necessary as the blood drained from his face. Making no further movement, his eyes were fixed firmly upon a shadow that had no right to be there.

Looking at the thicket of swaying trees, he saw a tall figure, darker than the night around it with eyes that instilled fear into the core of his very being.

'My security!' he quailed, seeing the cold, unblinking white eyes fixed upon him as though he was its prey. 'It's stronger than my defences!' he panicked, temporarily frozen with inaction.

Very slowly, he lowered his arms and then jumped in fright as his magickal protection finally responded. Alongside the alarm in his mind, the first of his defences washed away all illusions so that whatever the threat was, it was in its true form. Also, the knowledge as to the nature of the threat so that he could prepare and counter it more effectively.

'Death,' said the same voice that had awakened him, causing his face to twitch as the sickly feeling of dread swelled in the pit of his stomach.

'Gilga's balls!' he gasped as his second defensive measure failed to react.

This was one of containment, designed to trap the unwanted guest before entry could be made into his home. To this end, he had grown hawthorn bushes all around the property, magickally imbuing them to hold any who trespassed, even the undead.

As the wizard watched, the shadow passed through his treacherous bushes unharmed before the final of his defences sprang into action.

Fire engulfed the creature, encasing it within a sphere of intense heat that he himself could feel through the large pane of glass.

'What the...' he gasped, witnessing the impossible as the flames avoided the intruder, neither harming nor casting light upon its depthless frame.

After this final attack, he saw fanged teeth bared briefly, followed by a gesture of warning as it wagged a finger at him in time with a shake of its head.

Though manlike in appearance, that was where all similarity ended as the reflective, almost glowing white eyes glared into him coldly. He could see that whatever else this creature was, it was muscular, the definition of its physique highlighted somehow by some cold, unknown light.

Diving to his left, he reached for the wall and placed his hand upon it, sending his magick out around the house in an attempt to shield it.

'Sit down, Blue!' a thunderous voice growled, speaking in time with a deafening clap of thunder from above and a flash of lightning that lit up the room with its sudden brilliance.

Jumping in fright, David broke wind as his instantly released adrenaline attempted to empty his bowels.

'Gilga's balls!' he cried, instantly raising a shield of protection.

Towering over him, the black creature threw back its head as dark laughter reverberated around him.

Looking up at this amused nightmare, David saw the vicious incisors as the creature continued in its mirth.

With an incredulous look upon his face, he began bobbing on

his toes and swinging his arms rather awkwardly at his sides, waiting for this shadowed thing to recover itself.

At last, the amusement ended, and the cold white eyes settled on him once again.

'If I wanted you dead, you'd be dead. Now, please...' it rumbled, pulling his chair out from behind his desk, 'sit down.'

Staying where he was, David studied the creature, never having seen anything like it before in all his long years.

*'What the hell is it?'* he wondered, feeling the sense of danger recede from him a little.

'Move away then!' he replied testily, cursing his frightened, high-pitched tone of voice.

Raising its arms for peace, the thing stepped back to allow him safe passage.

Goose-stepping gingerly to his chair, the wizard lowered himself slowly before placing his hands flat upon the table.

'Sitting,' he confirmed, croaking out the word in a desperate attempt to lower his pitch.

Taking a seat opposite him, the massive creature lowered itself tentatively as though expecting the chair to fail under its weight.

Spreading his hands with impatience, David saw the creature bare its fangs at him again and with shocked understanding, he realised that it was smiling at him.

With a frown, he leant forward a little to inspect his visitor further.

'Am I that different, old friend?' it asked, running its depthless hand through its mane of long black hair.

'Gilga's balls!' David cried, peering at the creature as though for the first time. 'What the hell... Daire?' he asked, rising abruptly from his seat. 'You frightened me half to death!' he howled, his white face flushing with relief.

'Well, your enchantments took away my illusion, so...' Daire defended, shrugging his huge shoulders. 'I did try to smile at you, but you went into a hissy fit and ran to the wall,' he replied, chuckling deeply at his friend's discomfort.

Growing haughty at the implied cowardice, the wizard defended himself just as the other knew he would.

'I ran to shield my home! I didn't run like you are suggesting!'

he grumbled, slumping back down in aggravation.

'If you say so, Blue,' Daire sighed but then grew more serious. 'But then you sharted!' he pointed out, pulling a disgusted expression that made the wizard smile. 'Bit awkward now, to be honest,' he added, looking at his long-nailed fingers with disinterest.

'Shut up… and it's David, these days, thank you very much,' the wizard barked, taking in his friend's appearance with a calmer frame of mind. 'What the hell has happened to you?' he asked, his brow furrowing in concern.

'I need you to help figure that out,' Daire replied, turning his hands over to study them. 'Though I need to tell you what happened to me first,' he continued sombrely, flicking his eyes back upon the wizard.

Lighting a cigarette, David inhaled the smoke deeply before blowing it high into the air.

'Does this have anything to do with the wizards wanting to get to your house?' he asked, taking another long drag.

Narrowing his eyes, Daire stared long and hard at his friend, which made the wizard fidget in his seat.

'One came to me to help them get past your web!' he defended, holding his hands up in innocence. 'Though I did let slip that it was your house,' he confessed, swallowing hard as the shadows seemed to intensify around his legendary friend.

'Did you indeed?' Daire asked, his deep voice lowering into a rumble that the wizard could feel in his chest.

'I didn't want you killing him, and I thought that the mere mention of you would cause them to back off,' David explained, his voice sounding dry even to himself. 'They had the wolves with them,' he added, nodding his head as though this fact alone was enough to justify his actions.

Throwing his head back, Daire laughed with genuine amusement, which seemed to cause the gathering darkness to recede once again.

'I'm glad I amuse you,' David grumbled, causing his friend to nod as he wiped at his eyes.

'Be thankful that you do, Blue!' Daire rumbled, staring at his friend seriously. 'I nearly lost control of it then… which would not have been good for you!' he whispered, causing the wizard to pale.

Closing his eyes, he reopened the box that held who he was and drew upon the essence within his ring. Appearing more human, he smiled apologetically before continuing.

'My time is nearly up, Blue!' he sighed, shaking his head with a rare look of fear. 'I taught Kris how to use magick, and now all hell is breaking loose!' he sighed, moving on with the story.

Breathing out slowly, David had never felt afraid of his friend until that moment. He knew many who were, but he had never even had a crossed word with the man until now.

Taking a long, nervous drag of his cigarette, he tried to shake the feeling now that his friend appeared more human.

'I thought you had decided to keep it from her?' he replied, blowing the smoke through his nose.

Shaking his head, Daire waved off the question with a gesture of his hand.

'I hid her, but she left a book out for the kids to find,' he replied, irritation causing the thunder to return to his voice. 'Needless to say, I was not there and therefore couldn't hide them in time. Now all the bloody factions of man and vampire are trying to find them,' he growled, sounding more beast than man himself.

Taking another drag of his cigarette, David nodded as he absorbed the news in silence.

'So I took steps to protect them,' Daire continued, speaking then of what had been done to him by the elements.

Looking at what was once Daire, David felt a mixture of sadness and uncertainty for his old friend, but there was now fear there, too, after what had occurred.

'They actually killed you?' he asked, secretly wondering if this was truly his friend sitting before him.

Nodding his head, Daire shrugged before spreading his arms in frustration.

'I don't think they see it that way... they only see my ascension,' he replied, waving the issue away.

Leaning across the desk, David studied his friend with a look of wonder.

'How do you manage to look more human now?' he asked, genuinely intrigued by how it was done.

'More human? Isn't it convincing?' Daire asked, looking at his hand before showing his friend.

'Nope, you look like an animal trapped in a man's body... you look lethal!' David answered, sitting back with a sigh, 'And it's not just the eyes. You move too... smoothly!' he explained, shaking his head again.

'What's wrong with my eyes?' Daire complained, widening them theatrically.

'They kinda look like a cat's when it's stalking something. Maybe your pupils are too big, I don't know, but you look like a predator!' he explained, nodding his head as though he agreed with his assessment.

Dropping his illusion of humanity, Daire smiled in satisfaction when his friend had a fit.

'Gilga's balls!' David cried, jerking back so fast that he and his chair fell over backwards.

'Classic!' Daire roared, his deep laughter causing the wall of glass to vibrate in its frame.

Looking totally unamused, David reseated himself carefully with a look of resentment.

'Come on!' Daire sighed before chuckling again. 'I'm sorry,' he apologised, spreading his arms wide. 'How do I look now?' he asked, leaning forward slowly.

Leaning forward himself, David stared at his friend without emotion.

'I can't see any definition to you... it's like you're not really there. You look unnatural, mate,' he assessed, giving his critical view. 'If you, yourself, created this body, then why is it black like that? I mean, shouldn't you look... normal?' he asked, raising his eyebrows questioningly.

Returning his gaze to his outstretched hand, Daire nodded his agreement and then stared back at the wizard with more to tell.

'I wish that was all it was, my friend, but something has changed inside me also, and though I fight it, I know I will succumb to it soon. I need you to help me figure out what the hell went wrong and how to fix it.'

With eyes closed, David placed his hands at either side of his friend's head in an attempt to search within.

'You're definitely not human, mate,' he observed, seeing the ball of energy in his mind.

'That, I know!' Daire snapped, instinctively reacting to the other's probing mind. 'Sorry, please continue,' he added lamely, struggling to keep control of his natural urge to repel the intrusion.

Several moments passed before the wizard spoke again.

'Well, you're not like anything else on this earth that I've ever come across, but it's more than that. You feel unnatural,' he stressed, shaking his head with a frown. 'You said that when you created this body, you drew the essence from your human body?' he asked, confirming what he had been told.

Feeling the legend nod beneath his hands, he continued swiftly. 'You felt something different in it though, and randomly chose to enhance it?'

Again, the nod, and the cold light of what had been done brightened his friend's eyes again.

Dropping his hands, David sighed and moved back to his chair.

'Can you see that same quality in me?' he asked, seating himself with a wistful glance towards the desk drawer.

The reflective eyes bore into him, freezing the wizard momentarily before the moment passed as his friend sat back with a nod of his head.

'I see the same in you, yes,' Daire confirmed, closing his eyes for the other's benefit, 'but less so than it was in me,' he finished, pursing his lips in thought.

With a flick of his thumb, David lit his addiction before tilting his head back to blow out a huge plume of smoke that hit the ceiling like a billowing storm cloud.

'I wonder...' he began, but was cut off before he could continue.

'Gail is free of it,' Daire interrupted, giving his friend a tight smile.

Totally taken aback, David could not help but marvel at the power required to scan someone from so far away and to do it so quickly.

'Gilga's balls!' he whispered, clearly impressed. 'So it's a magickal taint,' he reasoned, leaning back to ponder the problem. 'That would explain your extra power, although that could also be from what the elements did to you... it also doesn't account for why you look like a bloody monster!' he stressed, scowling at the legendary killer.

Raising an eyebrow at the inspired picture of evil that flashed in his mind, Daire shrugged, thinking it more or less an apt description.

'Suggestions?' he asked irritably, leaning back in his chair.

Shaking his head again, David sighed and spread his arms helplessly.

'Too many things have happened to you to know for sure. It's either the elements, which I doubt, or what you did when creating this body, which is the more probable, but if it is in me too...' he replied, trailing off with another shrug of his shoulders, 'maybe you should seek out a higher form of help,' he suggested, shrugging again with helplessness. 'Have you tried talking to the elements? Maybe try to summon one of those elusive gods the witches pray to?' he asked hopefully, not knowing what else to say. 'They might actually hear you now... who knows?'

Closing his eyes in resignation, Daire tried to control his anger at wasting his time ever coming here.

'The elements warned me that I was corrupting myself,' he confessed, raising his hand before him again. 'If I have enhanced in me what also resides in you, then it would mean that our magick is born from something very dark indeed,' he whispered, staring at the depthless hand before him.

'Okay. Thanks for your help,' he said, sighing in defeat and disappointment before rising slowly to his feet.

'There is one more thing you should know,' David blurted, causing his friend to pause in the act of straightening. 'My instinct... my very soul... tells me that you are my enemy,' he confessed, feeling a fresh wave of fear as the legend straightened up to his full height.

'Your enemy?' Daire asked, looking deep into the wizard's eyes. 'That's the sense you get?' he asked, his reflective eyes looking almost luminous as the room darkened once again.

Seeing the light in the room seeming to absorb into the hulking mass of his friend, David smiled apologetically and instantly regretted the comment, wishing desperately that he could take the words back.

'What I mean is, your approach here woke me up! I suppose the best analogy would be if I was swimming in the ocean and a fin popped up. My entire being cries out to be away from you,' he explained, wishing that he understood the reason behind it.

Saying nothing, Daire nodded slowly before turning to leave, but a final question stopped him at the door.

'Can the elements keep the Bloods away?' David asked, knowing that he was treading on very thin ice.

Without turning, his friend appeared to consider the question before finally lifting his head a little as though having decided upon something.

'I sincerely hope so, for if my children fall, I will burn this world down to its foundations,' he answered. And without another word, he melted into the darkness, leaving a deathly silence in his wake.

After several moments had passed, the wizard sent out his awareness but sensed nothing of his friend and knew for sure that he was gone only when the hairs on his neck settled back down.

Letting out a shaky breath, he reached for another cigarette but fumbled with the lighter in his nervousness. A cold reality settled upon him, and he knew with dread that he had only been able to sense his friend when he had been allowed to do so.

*Just like a vampire,'* he thought, fear rising in him anew at what would happen if the legend's children did indeed fall.

# CHAPTER SEVEN

The world blurred past him, and it took but a moment for the woods to give way to the mountainside.

Lost in his rage, he, who had at one time been a man, finally gave in to the darkness within. No longer fighting against it, he roared his fury into the night and relished the feeling that accompanied it.

The elements were with him, his pain their own, but they spoke not while the corruption held sway.

'Bloods!' he roared, sounding bestial and full of wanton destruction.

Suddenly, without thought or intent, he shifted from where he was to where he desired and crouched low after the crossing. Looking around wildly, he saw that he was in the forest again, his forest, and took a moment to centre himself.

Throwing out his awareness so that he could get his bearings, the forest came alive in his mind, and with a snarl of absolute hate, he searched for those that were not.

'I see you!' he hissed, sensing the undead creatures that moved amongst the trees.

A small part of him knew that he should not be able to sense such vampires, but the more dominant part took little heed of it.

With his face suddenly contorting in fear, he threw out his awareness towards his children, but he had made the house strong, giving it life and a will of its own so that it could protect them as vigorously as himself.

Sensing his children asleep in their beds, he breathed out slowly before turning his mind back to those that hunted them. Lowering his head, he left his body and set his spirit free from the chains of physical restraint. He felt surprised at the ease of it, for no sooner had he thought of entering the astral realm had he found himself there.

Floating high above the trees, he looked down upon his enemies and saw that they were spread out in a crooked half-circle, working together to navigate against that which had held them at bay for so long.

It was slow going, he noticed, his magickal web pulling them off course more often than not, but slowly and surely, they made their way despite it.

The elements, too, had worked to turn them aside, changing the land to assist in the confusion, and would have been successful but for this new tactic that took them ever closer to their quarry.

Counting more than fifty Bloods, a number that would strike fear into all of the combined factions of mankind, Daire smiled confidently, for he was a man no longer. Rising to his feet, he drew the elements to him with one question in his mind.

*'Are you ready to wage war upon these creatures?'* he asked, wishing suddenly to know their minds.

*'We fight for your children as promised,'* they answered, their different voices mingling into one deafening answer in his mind.

*'After this night, they die on sight of this place,'* he seethed, letting out a roar that silenced all but the dead within the darkness.

***

Stalking silently through the trees, the vampires would not be turned away again, not this night. For too long had they been thwarted by the cursed forest around them, unable to feed until they had come to do what they had been sent here to do.

The first to come was one who had been called Andrew when he was mortal, a vampire of rising renown, intent on raising it higher. Not yet a lord, his bloodthirsty reputation had set him on the path to be just that. A Blood Lord beyond such identities as man or woman, for he would be a lord, and such was the way in regard to their kind.

Upon entering the forest, the scent of the ones he sought had been intoxicating, but the deeper he went, the more confusing their essence had become, and after a couple of days of aimless wandering, he had found himself walking out again the way he had entered. All sense of direction had been lost to him within the trees, and upon seeing the forest beginning to thin in the distance, he had moved at speed to free himself from this accursed place.

As his continuous attempts failed in much the same way, more of his faction had come in groups of three, but even they had been turned back, and it had fallen to him to propose this winning strategy. Now numbering nearly seventy strong, they worked together to form a line that would hold each other in the right direction.

'Soon,' he breathed hungrily, thinking of how they would leave this forest to stand before those who must think themselves safe. At the sight of seeing so many of his kind approaching, *'They will scream, and they will die!'* he thought lustily, his face snarling in anticipation of his imaginings.

The new-bloods were to be taken and turned into vampires, but that was before this hateful forest had ensnared them so. Now their only wish was to kill the ones who had placed this curse upon them. Having not eaten for quite some time, the vampire licked his lips in eagerness.

'Soon,' he whispered again, knowing with a savage certainty that they were getting closer to that end.

A sudden roar filled the night, a sound so evil and so full of hate that it froze his already cold blood in his veins. The forest became deathly silent in the roar's wake, as if all life froze in that singular moment.

A growl was heard from behind and then to the side, causing the unsteady line of vampires to close ranks swiftly. Abundantly clear that they were being stalked, they felt like sheep being hunted by some unseen wolf.

*'What made that sound?'* a question pulsed into Andrew's mind.

*'Be silent!'* he sent back, the dread in the question feeding his own.

'There!' another hissed, flinching at his side, and Andrew could literally smell the fear emanating from it.

'We are vampires!' he roared, growling out the words for all to hear. 'We are those who inspire fear,' he stressed before vanishing without sound or struggle.

Those closest to him hissed and backed away as something small landed at their feet, rolling for a moment before lying still.

'It's his head!' shrieked the nearest vampire, backing away in panic.

Though the darkness was almost total within the dense forest, the vampires, with their unnatural sight, saw everything except that which hunted them.

Sending out their senses in an ever-increasing circle, they scanned the area for a sign of what it could be. Not used to being on the receiving end of such a hunt, they simply stood there and waited for something else to happen.

Hissing as a black shadow began to rise out of the ground before them, they cowered before it as though it was death itself. Blacker even than the darkest of shadows, the hunter towered over them with a guttural growl emanating from its chest.

Two luminous white eyes opened, fixing upon the nearest vampire before the being hissed through fanged teeth at these so-called creatures of the night.

'Why hunt us?' the vampire asked, its own teeth bared in fear.

The reflective eyes narrowed, and the vampire was instantly wreathed in flame, consuming it utterly before leaping to another, spreading quicker than wildfire as it ate into the undead.

'*Y Blaidd Tywyll!*' the creature roared, speaking the ancient name that they themselves had given.

Hissing through its teeth again, a sound more from a furnace than from any living thing, the reawakened legend tore into his enemies with an unholy efficiency.

Upon hearing the ancient name, the remaining vampires turned to flee, for nothing could have prepared them for what stood against them now.

'The Dark Wo...' a cry was heard before being savagely cut off – the name screamed by one of the younger vampires in the modern tongue.

There was total discord among the vampires as they raced through the trees, the furtive glances over their shoulders adding to their terror as the fire could be seen pursuing them, carried now upon the wind which had lifted at their backs.

Those who were the first to flee began to take a lead on the carnage behind them, so it was with total surprise that the land rose up before them like a cavernous mouth to swallow them as they ran headlong.

Those not killed outright were left crippled upon the cold forest floor, twitching and broken until the flames sought them out like a fiery serpent intent on its feed.

The last three sped on heedlessly, uncaring of the screams and cries of those left behind. At last, they came upon a wide riverbed and felt relief at seeing the open sky through a parting in the trees.

Launching themselves high into the air to clear the distance in one mighty leap, they were caught mid-motion by the river itself as it frothed up to encase the trio within a cocoon of near-freezing water.

Held in the air by the steady stream of water, the vampires struggled desperately until finally resigning themselves to their fate.

After a time, they saw the steadily increasing glow from the fire that, even now, continued its pursuit. Within its flickering light, they saw the figure of their nightmares come to stand before them.

The cold eyes fixed on them with pure hatred, and after only a moment's thought, the order was given.

'Die!' Daire whispered, his reflective eyes showing neither forgiveness nor pity after the intended transgression upon his children.

Glowing embers drifted forward as though carried upon a breeze, dancing before each of the vampires in turn.

Pausing before two of the vampires for a moment, they seemed to hover before swelling into balls of swirling magma as they slowly entered the water.

The one remaining vampire could only watch as its brethren died within the steaming water before it was moved within reach of its legendary enemy.

With a growl like thunder, a depthless black hand seized the undead creature by the throat, ripping it free from the imprisoning element.

'This is my land,' Daire seethed, causing the last vampire to flinch in response. 'You shall not come back,' he commanded, pulling the Blood's face to his own.

The vampire merely hung there, limp and unresponsive in the wake of what had happened to the others of its ilk.

'Say it!' Daire roared, pulling the face closer until their foreheads touched.

'I will not come back,' the Blood echoed, dread shining clearly in its eyes.

'Do not awaken me again,' Daire warned, growling in time with the spontaneous eruption above. 'I have been lenient thus far, but if you come to me again, I will take the fight to you,' he promised before throwing the vampire to the far side of the riverbank.

Watching the vampire fall, he had to quell the urge to give chase and rip the life from the loathsome creature.

'Harry him,' he whispered, watching as the elements gave chase before he threw back his head to roar into the night.

***

Awaking with a start, Kristina felt panicked, but by whom or what she did not know. Looking around the room, her eyes darted about frantically for the source of what had awakened her before laying back down in relief.

Cold sweat clung to her body, making her skin feel clammy and unclean. Reaching down, she felt the bedsheets and groaned at finding them soaked in perspiration.

'Oh, man!' she whined in a high-pitched tone before getting stiffly out of bed with a grimace.

Scowling irritably, she tried to remember the dream that had ripped her from sleep but could only recall the scream that had mixed in with the sound of thunder.

Walking to the window, she opened the blinds and peered out over the forest treetops.

*Is that fire?* she wondered, seeing faint flickers of golden light shining through the trees some distance away.

Opening the window wide, she sat on the chaise to see more clearly, but the cold night air made her shiver as it touched her moist skin.

Closing it again, she returned to the bed to remove the bedsheets and as silently as she could, she walked to the bathroom to retrieve a clean set.

After towelling herself dry, she returned to make the bed anew before slipping into a clean nightdress with a dressing gown added for good measure.

Returning to the window, she reopened it and sat again to watch what was happening. Tilting her head slightly, she was positive that she could hear people crying and could definitely see the spontaneous glow of fire this time.

Upon hearing the thunderous scream again, she knew immediately that it was the same sound that had awakened her, but thought it more of a roar now that she was fully awake.

Deeper than a lion's, it sounded to her more like something she had heard in some horror movie but far more sinister because it was coming from something real.

'*Is this his protection at work?*' she wondered, hoping that it wasn't, for if it was, whatever was happening out there was far too close.

She wished then that Daire was home, the sudden emotion catching her by surprise and making her feel weak.

'Get a grip, Kristina!' she growled, chastising herself for her weakness.

Sensing movement behind her, she turned to see her daughter padding towards her, bleary-eyed and with tears on her cheeks.

'What's wrong, baby?' she asked, her tone hushed and soothing.

'I had a bad dream,' Francesca replied, sobbing a little as she wiped at her eyes.

Wrapping the girl in her arms, Kristina whispered secretively into her ear, 'Sleep with me tonight,' kissing her daughter on the head.

The child said nothing, but Kristina felt the movement of her head as she nodded her agreement.

Reaching out to close the window, she led her little girl to her bed to cuddle under the covers. Running her fingers through her daughter's hair, Kristina made soft, soothing noises to chase away her fears.

'What did you dream about?' she asked after a while, seeing that Francesca was far from sleep.

Looking at her mother with her blue eyes wide, Francesca's

lip began to quiver again.

'I dreamt that Daddy was fighting a big black monster, and he was screaming! He was screaming!' she cried, causing her mother to stiffen before looking fearfully back towards the window.

# CHAPTER EIGHT

It was clear to Kristina that something terrible had happened that night, for it had now been well over a month since the scream, and there had been no sign of Daire in all that time. Only the fear of what she would find had stopped her from going to investigate – the promise made now long forgotten.

Francesca was still fretting, however, unwilling to let the matter drop as to where her father was and going into fits of rage at her mother's dismissiveness.

'Where is he?' she whined, her voice sounding high-pitched and worrisome. Even Lucian, who normally accepted things as they were, began sitting silently and withdrawing into himself at his father's prolonged absence.

Knowing that he, too, was thinking of their father, Kristina could think of nothing to say that would ease their pain and so said nothing at all, deciding to wait for their mourning to pass.

*'They'll get used to it,'* she told herself, shrugging off the situation as she did with most things.

The only thing that gave her some sense of peace was that the land still seemed alive and very much aware.

*'Surely that means that we are still safe, doesn't it?'* she thought, nodding her head as if in answer.

Daire had said there would come a time when she would need him, but the more time that passed, the more she wanted him to stay away and felt little guilt for ever thinking it.

Loving her life as it was now, she felt independent and free for the first time in years.

*'If not for them reading from that bloody book!'* she thought bitterly, annoyed at the 'butterfly effect' from that one simple act.

So she would console her children and let him fade into memory.

*'Time, after all, is the great healer,'* she thought, smiling to herself. *'Is that selfish?'* she wondered before shrugging the question away. *'It will all turn out fine in the end,'* she assured herself, waving off her already fading concerns.

Still furious with her daughter for reading the book and doubly so for using it, Kristina thought again of the promised danger that never came.

'They will come for them. They will all come,' she whispered, remembering their father's words.

But they had not come. They had been left in peace as she had hoped they would be.

Pulling out her mobile phone, she called her best friend, thinking it well past time to inform her of what had truly happened, for she had felt too afraid to tell her anything while Daire had been around. But he was gone now, possibly even dead, and she now felt free to do as she pleased.

'Hi, Kiki. What's up?' Janet asked, calling Kristina by her childhood name.

'Can you come over, Jan?' Kristina asked, feeling her composure slipping in the moment.

'You want to try and teach me magick again?' Janet asked, her voice rising with excitement. 'I'm sure it's only a matter of time before I can do it,' she continued, sounding more than a little desperate on the other end of the line.

Believing that the Bloods were now held at bay by whatever had been done, Kristina had tried to teach her friend the forbidden art, but try as she might, Janet could not influence the flame, and she began to wonder if she would ever be able to... maybe her friend just did not have the knack, or the 'gist', as Daire had once called it.

'I've found a way around getting noticed by the vampires, too,' Janet blurted smugly, clearly unwilling to accept that she would fail in her endeavours. 'You are talking to the newest member of the "Witches of Rhyme". I've joined them, so when I light my first candle, I will already be hidden within a coven. Like it?' she asked, finally pausing for breath.

Remaining silent for a moment, Kristina's emotions almost overwhelmed her.

'They've been practising in secret, Jan!' she sobbed at last, her tone soft and whispering.

Stunned into silence, Janet wondered what her friend was talking about.

'You mean the kids?' she asked, her tone hushed and shocked

at the implications.

With her lip quivering, it was all Kristina could do to stop herself from breaking down completely.

'Yes,' she answered in a small voice, tears brimming in her eyes.

'Oh my god, Kris! I'm on my way!' Janet replied, hanging up the phone.

Having been surreptitiously telling her friend all about the secret world of magick, Kristina had been forced to show her the candle-lighting to convince her of the truth of it and, after only a little resistance, had proceeded to teach her how it was done.

Fascinated by this hidden world around them, Janet had delved into the book and now knew all of the theory behind it. The only thing Kristina had not told her was the situation with the children, fearing a backlash from their father.

*'But he's dead now,'* Kristina thought and then shrugged, considering herself unbound from the promises she had made.

An hour or so later, Janet let herself into the house to find her friend snuggled up on the sofa, looking worried and out of her mind.

Striding quickly across the room, her tall, slender form covered the distance quickly.

'Oh, Kris,' she whispered, seating herself beside her before holding her friend close. 'What happened?' she asked, giving Kristina a little squeeze.

Composing herself with a deep, shuddering breath, Kristina leant back to look at her.

'Francesca somehow got into his room, found the book and then read it!' she cried, the words tumbling from her as she fought for control.

'Just read it?' her friend asked, seeing Kristina's eyes fill again as she shook her head.

'They've both been practising!' she wept, placing her face into her hands

Letting her friend cry it out, Janet began to rub her back with the palm of her hand before stopping to brush a lock of wavy blonde hair from her eyes.

'Let's shield them!' she blurted, watching her friend intently. 'Join the coven with the kids. They will be shielded automatically!' she explained, staring at Kristina with wide, pleading eyes. 'With us all in the coven, we number thirteen! It's fate! A witch circle needs thirteen witches!' she continued, squeezing Kristina's shoulder as she spoke.

Immediately shaking her head, Kristina looked up and wiped the tears from her eyes.

'He has already hidden and protected them, and it changed him into something terrible… it's why he left,' she answered, feeling totally dejected by the will of their father. 'This all happened a while ago,' she sighed, covering her face with her hand.

'Join the coven with me, Kiki! You'll have more support than you can handle!' Janet persisted, nodding her head eagerly.

Dabbing at her eyes, Kristina stared up at her friend doubtfully for a moment before shaking her head.

'If he lives, he will never allow me to do that,' she answered, regret thick in her throat. 'He told me as much before he left,' she continued, feeling reluctant to pursue this line of thought even though she believed him to be dead. *What if he isn't!'* she quailed, fearing his promised retaliation.

Squaring her shoulders bravely, Janet's face set into a confident glare.

'Once it's done and our circle complete, there's no breaking it! Oh, he can bitch and whine all he likes, and so can the factions, for all I care! But once it's done, it really would be done, and we'll have our own power to defend ourselves with! No more hiding in his shadow!' Janet paused; her eyes still locked on Kristina. 'He's not here, and to be frank, I don't think he ever will be again. We, however, are here, and so are the vampires. We need to act!' she stressed, placing her hands firmly upon her friend's shoulders.

'You think that your coven will agree?' Kristina asked, causing Janet to smile knowingly.

'With the completion of their circle? I know they will!' she assured, taking Kristina by the hand. 'The Bloods *will* come, Kris!' she whispered, speaking in a frightened tone with a glance towards the window. 'Don't you realise how powerful we'll become? But we need to do it now. We haven't a moment to lose!' she stressed, the words tumbling out of her mouth with an added little shake of her friend's shoulders.

Wiping her tears away, Kristina's face hardened in determination.

'Okay,' she agreed, believing that it fell to her now to protect her family.

Nodding emphatically, Janet smiled in triumph before giving her friend's shoulders another squeeze.

'We'll be able to defend them ourselves, Kiki. No one will ever go against a witches' circle,' she declared, smiling with an almost mad glint in her eyes.

Feeling impassioned by her friend's assurances, Kristina nodded again, more decisively this time, and began laughing through her tears.

'Okay,' she said again, nodding emphatically.

Pulling out her mobile phone, Janet thumbed through her recent call list before pressing her thumb down on the desired number.

'Let's do this!' she said, smiling tightly.

*** 

The following day there came a rare knock at the door, and after answering it, Kristina was shocked to see an elderly woman standing just outside.

The woman looked to be the epitome of love, her caring blue eyes widening a little with a warmth reserved for grandchildren. For that is what Kristina thought she looked like, a caring grandmother with half-moon spectacles perched on the end of her nose, straight out of a Grimm's fairy tale.

'Oh, Kristina, I am so happy to meet you at last,' the old woman greeted in the softest of voices, causing Kristina to flush with emotion. 'My name is Jacky, the priestess of my coven,' she continued, embracing Kristina in the doorway.

'Oh... hello!' Kristina stammered, totally taken aback by her appearance.

She had not really thought about what a priestess should look like but had clearly not expected such a motherly-looking woman to be the head of an order of witches.

'Please, come in!' she continued, stepping back with a gesture of her arm.

'Oh, thank you, dear,' Jacky replied graciously but paused in the doorway for a moment as though having second thoughts.

'Everything okay?' Kristina asked, frowning in confusion.

'Oh, yes, thank you,' Jacky whispered, seeming to shake herself off before finally entering.

Seating the priestess on a sofa, Kristina handed her a mug of tea and then took up the seat opposite her with an awkward smile.

'So you know of my... situation?' she asked delicately, causing Jacky to chuckle good-naturedly.

'Oh, yes, dear. I have been told,' the old woman answered, eyeing her over the rim of her mug.

Sipping the hot brew, Jacky made a complimentary sound before drinking a little more.

'Then you know, too, who their father was?' Kristina persisted, smiling nervously as though this fact alone might frighten the woman away.

Failing to keep the seriousness from her expression, Jacky nodded gravely as she lowered her mug.

'Indeed, I do,' she answered, all levity driven from her face. 'The wolf,' she announced quietly, unconsciously rolling the mug between her palms. 'I had thought him a mere legend, a story to scare the children, so to speak. I have to say, though, dear, I am glad that he has moved on to pastures new, if you catch my meaning?' she continued, finally putting the mug down with a nervous smile.

Intrigued by her manner, Kristina wished for nothing more than to quiz the woman about her legendary ex, but the priestess continued quickly in case she had caused offence.

'I am descended from a very long line of witches, and though I don't look it, I am very much older and far more powerful than I appear,' Jacky began, nodding her head seriously, 'but if the Dark Wolf were alive today, we would not be having this conversation,' she confessed, settling herself more comfortably into the sofa.

A sudden chill entered the room, causing the priestess to look about wearily before stiffening a little at what she had sensed.

'I feel his essence here, sense it in the very walls of this place. I have also witnessed the change in the elements, but for what reason I couldn't fathom, until I was told of you, that is. I believe now that in bringing on this great change, he lost his place amongst us,' she continued, sipping at her tea again.

Folding her arms around herself, Kristina leant forward a little in her seat.

'You think he's gone forever?' she asked meekly, twiddling her fingers nervously.

Narrowing her eyes in understanding, Jacky smiled reassuringly before nodding her head.

'Don't worry, dear, he's gone. I bet my coven on it,' she answered, smiling warmly.

Colour flushed into Kristina's face, turning it crimson in an instant.

'I think you misunderstand me, Jacky. I'm not glad that he's gone! He was a good father and…' she stormed but trailed off lamely at the other's arched eyebrow.

'And a good husband?' the priestess asked, looking her right in the eye.

'That is not your concern!' Kristina snapped, causing Jacky to hold a hand up in apology.

'I am sorry, dear, it was not my place. I overstepped,' the witch replied, smiling apologetically. 'So where are these beautiful children I've heard so much about?' she asked, quickly moving forward.

Letting out a long breath, Kristina let the matter drop in one drawn-out sigh.

'They're upstairs… practising,' she answered, sighing out the words in resignation. 'It is, or was, his wish for them to be able to defend themselves,' she answered, rolling her eyes and shaking her head.

Widening her eyes in surprise, Jacky was taken aback by the unsupervised practises but fought to keep her disapproval from her face.

'Are they indeed?' she chuckled, rolling her eyes as though to explain away how unruly children could be. 'I would dearly like to meet them,' she asked, her eyes brightening in anticipation, but no sooner had she spoken than the door to the hallway slammed shut, causing them both to start in surprise.

'Old houses,' Jacky chuckled offhandedly, but the fear in her eyes did not go unnoticed.

'Maybe next time,' Kristina responded, feeling a cold uneasiness seep into her bones.

Shrugging sadly, Jacky said nothing and finished her tea in one large gulp.

'It's time that I was leaving anyway,' she said, clearly unsettled by the slamming of the door and the progressive change in the atmosphere.

At her words, the door flew open again, as did the one to the front of the house.

'Oh my god!' Kristina exclaimed, tipping the remainder of her tea over herself. 'Bugger!' she cried, the hot liquid causing her a little pain.

Saying nothing more, the priestess rose swiftly and walked quickly from the house, leaving a startled-looking Kristina in her wake.

Just outside the doorway, Jacky let her held breath out, feeling the oppressiveness of the house lift immediately.

Surprising Kristina, who had followed from behind, she opened her arms for a hug of farewell and turned her head to whisper as she did so.

'This house has been tainted by him. Be wary,' she whispered, stepping back once again. 'If it is what you desire, dear, then I would be only too happy to welcome you into my coven,' she said aloud, stepping back as though expecting something to happen and shrugging when nothing did. 'All of you,' she added before ambling away.

\*\*\*

As the weeks passed, Kristina saw more and more of the priestess and began to think of her more as a friend than the head of her would-be order.

The house, however, seemed to be getting angrier and ever more blatant in its show of disapproval, even showing signs of annoyance when Janet came to visit, refusing her entry even when using her key.

The latest sign of discord happened when both Jacky and Janet had arrived together to discuss the completion of the circle.

After struggling to get into the house, the temperature had plummeted rapidly, and an eerie silence had settled on the room.

'What on earth is happening here?' Janet asked, unable to sense the malice that the other two could.

Believing that the house was intentionally sucking the heat up the chimney, they were eventually forced to step outside to discuss the arrangements there.

Fearful that the house would eventually turn hostile, Jacky and Janet both tried to persuade Kristina into bringing the children to the priestess' home to complete the circle there, but Kristina had been resolute, insisting that it would be done at her house or not at all.

Becoming something of a recluse, she even took such steps as to order all food and essentials online, having them delivered rather than going out.

'You've become a hermit, Kris! A prisoner in your own home!' Janet admonished in frustration, taking Jacky's side on the matter completely.

'Better to be safe than sorry,' Kristina replied, thinking that any risk to the children was one risk too many.

\*\*\*

A knock at the door caused Kristina's head to jerk up from the book of magick and stare out towards the hallway in alarm. No one had knocked on her door in months, not without her expecting it.

Heaving herself up from the sofa, she walked to the door and took a deep, composing breath before looking at herself in the hallway mirror.

'Not the best I've ever looked,' she sighed to herself before shaking her head tiredly.

Taking another deep breath, she cracked the large black door open and peered out nervously.

'Hello?' she called, readying herself to close it again immediately.

Squinting up at her, an elderly man of maybe seventy years backed up a step to ease her clear show of fear.

'Good day to you,' he replied, doffing his trilby hat in greeting, presenting her with a well-tanned bald head.

Sighing in relief, Kristina smiled immediately, loving the men of his era.

*'Real men,'* she thought appraisingly, taking in his weathered complexion.

'Oh, hello,' she answered, slowly opening the door, which caused the old man to smile as he replaced his hat upon his head.

'I'm sorry to bother you, young lady, but I was wondering if you'd like to buy some logs off me?' he asked in a deep but softly spoken tone of voice. 'For the fire,' he clarified, gesturing up at the chimney.

Reasoning that if the man could come all the way here without falling prey to the magick outside, Kristina believed that he must surely mean them no harm.

Staring at him, she noted his heavily lined face and small but lean stature, thinking he looked almost frail in his 'old man' clothes.

Raising his eyebrows, he smiled awkwardly at her lack of response and started to wave his arms slightly as he bobbed on the balls of his feet.

'Oh, I'm sorry!' she blurted, laughing embarrassedly at her silent appraisal. 'Yes! I would love some wood,' she finally answered, peering at the wheelbarrow that was left just outside the gate.

'Excellent!' he replied, his grey eyes lighting up with relief. 'I thought that you'd have enough, what with the forest on your doorstep,' he said, rubbing his hands together in anticipation of the sale.

Staring at him again, Kristina's smile faltered a little as her suspicions began to rise.

'Where have you come from?' she asked, looking around nervously for a sign of danger. 'This is the only house for miles,' she continued, stepping back further into her home.

'I've come from the forest, just down the road,' he answered, stepping back to show that he meant her no harm. 'My name is John, but my friends call me Jack. I've been cutting logs to sell in the village for years,' he continued tiredly, showing her his heavily calloused hands.

Unconvinced, Kristina frowned at him and backed away further.

'Then why have I not seen you before?' she asked guardedly, her words clipped and precise.

Pulling a hanky from his pocket, Jack wiped his brow with it before responding.

'I never thought to ask, since you live here,' he replied, spreading his arms at the position of her house. 'I only ask now because I'm overworked and feel too tired to lug these logs back into the village,' he continued, nodding back towards the gate.

Studying the old man, she tried to decide if he was genuine or not and whether he was to be a friend or foe to her.

'He does look tired,' she thought, looking him up and down with a critical eye.

'If I have alarmed you, missy, then I apologise and bid you a good day,' the old man conceded, stepping back to the path with a tired sigh.

Shaking her head in frustration, Kristina rolled her eyes at her insecurities.

'I'm the one who should apologise,' she replied, stopping him at the gate. 'I'll buy all you have!' she blurted before wincing. 'Bugger!' she exclaimed, rolling her eyes again. 'I have no money! Well, I do have money, but no cash,' she explained as Jack looked back vacantly.

'I beg your pardon?' he asked, clearly not understanding her predicament.

'Can I transfer you the money?' she offered, her eyes widening in hope.

Staring at her with his blank expression fixed firmly in place, he finally shook his head in confusion.

'Is that not how it has always worked? I transfer you my wood, and you transfer your money into my hand. How else do you propose to "transfer" it to me?' he asked, frowning at her.

Smiling indulgently, Kristina understood that he did not, in fact, understand, and began blushing a little at the awkward situation she had created.

'I'm sorry, I have no money at the moment,' she replied, shrugging apologetically and spreading her hands helplessly.

Smiling mischievously, Jack's eyes brightened as he chuckled in amusement.

'You can transfer me the money. I may be old, but I'm not *that* old. Not yet, at least,' he replied, laughing quietly at her expression of shock.

'Oh, you bugger!' she admonished, bringing her hand to her mouth and giggling in a high-pitched tone of voice.

\*\*\*

As the weeks passed, the season began to shift from the freshness of spring into a drier, warmer climate as summer finally took hold.

The old man had become a regular visitor during this time, popping in often and always unannounced, never sticking to any kind of routine or timetable.

Loving the welcome distraction, Kristina always bought whatever wood he had to sell, but there was something keeping her from inviting him inside, whether a sixth sense or just her fear, she did not know.

'Where do you cut the wood?' she asked as he stood before her again.

'In the forest, of course, where else?' he answered, scowling up at her grumpily.

'I thought so,' she replied, putting her hands on her hips in annoyance. 'The reason I asked, you cantankerous old git, was because I was thinking that you could use my tool shed. It has a vice and everything,' she said, smiling at his shocked expression.

'And everything?' he asked sarcastically, widening his eyes playfully before smiling wickedly. 'That would be a great help, Kris,' he continued, dipping his head appreciatively. 'I'm really tired of all the lugging about, to be sure,' he continued, rubbing his shoulder as though to prove his point. 'I won't be charging you for the wood anymore, then,' he announced, holding up his hand before she could refuse. 'I will be tending to your garden as well,' he continued, scratching at his stubbly white chin ponderously. 'As payment,' he added, giving her a no-nonsense kind of look.

Looking at him sternly, Kristina stepped back from the door before shrugging to herself.

'We shall discuss it over tea,' she replied, opening the door a little wider.

'Very well,' he answered agreeably, looking up at the house momentarily before taking a tentative step over the threshold.

# CHAPTER NINE

The tall man walked casually down the cobbled streets, idly browsing the wares displayed in the numerous shop windows. He had been in the town for quite some time, watching and waiting with more patience than he was known for, but it was now clear to him that whom he waited for was not going to come.

Frustration gnawed at him, for patience had never been his strong suit, and now, after all this time, his irritation was beginning to show.

Running a hand through his curly dark hair, he considered his next move carefully.

*They have to eat, damn it!'* he thought, shaking his head as he wondered what he was missing.

Hunger gnawed at him, and he knew that he had needed to feed for quite some time. His mind felt slow, and the call for sleep made his wits even more sluggish.

*'Not until I've fed,'* he thought darkly, knowing that to sleep while so hungry would weaken him further. 'What to do?' he sighed, pursing his lips as he stared up the valley to the forest that dominated the horizon.

A screech of tires dragged him out of his contemplation, annoying him further as he snapped his head towards the source of the disturbance.

Scowling, he saw a drunken man in the street, giving a van driver an obscene gesture before staggering across the vehicle's path.

*'Clown!'* the tall man thought, about to follow before he turned back to the van. 'Of course!' he whispered, his dark eyes squinting in thought. 'Clever, very clever!' he conceded, a smile of respect spreading across his handsome features.

Moving to the driver's side, he signed for the man to lower his window and locked eyes with him as he did so.

Red-faced and full of anger, the driver pressed down the

switch and then stared back rather vacantly.

'Where are you delivering to, Driver?' the tall man asked, his tone soft and unoffending.

Looking back with his eyes glazing over, the man blinked slowly before responding.

'I deliver all over,' he answered, his face returning to a more normal shade.

'Up the valley?' the tall man pressed, his dark-eyed gaze fixed and unwavering.

Nodding dumbly, the driver felt a strange compulsion to answer whatever the tall man asked without thought or hesitation.

'Up to the house that backs onto the forest?' the tall man prompted and smiled again at another muted nod of response. 'The next time you go there, you will want to give me a call,' the tall man informed. It was not a request.

Nodding obligingly, the man stored the mobile number given to him.

'Thank you,' the tall man finished with an appreciative smile before dismissing him to go about his business. *Time to feed!* he thought, smiling coldly.

*** 

The night was a warm one, and because of it, the city's nightlife was in full swing earlier than normal. The long street was heaving with people of various ages and ethnicity, all standing about with bottles in hand as they prepared to end their night of revelry in their chosen club of choice.

Breathing in deeply, the tall man smelled the testosterone in the air and smiled knowingly at the cause of such a scent. Eyeing the scantily clad females parading up and down the street, the tall man smiled wider at the effect this simple act was having on the men in the vicinity.

He had come to the city of Swansea because it was the closest to the valley, and only a place with a mass population could sate his hunger and supply the energy he needed.

Slowly prowling the city centre, he had come upon this street and found that it housed almost all of the city's nightclubs.

'Wind Street', the sign read, but he had heard the locals refer to it differently, pronouncing it as 'Wine Street', and he thought the wordplay rather apt.

Turning his head, he sniffed at the air again and caught the scent of pheromones as the expected fight began to break out. A large, heavily-muscled youth had ripped off his shirt before dancing back and forth like a would-be cage fighter.

The smell of energy from the spilt blood caused the tall man's pupils to dilate exponentially, giving him a shark-like look that gained him several weary glances from those who passed by him.

Drawn by his hunger, he found himself amongst the brawlers and within the circle of conflict just as the 'cage fighter' threw a wild punch that connected with a random man's head, causing his unsuspecting victim to crumple without a sound.

Without saying a word, the youth turned and let fly with a second punch aimed at the tall man, who felt a cold fury seep into his stomach at the unprovoked attack.

Catching the fist in one hand, he gripped his attacker by the throat with the other and lifted him onto his toes so they were now eye to eye.

'That will cost you,' the tall man hissed, draining the young man of his much-needed energy.

Strength leached from his assailant, ripping from his throat into the hand that held him, and there was nothing to be done to stop it, for it was over almost as quickly as it had begun.

Laying his victim down upon the ground, he placed him in the recovery position as the unconscious body began to convulse at the violation wrought upon it.

'What the...' an onlooker gasped, seeing something he could not explain.

Energy flowed through the tall man, his fatigue all but a memory as he walked on through the parting crowd before him.

Contrary to popular belief, vampires of his ilk did not need to feed often, so long as they did not expend more energy than was necessary. Draining this youth of a year's worth of life would now feed him for that exact amount of time unless, of course, he was to burn up said energy more quickly.

Walking the street again, he waited for the right time of night and the right type of venue to present itself to him.

A little after midnight, he paused before a door and breathed in what he sensed from inside before finally finding what he had been searching for.

*'The place to be,'* he thought, smiling to himself.

Every city in the world had one, a venue where everyone wished to go to end their night.

*'Time to feed!'* he thought, feeling his excitement build.

Looking up, he read the name above the door and smiled wider still.

*'Time and Envy,'* he read, understanding immediately that this was two clubs joined as one.

Approaching the door, he saw that the queue to get in was ridiculously long, stretching up the street and around the corner to god knows where.

Switching his gaze to the doormen standing close by, he heard them barking orders to keep the patrons in line. Now and again, these 'bouncers' would drag someone out of the queue and send them on their merry way, ending their night earlier than expected.

'ID?' shouted a tall, muscular black man who was clearly the head man at the door.

'I'm nineteen!' protested a pretty young blonde girl, fearful desperation shining in her eyes, but with a dismissive gesture of his hand, the head doorman waved her away, grimacing at her plaintive cries of innocence.

'Professional,' the vampire approved, stepping forward and ignoring the queued clubbers completely.

The tall man locked eyes with the head doorman, and after a moment only, the man smiled, beckoning him forward with a quiet chuckle of recognition.

Stepping into the club, the tall vampire walked down the many steps and passageways that led to the cellars of what was once an old supermarket. Halfway down, he came upon a landing area and was instantly stopped by yet another of the club's security.

'Empty your pockets!' barked the black-clad figure automatically before looking up into the tall man's eyes.

Without another word, they appraised each other with a growing smile spreading across their faces.

The vampire took in the doorman's appearance, noting the piercing dark eyes that had glared at first but now softened in recognition of what they both were.

The tall man took in the smaller man's lithe frame, thinking him too small to be a traditional doorman but not small by any other standards. The doorman bobbed up and down lightly on the balls of his feet as they continued to study each other.

Though smaller than himself, the tall man recognised the same sense of danger from the doorman as he was sure could be sensed from him. After the moment had passed, again came the nod of approval, his admittance granted for the second time.

'Have a good night, brother!' the doorman called, causing the tall man to look back and smile.

'You too, and watch your back,' he replied, giving the man a wink of camaraderie before walking on.

'Always do,' he heard as he descended into the bowels of the building.

*'What better place to feed than a nightclub,'* the tall man thought, remembering when he had been a bouncer himself for a time.

*'Bouncer,'* he thought, unable to think of the doormen as anything else, a term now frowned upon by the government in favour of the more respectful 'Doorman' image.

Entering the club felt to him like coming home, and on hearing the bass of the music getting louder, his smile had grown along with it. On reaching the bottom-most level, he could feel the energy hitting him in waves of ecstasy and with a sigh of pleasure, he opened himself up to it, drinking in the energy that was so wastefully released, soaking it up like the absorbent he was.

Many times he was glared at by the more unsavoury of the club's clientele, and he was only too happy to drain more than what was needed from them, knowing that the better the vibe in the club, the more the energy would feed him.

To this end, he put his mind to the task of ridding the building of those that would undoubtedly bring the atmosphere down, for he needed it at fever pitch to provide all the energy he required. Walking around in the darkness, he revelled in his creation and the harmony he had cultivated.

The only light cast at this low level was from the large bars at either side of the building and the strobe lights that flashed upon the dance floor.

Looking around, all the old feelings came rushing back, and he remembered the one rule back in his day.

*My way or the highway.* Make a decision and stick to it, right or wrong, for he knew from his wealth of experience that showing compassion or regret over a decision ultimately led to the witnessing lowlifes believing it to be weakness, which ultimately made life harder in the long run.

Midnight passed, and the music had the revellers gyrating on the dance floor, lost as they were within the beat of the music. Girls danced seductively, raising their arms sensually into the air as the young men danced close by, barely restraining themselves from making the desired contact.

Reminded of a religious teaching, he acknowledged the sentiment with a sardonic smile.

'Look, but don't touch,' he scoffed, shaking his head at the foolish notion. *'I touch!'* he thought darkly, for this was the time he had been waiting for.

He had cast his web within the club, removing all the elements that would disrupt what was to happen, and he would now reap the rewards of his labour.

Sexual tension was his energy of choice, for it was the most intoxicating to him, and since these humans lived by such religious codes of denial, that energy was now beginning to flow.

Standing there like a god among mortals, he stretched out his arms to absorb it all before snapping his eyes open at something amiss.

Already brimming with more than enough energy, he had stayed simply for the pleasure of it, but that time had now passed, so he turned his attention to the cause of the disturbance.

Positioning himself against the outer wall, he scanned the club before suddenly feeling eyes upon him. Looking up, he saw all the doormen lined up along the railings of the balcony above, looking down upon him with grim expressions.

Gathering his power about him, he was about to cast his shield when he realised that he was not the cause of concern. Catching the eye of the doorman who had spoken to him on the stairs, he raised his chin enquiringly.

A cold few seconds passed between them, all previous camaraderie lost, before the doorman slowly nodded his head as though deciding upon something.

'Bloods!' he mouthed, staring down with white-faced anticipation.

Instantly shielding himself, an invisible sphere of protection expanded out from him to push those closest to him off their feet, sending them sliding away across the glass-strewn dance floor.

Though unseen to the naked eye, a circle of space cleared around his position as the drunk and drugged alike were cast from him.

The club was near to capacity, the patrons packed almost shoulder to shoulder, and as he made his way slowly through them, it appeared from above as though he were a shark, with the fish around him desperately keeping their distance.

The doorman's eyes never left him as he moved through the crowd, waiting to see his response to the hidden threat.

Looking up at the doorman, he mouthed a question in the knowledge that he would be understood.

'Where?' he asked, unable to pinpoint where the dread was coming from, an emotion he could almost taste in his mouth, but the doorman shook his head, as oblivious to its origin as he was.

'*Of course, the Bloods would be here!*' the tall vampire admonished himself and thought himself foolish for not expecting it.

It was pointless trying to sense them, for all vampires were hidden from such attempts, so instead, he cast his awareness into the crowd, seeking the source of the fear instead of what caused it.

Towards the rear of the club, the taste became more palpable in his mouth, so after another glance at the doorman, he headed in that direction.

'Toilets,' he mouthed, seeing all the doormen stiffen in

response.

Turning back to the task at hand, he pushed open the door that read 'Gents' upon a silver placard but then paused and cocked his head to one side. Stepping back, he moved on before entering the door that read 'Ladies'.

The door opened with a louder whine than he would have liked as the rusty spring mechanism resisted the movement before he let it go to slam home behind him.

Mirrors dominated the entire far wall, with many sinks lined up underneath. On his right sat several cubicles with solid-looking wooden doors painted a dark green, all closed but not tightly after the locks had been broken off at some point in the past.

What was once a cream-tiled floor was now corrupted with the darkness of blood that looked burgundy in the dim light, giving the room that unsettling, straight-out-of-a-horror-movie appearance.

A couple of girls stood trembling to the left of the sinks, standing with their backs against the wall with wide, crazed eyes that stared towards the cubicles.

Placing a finger to his lips, he gave them the gesture for silence, though he suspected they were too petrified to do anything but whimper.

A grunt, not unlike that of a pig, issued from one of the cubicles before they heard the sound of a dead weight being dropped. An instant later, one of the green doors burst off its hinges, crashing against the far wall with a large splintering crack running right down the centre of it.

As the tall man watched, the shapely form of an original vampire stepped out confidently.

He took in the long, well-muscled legs before noting the cold blue eyes fixing upon his own with sudden interest.

He thought that she would have been beautiful, but for the gore dripping from her chin, and as though sensing his revulsion, she casually wiped it from her chin with the back of her hand.

The smile grew on her face, and he saw a fang suddenly protrude a little from the right side of her mouth, causing him to frown again.

The 'Blood girl,' for that is what she appeared to be, looked no older than twenty years of age as she took a long-legged step towards him before stopping to wiggle her hips in anticipation.

Though he knew exactly what she was, he could not help but notice her enticing attire and sexy appeal.

'What do we have here?' she asked huskily, eyeing him up and down appreciatively. 'I do hope that you've come to stop me, handsome,' she continued confidently, licking blood from her lips before sucking at her fingers.

'That I have,' he answered, taking a step forward himself.

Knowing from experience how much faster her kind was than his, he knew that when her attack came, it would be faster than that of a cobra.

Spreading her arms, she shrugged apologetically.

'Have I done something wrong?' she teased, playing her character well. 'Things are about to change, cousin,' she continued, smiling at him sweetly. 'We are about to be so much closer, you and I,' she whispered, crouching low as she readied to pounce.

Behind him, the door burst open, slamming hard against the white-tiled wall as men in black spread out cautiously to bar any attempt of escape. Not known for their conversational skills when things truly hit the fan, the doormen reacted on instinct and attacked without warning.

The first threw a blindingly fast punch at her face, which she caught at the wrist before twisting it hard to send her attacker to his knees with a cry of pain. Striking out at her second attacker, she front-kicked him in the chest to launch him back through the door he had just come through.

The first attacking doorman cried out again as she forced him down to the blood-smeared floor, face first with his arm bent impossibly behind him.

The door crashed open again, and, without turning, the tall man held up a hand to stop them. Whether it was his manner or some hidden authority he seemed to exude, the doormen silently came to a stop behind him.

Glaring at him with a sadistic lust in her eyes, the girl tensed suddenly, but he read her intent before she could carry out the deed.

'If you kill him, you die,' he warned with finality, meaning every word. 'If you hurt him further, you die,' he continued. 'In fact,' he added, as though in light conversation, 'you are going to have a hard time staying alive at all,' he finished, smiling with the same confidence he had seen in her.

'At some point,' she replied, her eyes looking black and full of lust, 'I'm going to have you all to myself,' she breathed, unconsciously licking her lips at the prospect.

With her eyes locked onto his in a battle of wills, she sensed no weakness in the dark, brooding eyes and felt all the more excited for it.

Sighing at last in resignation, she smiled at the tall man warmly before kicking the doorman away.

Without warning, the tall man's arm shot out, throwing her back against the wall with his mind alone, pinning her there off her feet. The force of the impact sent a low thump of vibration reverberating dully around the room, the tiles cracking into what looked like a spider's web behind her as fragments of white dropped to the crimson floor beneath her feet.

With eyes widened in shock, she was clearly unprepared for this kind of attack and simply hung there for a moment with her fierce blue eyes still locked on his.

Recovering quickly, she braced herself against the wall before delivering her response.

'I think not,' he said, seeing that she was not yet defeated, and with a gesture of summoning, she floated effortlessly towards him.

'An ancient!' she cried, looking overjoyed despite her predicament. 'Who would have thought,' she remarked mockingly, speaking the words slowly. 'I will enjoy you all the more for this,' she continued, hanging impotently in the air. 'With those luscious brown locks of yours, you just have to be Cristian,' she surmised, cocking an eyebrow at him to see if she was right.

Dipping his head in acknowledgement, Cristian half-smiled with the right side of his mouth.

'At your pleasure,' he confirmed, broadening his smile.

'Oh, indeed it shall be,' she promised, clapping her hands in slow appreciation. 'I am Lore,' she introduced, winking at him seductively as she awaited his response.

He had heard her name before from his father and knew her to be as deadly as she appeared to be.

'A Blood Lord, no less!' he remarked, looking her over with a wandering eye. 'I must say that others of your ilk have been less...' he continued, pursing his lips as he sought the right word.

'Attractive?' she offered, reading the desire he had for her and smiling when he did not correct her. 'We are not all as sexless as you have been led to believe, and though a lord I be, I am clearly a lady!' she informed, showing him a rebellious streak even against her own kind.

'That title would be more fitting,' he agreed, causing her to laugh throatily.

Seeming to relax a little, she folded her arms before crossing her legs as though sitting in an invisible chair, and even suspended as she was, he found her more than alluring in her tight-fitting clothes as his eyes roamed over her curves again.

'Oh, we will have such fun together, Cristian,' she purred, nodding at him assuredly. 'But you have forgotten one fateful thing, my love,' she chastised sweetly, wagging a slender finger back and forth, 'there are always, always...' she began, pausing for effect, '... three of us.'

At her words, Cristian heard a great commotion from behind and spun on his heel to see two large Bloods fighting their way through the doormen.

The fight was quick and decisive, the Bloods having already downed a couple of the doormen with immense, bone-shattering blows.

The large black doorman from the front door was thrown hard against the line of mirrors, shattering them and caving in the brickwork that lay behind.

Pulling up his shirt sleeve, Cristian placed his hand over a silver tattoo etched into his forearm.

Looking to be a silver crucifix of some kind, the silver cylindrical object ran from wrist to elbow, but the cross-section appeared far too high, making it look more like the letter 'T' than a cross of Christianity.

Without deliberation, the ancient warrior closed his hand around it and pulled forth a silver sword of such deadly grace that the very sight of it was enough to give the Bloods pause.

Widening her eyes at the sight, Lore's once unwavering confidence began to fade into fear, for she had heard of the fabled Swords of Power but never once in her wildest imaginings had she believed them to be real.

An eerie light seemed to emanate from the weapon, casting a silvery glow about the room before flashing like lightning as it suddenly struck out. Impaling the first vampire through the heart, the blade spun masterfully before beheading the second.

Turning with the sword raised in defence, Cristian had anticipated an attack from Lore, but the space she had occupied stood empty, causing him to spin again before cursing her escape.

Finally stopping his dance of death, he surveyed the carnage before him and made doubly sure that the speared vampire was, indeed, dead.

The doormen, battered as they were, began to rise and dust themselves off, and the one he had saved stepped forward to grip his forearm tightly in a warrior's greeting of respect.

'Warren,' he announced fiercely, giving the ancient vampire his name. 'And thanks,' he added, the glow of kinship shining in his eyes.

Clamping his free hand upon the doorman's shoulder, Cristian smiled and accepted his gratitude.

'It was my pleasure,' he replied, giving the shoulder a squeeze.

'Pull me out of here, War!' called the hulking form of the head doorman, his rear end still buried deep within the hole he had made above the sinks.

Chuckling at his leader's predicament, Warren pulled the giant free, and then looked back at the swordsman.

'This is Geez,' he introduced, slapping the large ebony-skinned man on the back. 'No need to explain why we call him that,' he added, smiling up at his elder, who referred to almost everyone in that way.

Glancing about the room, Warren then proceeded to point out other people of note.

'The tall blond guy over there is Aled, and that mean-looking guy next to him is Bishop,' he continued, gesturing around the room.

The big bald man smiled, but Cristian could see that he was being gauged, seeing a wealth of experience in his unsmiling eyes.

Two more doormen entered and looked at the scene in dismay.

'Why didn't you call us?' asked the smaller of the two before his eyes fell on the swordsman.

Barbed wire tattoos ran all about his neck and head, giving him a wild, psychotic look, but there was intelligence in his eyes and a military sureness to his manner that marked him a veteran.

'That there is Lee and Wayne, or "Jedi", as we call him,' Warren continued, nodding at the quieter of the two.

Wayne nodded back but said nothing, his slightly slanted eyes showing little emotion as he looked at the newcomer.

'That big chatterbox over there is Rob, and that's Darren standing next to him,' Warren went on, finally finishing the introductions.

Not knowing which was which, Cristian saw that both men had turned at hearing their names and that both were bald, muscular and looked every part the doormen they were. In fact, the only difference between them that he could see was that one looked friendly, and the other did not.

Warren then put his hand on Cristian's shoulder and introduced him to the roomful of bouncers.

'This is *Cristian!*' he said reverently, smiling broadly up at the ancient.

Not knowing what to make of this unusual group of doormen, Cristian, nevertheless, felt intrigued as to their origin.

He had sensed that they were of the Egni upon approaching the door and knew that they had sensed the same of him, but what he could not understand was why he had not known of their existence until now.

Spinning the sword in an intricate manoeuvre, he returned the weapon to its magickal sheath in a blur of silver light before noting the look of shock registering in the others.

'You look like you haven't seen magick before,' he observed, looking at them all in turn before Wayne stepped forward with his hands clasped in a meditative manner.

'I can move stuff with my mind,' he said, nodding assuredly as though expecting to be disbelieved. 'It's why they call me *Jedi,*' he informed, smiling at the eye-rolling of his friends.

Scoffing out loud, Lee, the tattooed doorman, shook his head in disagreement. 'It's why *you* call yourself that, you mean,' he corrected, slapping his friend hard on the back.

Ignoring the banter, Cristian looked seriously at them all and began to realise the truth of the situation.

'You can all do it, and so much more besides! We, the Egni, have great magick at our disposal,' he announced, looking at the vacant, disbelieving stares before him.

Frowning, he felt irritated by their lack of understanding and sought to get to the bottom of it.

'Who is your elder?' he demanded, seeking to find the one who had broken his faction's law.

The doormen looked at each other, becoming tight-lipped suddenly until, finally, Warren shifted uncomfortably before clearing his throat.

'The one who made the first of us?' he asked tentatively, causing Cristian's eyes to fix upon him.

'Yes!' he snapped in irritation, his anger mounting.

Shifting his weight uncomfortably from one foot to the other, Warren briefly looked at Geez before finally responding.

'Maybe fifty or so years ago, a club owner made Geez here, and so I guess he is our elder,' Warren answered, standing to attention with his hands clasped behind his back.

Snapping his eyes to the giant, Cristian cocked an eyebrow at him.

'I guess he wanted a doorman that would be unbeatable,' Geez began, anger flashing suddenly in his dark eyes. 'He started to teach me things before he got bored and left... but he left a book of our history behind for me to read,' his deep voice informed, clearly harbouring a deep resentment over the matter.

Regarding him in silence for a time, Cristian felt a sudden pang of pity for the man being left in such a way.

'Is this all of you?' he asked, gesturing around the room.

Geez looked around the room and could not hide the smile from his lips.

'No,' he answered softly before sensing that it was the wrong answer. 'There are others,' he added, shrugging his huge shoulders uncaringly.

With a sinking feeling in his stomach, Cristian closed his eyes as though pained by the answer.

'How many?' he asked, dreading the answer.

The huge doorman took a step back as though expecting a fight, and gave a warning shake of his head for the ancient to calm himself.

'You need to understand that the Bloods came and nearly killed me,' he replied defensively, seeing the cold expression washing over the swordsman's face.

The bathroom became silent, and Cristian knew all too well that this was the calm before the storm should he accuse them of any wrongdoing. He was not afraid, however, for he knew that his might dwarfed theirs many times over. He just knew it would sit ill with him if he were to wipe them out for no good reason.

Suddenly noticing that the music had stopped playing in the club, a deadly tension hung in the air as they awaited his response.

'I am angry,' he confessed, clenching his jaw tightly in an attempt to control it. 'I am seething, but not at you. I am angered by the way you have been treated,' he continued, unable to believe what he was hearing.

Turning again, he looked towards the door with a tilt of his head.

'What's happened to the music?' he asked, causing Warren to come to life again.

'The club is empty. Lee and Wayne don't mess about when things turn to shit,' he answered, looking at his friends with respect.

'Damn straight!' Lee agreed as his friend merely nodded sagely at his side.

'Good,' Cristian replied, his respect for them growing at their no-nonsense approach. *Secrecy is paramount to them,'* he realised, looking at these men in black and thinking of the hardships they had endured. 'Good,' he repeated, turning back to Geez. 'You have inadvertently created a new faction. You know that, right?' he asked, shaking his head tiredly. 'So how many of you are there?' he asked, causing the black man to smile before turning once again to his second.

'War?' he asked, lifting his chin a little.

Standing to attention again, Warren looked up to his right for a moment before giving the answer.

'All told, we number maybe fifteen...' he began, but a sigh of relief caused him to glance at Geez again with a grimace.

Seeing the shared look between them, Cristian closed his eyes in depression.

'Fifteen hundred,' he whispered, shaking his head in misery.

Clearing his throat again, Warren corrected him rather awkwardly.

'Thousand,' he announced, looking straight ahead at no one in particular.

'Thousand!' Cristian cried, his face now white. 'Thousand?' he asked, at which the doorman nodded curtly before continuing his military stare ahead.

'If you don't like it, then leave!' Lee growled testily, shrugging off a restraining hand from Wayne. 'We've been doing fine without you. Those bloodsuckers keep coming, and we need the numbers,' he growled, glaring back aggressively.

Realising that he needed to make a point, Cristian knew just who to make it with.

'The Bloods are toying with you. They have realised that you are outside of the Egni faction and consider you sport for their amusement,' he replied, shaking his head warningly at the tattooed fighter, who raised his head in challenge.

'We don't need your poxy protection, and we are "sport" for no one,' he retorted, flexing his hands menacingly. 'So you killed a couple of Bloods, we've killed more! I think you're all talk!' he challenged, feeling fed up with the superior way of this newcomer.

A cold smile spread across the ancient's face, and he knew that this could only play out one way.

'Fancy joining me outside to find out?' he asked, and before his friends could stop him, the challenge was accepted.

\*\*\*

Standing on the dance floor with the main lights turned on, Cristian saw the remaining doormen spread out to watch how the fight would unfold.

Ripping his shirt from his powerful-looking body, Lee's barbed wire tattoo was now visible in its fullness, running down his entire torso and crossing at his waist.

Chuckling at the failed attempt at intimidation, Cristian shook his head before gesturing the shorter man forward.

Immediately obliging, Lee launched himself forward with a flurry of punches blurring towards Cristian's head.

Skipping back a couple of steps, Cristian held up a hand to lift the fighter off his feet as he had done to Lore.

Taken completely by surprise, Lee ran on the spot for a moment with his arms still lashing out before he screamed in rage after hearing the chuckles coming from his friends.

'It's not my intention to humiliate you, Lee. I admire your courage, but courage alone will only get you killed,' Cristian said, motioning the remaining doormen to attack him.

It was Wayne who was first to hit his shield, the force of the impact causing the barrier to whiten before driving the doorman back to skid across the floor.

'The Bloods are naturally stronger and faster than we are,' he informed, gesturing for more to attack. But his point had been made, it seemed, for the remaining doormen held back. 'Up to this point, they have been testing you, probably to see if there were any repercussions for their actions against you, and believe me when I tell you, they will kill you all in the end,' he paused, letting the truth of what he was saying sink in.

Looking around the room, Cristian shook his head, saddened as a cold reality occurred to him.

'The Egni will also kill you if they learn of your existence,' he whispered, glancing at the head doorman who spread his arms.

'Why, Geez?' the man asked in a pained tone of voice, causing the ancient to feel a great deal of sympathy for him.

'Because of your numbers, because you have not been taught, and because of the risk of discovery you pose,' he answered, giving them the cold hard truth of the situation.

'So, are you going to kill us?' Lee asked, with a sad and somewhat defeated tone in his voice.

Pursing his lips, Cristian slowly shook his head with a sigh of resignation.

'I came here for another reason tonight, a reason I am now forced to postpone,' he answered, holding their attention with every word he spoke. 'I will give you one month to get yourselves proficient in the use of magick. One month, so that you can defend yourselves against all who would wish to kill you,' he announced, smiling grimly at the appreciation in their eyes. 'I am going to teach you to become what you were always meant to be,' he whispered, silently fearing what retribution would be taken against him for doing so.

# CHAPTER TEN

A knock at the door caused Kristina to breathe out nervously, for the time had come for the coven to create a witches' circle. Opening the door, Jacky stood with her witches in tow, her pale blue eyes full of warmth as she stepped in to hug her.

'Everything is prepared, and we shall cast our circle shortly,' she whispered, giving Kristina another excited hug before moving past with a wary eye at the house as she did so. 'We'll ask for a goddess to bless us and seal our circle. Between me and you, I hope it's the Queen of Air who comes,' she confided quietly, the words trembling from her mouth.

'The Fae Queen?' Kristina asked, having read much about such things since studying witchcraft. 'Aren't there any deities from this world that could bless us?' she asked, intrigued as to why the priestess would wish for any other.

Shaking her head, Jacky smiled patiently and paused in her preparations to explain.

'The gods of this world rarely show themselves. It's almost always those from the other realms that add their might to ours, and, in turn, all we have to do is perform certain rights for them,' she replied, sounding very confident in the way it all worked. But on seeing the look of confusion on Kristina's face, she realised that more of an explanation was needed.

'I'm not completely sure why they require this of us, but it seems to me that we get the lion's share of the bargain,' she added, shrugging her shoulders a little.

'Do they ever ignore the summons or refuse the blessing?' Kristina asked, wanting to understand it all.

'There have been many times when a circle was ignored and a singular time that I know of when a circle was refused,' Jacky replied, her expression tightening. 'It's far better to be ignored than refused,' she added, her smile suddenly faltering.

Walking into the room, Kristina placed her hands on her hips and waited for the priestess to continue.

'A circle refused means death to the coven,' Jacky stated, holding up her hands at the expression of alarm on Kristina's face. 'Only the worst kind of witches have ever been refused, those who don't deserve to live in the first place,' she stressed, smiling more reassuringly. 'I have been in other covens before and other circles, so believe me when I say that we will be blessed,' she added, nodding her head assuredly before ambling away.

Watching them prepare, Kristina wished that she had more time to think about joining the coven. Doubt gnawed at her for the very first time, and she began to feel trapped as the preparations neared completion.

'Are we doing the right thing?' she blurted, causing the priestess to round on her angrily.

'Of course, we are!' she stormed, her tone harsh and totally out of character.

Taken aback for a moment, Kristina just stared with her face flushing crimson.

Stopping what she was doing, Jacky walked over and placed her hands upon Kristina's shoulders.

'Kris, you are doing the right thing. *We* are doing the right thing. This is the only way to protect them… the only way for them to be safe, okay?' she said after a pause, her motherly expression now full of care and understanding.

'Okay,' Kristina whispered, her eyes brimming with fearful tears.

*'Please let her be right,'* she quailed, wishing with all her might that she was.

***

Sitting in a half-circle before Kristina and the children, the witches stared back passionately, but it soon became clear whom their attention was fixed upon, for not a single one had eyes for the mother.

Looking back excitedly, Lucian was clearly unafraid of what was about to occur, but Francesca had withdrawn into herself and appeared sullen as she stared at her mother with accusatory eyes.

Having told her children that they were to become witches, their responses had been quite different. Lucian had nodded emphatically at the news, but Francesca had questions, and many of them.

'Why do we have to?' she argued, her blue eyes searching her mother's face for the truth.

Having expected this, Kristina had rehearsed her response well and answered almost without thinking about it.

'Because once you've practised magick, you have to join a coven,' she'd replied offhandedly, but her daughter had frowned at her words, seeing through the deception.

'Is Daddy in a coven?' she shot back, causing Kristina to pause before answering.

'No, baby, only women are in covens,' she stammered, feeling her face flush at the continued lie.

Hands on hips, in a classic pose normally reserved for her mother, Francesca glared up in anger.

'Then why is *he* becoming one?' she stormed, pointing at her brother before lowering her hands into fists at her sides.

Feeling her face deepen with embarrassment, Kristina's emotion quickly turned to anger.

'Because most boys choose another path, but because he's so young, he is to come with us!' she replied, her eyes wide and staring.

Shaking her head, Francesca was unwilling to accept the feeble explanation after seeing the lie for what it was.

'What other paths are there, and why can't I choose one of those?' she asked, knowing in her heart that she was being manipulated.

Blood-red emotion flushed into Kristina's cheeks before she raised her voice in anger.

'Because you are too young. Because you stole Daddy's book and learned magick before you were ready! Now you have to join the coven with me or be taken away! Is that what you want?' she shrilled, placing her hands upon her own hips.

Staring back in anger, the colour drained from her daughter's face after being called a thief.

'I didn't steal it!' she shouted, her voice shaking with fury. 'I read a book! You left the door open!' she retorted, clearly having listened in on her parents arguing.

It was Janet who had spoken next, cutting off Kristina's angry retort.

'Cesca, you went into your father's room, and now this is what we need to do to keep you safe! Otherwise, the vampires will come and take you away. You don't want them to take you, do you?' she asked softly, but there was no warmth in her flinty eyes.

The children looked petrified and took hold of each other's hands in fear as they stepped away from her instinctively.

'Mammy, please don't let them get me!' Lucian cried, running to her and hugging her waist.

Crouching down with arms open wide, Kristina took him in her arms, shushing him while stroking his hair.

'Of course not, my handsome boy,' she soothed, guilty tears falling to her cheeks.

'Why would they come?' Francesca spat defiantly but was clearly unsettled by the threat.

'Because they want to eat you because you can do magick!' Janet snapped, incensed by her insolent tone.

Looking at her mother, Francesca pleaded with her to listen.

'Mammy, please! Find Daddy! Please, Mammy, please?' she cried, looking so desperate that her mother could only cry and pull her into her embrace.

'Please. This is the only way,' she whispered into her ear, her heart breaking at the pain she was causing. 'Please, Cesca? Until Daddy returns? If he comes back, you can do whatever you want,' she sobbed, reaching out to stroke her daughter's face.

Long moments passed before Francesca finally nodded, little knowing that the agreement had been witnessed and a deal had been struck.

*** 

'The coven is cast, one and three, accept these witches into thee,' the witches began, and the house came alive in response.

It started with a groan that got steadily louder, like some restless soul that was beginning to stir.

Flinching when the doors slammed closed, Kristina had a

sense that the house was fortifying the room or maybe that it intended to trap them there against their will.

Several witches looked up from their chanting, but a glare from their priestess made them return to their work.

*'Horns of the forest, Air of the Queen, we call upon thee to bless us clean.'*

The low, mournful wail began getting louder, vibrating up through the floorboards as though issuing out of hell itself.

The bright morning sky darkened ominously, casting the room into almost total darkness except for the illumination from the thirteen candles that shone upon their faces.

The wind outside gathered into a gale, driving a spontaneous bout of rain hard against the windows with force enough to break them.

After a brief pause, Jacky took up the summoning again, unwilling to be distracted at this pivotal point.

'Horns of the forest or Air to the Fae, we humbly beseech thee to bless our circle and grant us...' she continued but stopped again when her candle snuffed out.

The children shrank back, looking to their mother for support.

'Mammy!' Lucian cried but was instantly silenced by a finger to the lips.

Deciding to take up the chant, Janet opened her mouth to speak before her candle too extinguished with an angry hiss. And so it was for each of the witches until only the mother and her children remained.

Cast now in almost complete darkness, the trio of flickering lights did little to penetrate the blackness that seemed to solidify into an impenetrable wall of hate around them.

Steeling herself after a pleading look from the priestess, Kristina raised her voice over the sound of the rain.

'Grant us...' she began, but a hiss from below caused her to cry out in alarm as the flame appeared to coil like a viper readying to strike.

The flame appeared not to flicker any more, sitting within its bed of wax, intent, it seemed, on stopping her from completing the ritual.

With eyes widened in realisation, she knew in that dreadful

moment what it was she was truly seeing. This was *his* magick at work and his protection that seemed caught with indecision.

Feeling the flame's caged desire to hurt her, she finally understood that what he had called forth went far beyond the land alone, for not one but all of the elements had gathered about them, and she looked to the window to see two of them bombarding the glass.

'Air and Water,' she gasped, and in her hands was the element of fire itself!

Closing her eyes, she felt unwilling to look at the fury in her hands and the desire it had to harm her for what she was allowing to occur.

Feeling the vibration beneath her feet, she knew it to be from the land itself as it shook in anger.

*'Why hasn't my candle gone out?'* she wondered, opening her eyes to frown down at the naked flame. 'Of course!' she gasped, knowing the answer as a memory burst through her mind to enlighten her to what was happening now.

*'The protection is not just for them,'* Daire had said before he left that fateful night.

Staring at the flame, she sensed its desire to leap at her and instinctively angled it away before opening her mouth to complete the summons.

The fire's hiss erupted again, louder than before, as the ten candles burst suddenly into life once again, causing many of the hooded witches to drop them in alarm.

'GET OUT!' thundered a deep, terrifying voice, erupting from everywhere at once.

Some of the witches screamed, as others openly wept at the demonic-sounding command, for the voice was wrath itself, full of hate for those it deemed unwelcome.

A few of the women lost control of themselves, wetting their robes and the rug on which they knelt as they fumbled at their candles.

Cowering low from the angered presence, Kristina could feel it move among them in the flaming half-light as if readying to finally take form and smite them. Looking around frantically, she saw that all composure was lost among the witches, desperate they seemed now to leave this hateful place.

Turning fearfully towards her children, she saw that Lucian had buried his head into the crook of his sister's arm but that Francesca herself sat straight-backed with her eyes looking stern.

Angered by the expression, Kristina stubbornly refused to be controlled by the will of the child or that of her father and breathed in deeply before breaking her promise.

'Grant us our circle!' she screamed, holding Francesca's eyes in challenge as she did so.

Shaking her head, tears sprang from Francesca's eyes.

'You will regret this,' she whispered, the tears falling to her cheeks. 'You know what he promised!' she continued, her young face creasing with pain.

Erupting at her words, the walls began to tremble, and the doors opened with a thunderous crash only to close again to seal them in.

The candles the witches held flared, burning them about the neck and chin before climbing murderously up to their faces.

Screaming in pain, one of the witches ran into the kitchen to douse the flames from an upended pitcher, but the water inside refused to leave, fighting gravity itself in its refusal to help her, and howling in dismay, the witches burned as the fire began to consume them.

Looking on in horror, Kristina put her hands to her mouth, not knowing what to do, and so it was her daughter who was the one to act. Standing up with her brother still attached to her midriff, she raised her arms into the air and closed her eyes to concentrate.

'Stop!' she sobbed, keeping her eyes closed so as not to see what the firelight showed.

The fires instantly died, sending the room into almost total darkness, the two flames left burning casting an eerie light upon the children's faces.

Clutching his candle tightly, Lucian had unintentionally turned it into his sister's side, and on looking down, he snatched it away with a cry of concern.

'I'm sorry!' he apologised before frowning as he peered a little closer to see that not even her dress had been burned by the contact.

Tentatively passing his hand over the flame, he shook his head in disbelief after feeling not the pain nor the damage wrought upon the witches by the wrathful elements, and, in a moment of daring, he cast his hand into it with a wince of expected pain.

Oblivious to her brother's antics, Francesca looked at her mother and shook her head again.

'You caused this!' she accused pitifully, causing her mother to gather her into her arms.

'I'm trying to protect you! Don't you see that?' Kristina cried, turning her head to the sounds of pain hidden in the shadows.

'Did it work?' Janet shrilled, almost completely hidden within the gloom.

Struggling to her knees, Jacky closed her eyes and gritted her teeth against the pain before gathering what strength she had left.

'We beseech thee to bless our circle!' she intoned, finally completing the summoning.

An unsettling stillness descended upon the room, and the darkness seemed to deepen into a depthless, disturbing black.

A sense of movement could be felt but not heard or seen from the glow of the two candles.

The shadows seemed to dance, adding to the sense of movement, but there was now a feeling that they were no longer alone.

'My god!' Kristina whispered, seeing two glints of white appear in the fireplace.

Appearing side by side, they rose slowly, reflecting the light of the candles like the reflective eyes of a cat.

Coming to a stop where Kristina deemed someone's eyes should be, the shining glints narrowed and began searching the room until finally widening in her direction.

The two white orbs reminded her somehow of Daire after his transformation, for they glowed like the moon when they found what they were looking for.

The shadows around them condensed suddenly, and an outline of a figure began to take shape. Long-limbed and seductively female, the form stretched like a cat before the glowing white eyes narrowed again.

'Fear not, my children, for no harm will I ever intend upon thee,' the goddess purred, soft and full of warmth as she surveyed the scene before her.

The fallen witches rose immediately to their knees with a look of awe etched on their faces, the pain of their injuries forgotten for the moment.

Feeling a warm flush at the words, Kristina could not fail to hear the acceptance and love for her in the tone of the goddess.

'For you are his children and will be treasured in all of my forms,' the goddess continued, turning Kristina's elation to ice in her veins.

She understood then that the goddess spoke not to her at all but to her children, and the resulting fear swept through her like a winter storm.

Peeping out from behind his sister, Lucian looked at the goddess with an uncertain smile spreading across his tear-streaked face.

'I like your eyes,' he remarked innocently and opened his mouth as his smile grew bigger.

A deep, throaty laugh reverberated around the room as the shadowed goddess showed her amusement.

'As I do yours, young Lucian. And you, Francesca,' she purred softly, turning her attention to the blonde-haired child, 'a fairer beauty I have seldom seen,' she soothed, noting the pain in the deep blue eyes.

Flushing at the compliment, Francesca smiled shyly before opening her mouth to respond.

'Will you bless us?' Janet cut in, so desperate was she for the power to be bestowed upon her.

The Queen's eyes snapped to her in anger, causing the woman to shrink back in terror.

'I would have had you been pure and worthy to receive it, but...' she replied, her tone rising at the last.

There was a pause, and Kristina saw the eyes turning round in anger.

'You have manipulated, scared and guilted these children into completing your circle,' the goddess accused, speaking in a voice so powerful and so full of menace that it reminded Kristina of when the house had spoken.

Pausing again, the Fae Queen turned her glare upon Kristina and tutted softly with a shake of her head.

'There will be a reckoning,' she warned lightly, speaking again in that high, lilting tone.

Seeming to mull something over in her mind, the goddess narrowed her eyes again before sighing in resignation.

'You have, however, completed your circle without me and so shall reap the rewards of your labour,' she continued, breathing out the words tiredly, stalking forward to cause the witches to scramble back. 'For now,' she added wickedly, the threat of what would come evident in her tone.

Turning back to the children, the Queen of Air tilted her head with a look of fascination before glaring again at their mother.

'There will be a price to pay for your betrayal,' she thundered, shaking the room with the suddenness of her anger.

'Please don't take them from me!' Kristina begged, struggling to speak through her sobbing. 'I beg you. They're all I have,' she pleaded, shaking uncontrollably as her emotion threatened to consume her.

Regarding her in silence for a time, the goddess looked back without care or sympathy.

'That is not for me to decide, for if it was, I surely would, but I, unlike you, will honour his wishes and allow this circle that you have sacrificed so much of yourself to have... but bless it, I will not!' she replied coldly, turning her attention once again to the children.

Tilting her head to the side, her glowing white eyes narrowed again as she backed up into the hearth.

Raising her hand shyly in farewell, Francesca caused the white eyes to widen momentarily before the goddess spoke again.

'Until next we meet, Cesca. For we will surely see each other again,' she whispered, using her shortened name in the way her father used to.

Turning her attention to the priestess, the goddess glowered at her coldly.

'I am forbidden to you now! Call not upon me again,' she warned, closing her eyes as the two remaining candles finally snuffed out.

No one breathed in the dark aftermath, all eyes locked on

where the fierce white eyes had disappeared.

'Goddess?' Janet called meekly, but the Queen of Air had withdrawn and she began weeping in relief at her departure.

Gathering themselves up, the witches' previously forgotten pain returned with a vengeance, causing them to cry out in anguish.

'I can't see,' Lucian moaned, causing his candle to ignite and highlight the triumphant expression on the face of the priestess.

'GET OUT!' the house erupted, more venomous than before, as it came back to life.

A low growl rose up around them, and it was clear that the house was continuing where it had left off.

Screams erupted but were unceremoniously cut off, causing Kristina to hold her children close in an attempt to protect them. Squinting through the gloom, she adjusted her eyes to the darkness and inhaled sharply at the scene of outlined horror.

Several of the witches were wrenched from their feet as though by unseen hands at their throats and then left there to twitch in their fight for life. She saw Jacky scrambling desperately towards the door before being dragged back into the darkness, her nails scratching up the wooden floor as she did so.

'Make it stop, Mammy!' Lucian cried, his voice muffled as he pressed his face into her side.

As though in response, loud thumps sounded with gasps of expelled air issuing upon impact, and at the witches' sudden release, they took little time in racing from the house. Only the High Priestess hazarded a glance in the children's direction as she, too, fled, seemingly assisted by unseen hands.

Janet remained where she had fallen, her hands placed at her throat as she coughed blood onto the dark wooden floor.

'Oh, Jan!' Kristina cried, tears welling in her eyes again.

'Turn the lights on!' Francesca demanded in anger, unable to see clearly in the glow of her brother's candle.

The lights blinked on, seemingly of their own volition, and a stunned silence fell upon them at the sight before them.

Crumpled upon the floor with a hand at her throat, Janet

began whimpering again as something clamped onto her foot to drag her backwards towards the open doorway.

'Stop it,' Francesca demanded, her fists clenching at her sides.

Seeing her friend instantly released, Kristina realised that the children had some kind of influence over what their father had done to the house.

Bending down, she whispered into her daughter's ear and stood back to see what would happen.

'You are not to hurt Janet anymore,' the child commanded, looking up and around the room. 'Okay?' she snapped, impatiently awaiting its response.

The house groaned, and the living room door slammed shut as though in temper, followed by a door upstairs closing with a similar ferocity.

Kristina froze, realising fearfully whose room it was.

*Is that where he did it?'* she thought, feeling sick to the stomach at the thought of the presence emanating from where her daughter slept.

Rising shakily to her feet, Janet stumbled to a sofa before falling into it.

'Are you okay?' Kristina asked, hovering her hands over her friend worriedly.

'What do you think?' Janet shrilled, glaring up at her accusingly before closing her eyes. 'I'm sorry, Kiki. I just don't know why... why would it want to hurt me?' she sobbed, her bottom lip beginning to tremble.

'Daddy,' Lucian answered, speaking in an uncharacteristically insightful manner before leaning to the side to kiss the wall.

'I love you, Daddy,' he whispered, stepping forward to hug the brickwork.

'I love you, too, my little wolf,' the house growled, causing both women to scream.

\*\*\*

The following week passed without incident, and the nightmare of that night began to fade into memory. The house seemed calmer and somewhat subdued after the event, but there was still a sense of unease about the place, at least as far as Kristina was concerned.

Thinking constantly about what the goddess had said, she relived the conversation in her mind.

'His children,' the goddess had said, clearly referring to their father. 'So is he alive, or had she known him at some point in the past?' she wondered, believing the latter since she could now sense his essence deep within the forest.

It was a strange sensation, as though she could smell him there somehow, unmoving and slowly fading away, which only added to her belief that he had indeed died out there.

Shaking her head, she knew that a time would come when she could no longer stand the not knowing and go see for herself.

All had been quiet since the witches had fled that night, never to return, it seemed, and she could not blame them. What had been done to them was nothing short of evil, and if not for the persistent threat to her children, she would have followed them. The place felt colder to her now, as though all the 'homely' feel had gone, and she silently resented him for ever changing it.

She could still sense the house's anger as she could the elements', but believed it held in check, or more likely that they were simply forbidden to act against her out of some deep respect for Daire.

Looking across at her children, she smiled sadly and marvelled at their resilience, for they had risen from their beds the following morning as though nothing had happened.

'Amazing what a good night's sleep can do,' she thought, considering their mental recovery nothing short of miraculous.

Both seemed to tire more easily since the circle's creation, however, as though the circle was draining them in some way.

Closing her eyes, she could not help but feel that she had been played by the lot of them and that the only reason she had been accepted at all was because of her children.

Leaving them to play on their iPads, she walked into the kitchen to cook up some lunch. Removing a packet of pasta from one of the many cupboards, she placed a saucepan in the sink before turning on the tap.

Frowning when nothing happened, she thought that maybe the water had been cut off and, experimentally, turned the tap open fully.

'Hmm,' she mused, peering more closely just as a jet of cold water soaked her as it rebounded off the basin.

Coughing and spluttering, she turned the tap off, and stared at it for a moment before finally shaking her head at her overactive imagination.

Shrugging it off as just one of those things, she wiped her face with a dishcloth before continuing.

After dinner, she washed up and went upstairs to the bathroom, feeling the need to be clean before settling down for the night. Walking to the bathtub, she paused to look sceptically up at the shower head, feeling as though it was waiting for her to make the first move.

Tentatively this time, she turned the lever with a held breath, but the water sprinkled out in the usual way, and she shook her head with a chuckle.

'Get a grip, Kristina!' she admonished, beginning to undress.

Feeling invigorated and more than a little refreshed, she headed back across the landing whilst towel-drying her hair. Humming to herself, she was on the verge of entering her bedroom when a cold shiver ran up her spine a moment before the door slammed in her face.

Dropping the towel in fright, she slowly reached for the handle. Pushing the door with her foot, she held her breath as it slowly creaked open.

'Cesca? Lucian?' she called out nervously, having not heard them come upstairs.

'Yes, Mammy?' they answered simultaneously, their voices sounding muffled from down in the living room.

Another cold shiver ran through her before she nervously stepped inside, looking left and right for signs of an intruder as she did so.

'Don't worry,' she called back just as the door slammed behind her.

Yelping in alarm, she knew immediately that it was the house and not a vampire, though the enlightenment gave her little solace after witnessing what her home was capable of.

'I'm sorry,' she whispered, seeing her breath fog from her

mouth as the temperature dropped. 'I'm truly sorry for what I did,' she stressed, spreading her arms a little.

As though in answer, the cold chill receded, and the door creaked open again to let the warmer air brush against her skin.

Finally dried and dressed in her nightwear, she walked out onto the landing to descend the stairs when she heard the faint sounds of whispering coming from her daughter's bedroom.

Creeping to the room, she pressed her ear to the door to better listen to what was being said.

'You're sure I can kill them like that?' her daughter asked, causing her mother to hold her breath in fear.

*They're talking of killing?'* she thought in alarm before opening the door quickly to catch her children off guard.

Standing with her back to the door, Francesca stood alone with her back to the door as she faced the open window.

'Who are you talking to, baby?' Kristina whimpered nervously, scanning the room for any sign of her son.

Turning slowly, Francesca moved like she was sleepwalking, her expression vacant as she stared straight ahead.

'Cesca?' Kristina sobbed, fear making her voice shake.

Blinking rapidly as though to clear her eyes, Francesca smiled sadly and looked like she was ready to drop from exhaustion.

'No one,' she finally answered, turning back to close the window.

\*\*\*

The following morning while brushing her daughter's hair, Kristina asked the question that had plagued her all night.

'What do the voices say to you?' she asked, keeping her tone as light and as casual as she could.

Stiffening in response, Francesca seemed about to reply, but it was her brother who mumbled the answer.

'They teach me things,' he replied, speaking around a mouthful of toast. 'Really cool stuff like controlling fire and calling the wind,' he explained before pausing to look up at her. 'What do they say to you, Mammy?' he asked, his eyes wide and innocent.

Turning slowly, Francesca eyed her mother sadly.

'The elements don't talk to her,' she whispered, looking as though she was about to cry.

Looking up in surprise, Lucian turned to his mother with sticky breadcrumbs covering his mouth.

'Have you been naughty?' he asked reprovingly, frowning up at her.

Groaning and rolling her eyes in frustration, Francesca spoke her mind before she could think to stop herself.

'She forced us to...' she stormed, but the sight of tears in her mother's eyes stopped her from completing her rant.

Looking forlorn and utterly repentant, Kristina apologised in her softest voice.

'I'm so sorry, Cesca,' she wept, whispering the words so they could hardly be heard.

Leaning into her mother, Francesca started to cry, releasing built-up tension.

'I know,' she sobbed, having known her mother's mind for quite some time.

'I'm sorry,' Kristina cried, causing her daughter to turn and face her.

'Oh, Mammy, it's okay,' she soothed. 'I forgive you,' she added, holding her close.

Watching them intently, Lucian chewed his toast mechanically, not entirely following what was happening.

'But Daddy won't forgive you,' Francesca warned, causing Kristina to sob more loudly.

*'Daddy's dead!'* Kristina wanted to say, but there was a time and place for such a talk and the way of saying it needed to be far more delicate.

Feeling Lucian's eyes on them, they both turned and raised their eyebrows at the same time.

'I forgive you, too, Mammy,' he said, holding out his arms for his turn to cuddle.

Laughing through her tears, Kristina received him into her arms and hugged her children tightly until Lucian began to complain.

'Get off, Cesca!' he moaned, wanting his mother all to himself.

# CHAPTER ELEVEN

The promised month, and five more, had come and gone since that night in the club, but now Cristian was ready to leave them to their own devices.

'They are ready,' he sighed, feeling weary after his prolonged ordeal.

The doormen were now a force to be reckoned with and could stand their ground against any of the factions.

*'But not the ancients,'* he knew, thinking of his father suddenly. *'But who could stand against us?'* he thought, long believing that the only threat to them had died a very long time ago.

After calling a meeting with the heads of each vampire group, he thought it well past time to set them free and felt rather relieved by the fact, if truth be known.

Working around the clock, Cristian had elevated them to a level of magickal proficiency that should save them if push came to shove.

In six months, these abandoned, unaware vampires had become a true faction in their own right, having learned many of the ways of the Egni and the use of magick.

Relishing in the new and somewhat blunt way they viewed the world, Cristian felt a great deal of satisfaction at enabling these forgotten fighters to become a future power in the world.

They had taken to the task in much the same way they tackled everything else – they attacked it head-on and had achieved much in the time allotted to them.

He had first taught magick to the club doormen, who in turn had taught others. Referring to each other as brothers, the bond between them seemed stronger than anything he could have thought possible without the tie of blood.

*'Brothers,'* he thought, smiling at the seated men.

Standing before them now, he looked at these head vampires and nodded in satisfaction. Not liking the term 'vampire lords', the doormen preferred instead to be called 'head vampires' or, rather, 'heads of the families', and were here today to discuss their future.

Thirty head vampires sat around the table, each family consisting of five hundred seasoned fighters.

Having internally cringed when they had insisted on modelling themselves on the Sicilian crime families, Cristian had desperately tried to dissuade them, but the vote had been unanimous, so he had been forced to go along with it.

Seemingly not interested in crime or any other form of underhanded business, they chose only to remain in the nightclub industry. That said, Cristian believed they had 'coerced' many club owners into selling up, whether they had wanted to or not.

And so here they were, gathered in a very large room that appeared to be a little too grand for men of their profession.

The venue was the best in the area, and the room booked the most expensive, with elegantly engraved wooden panels fixed along the white-painted walls that stretched up to the high arched ceiling. Upon the floor, a deep red carpet stretched out like a sea of blood, matched by the seats of the high-backed chairs and the long-draped curtains.

Standing at the head of the large, ornate table of the same wood as the walls, Cristian placed his hands wide as he leant forward.

A hush fell upon the gathered fighters in anticipation of what he was about to say, all waiting patiently as he began to nod his head.

'The time has come,' he announced, pursing his lips in thought, 'for you to be seen and counted,' he continued, straightening himself to stand more casually.

Some of the men nodded their agreement, and one or two made agreeable sounds with their throats, but most remained silent, hanging on his every word.

'It's been a long month,' he remarked dryly, smiling a half-smile at his earlier goal.

Laughter burst forth from around the table, and he was forced to raise his hand to quieten them.

'You have made yourselves strong,' he said seriously, passion shining in his eyes. 'The Bloods have learned what it is to mess in your affairs!' he shouted, causing their cheers to resound around the room, and again, he was forced to raise his hand for silence. 'It is now time for you to choose on which side of the road you wish to stand,' he continued, pursing his lips again. 'It's only a matter of time before you are discovered, the Bloods were but the first, and you need to be ready for when the others find out,' he warned, looking at each of them again. 'You have a choice before you, and it's a choice you must make alone,' he continued, seeing some glance at each other doubtfully. 'Do you align yourselves with the vampires? Which means the Egni or the Bloods, or will you side with mankind?' he asked, putting the fateful question to them.

A heavily-muscled vampire stood up suddenly and cleared his throat noisily.

'Why do we have to decide at all? Why can't we just be neutral?' he asked, looking around for support.

The table murmured its agreement, aligning themselves with the intimidating man.

'That, Shaun, is the third option, but it does have its own risks,' Cristian replied, smiling back warmly.

The doorman was well respected among these men, and rightly so, for his deadliness in a fight was almost legendary. Cristian had heard that he had even killed a Blood in hand-to-hand combat, which was a feat unheard of throughout the ages.

'If that is the path you choose, you will need to show them all how strong you truly are, for you will be tested on all sides and must retaliate with zero tolerance. You must react immediately, lethally and without remorse. Only then will you be taken seriously, and only then... will you be left in peace,' he answered, looking once again around the room.

The silence lengthened after he had finished, so he seated himself and leant back in his chair to await their decision.

After a time, Warren stood slowly after conversing quietly with Geez, who gestured impatiently for him to get on with it.

'What we need first is a leader,' Warren began, his voice raised and as official as ever. 'What we need is one to govern the families. What we need is a Godfather!' he shouted, looking directly at Cristian. 'I call for a vote that this position be given to Cristian. He has relationships with these other factions and is stronger than all of us. Even you, Shaun,' he teased, causing the fighter to laugh and shrug his shoulders.

'Yet to be proven!' the big man growled, winking at the ancient warrior.

'Do I hear a second?' shouted Warren, and the room exploded with its agreement.

Closing his eyes, Cristian's face paled at this unexpected turn and rose to his feet with yet another hand for silence.

'I already belong to the Egni, as I have from the very beginning, and cannot belong to both,' he replied regretfully, looking apologetically at Warren.

'So? We're a secret organisation, aren't we?' Lee shouted from across the table, enjoying the vampire lord's discomfort. 'We're unknown, and our "Godfather" should be unknown as well. In fact, I think that maybe he should remain that way even after our discovery,' he continued, his tattooed hands slamming down hard upon the table.

Holding the ancient vampire's eyes, he nodded his head imperceptibly as though willing him to agree.

Running his hand through his hair self-consciously, Cristian looked at Geez for support, but the large man returned his gaze with a twinkle in his eye.

'You're our Godfather, Cristian,' he said, shrugging his shoulders before his smile began to fade. 'We need you!' he stressed seriously, gesturing for him to get on with it with a shooing motion of his hand.

Shaking his head at the ridiculousness of it all, Cristian rose once again to his feet with a scowl at the table. Sighing, he began to chuckle at the predicament he himself had brought about.

'So, what shall we call ourselves?' he groaned, causing the room to explode yet again.

Spreading his arms wide in mock appreciation, he bowed before them with a flourish of his hand.

'Thank you,' he acknowledged, feeling unable to refuse these men anything. 'So, our faction name?' he pressed, looking around for suggestions.

'How about the Dark Brotherhood?' a bald, lean-looking vampire offered, before shrugging rather awkwardly when all the attention fell on him.

Shaking his head vigorously, Cristian waved away the agreeable cheers with eyes widened in alarm.

'Absolutely not!' he replied, more sternly than he had intended.

'Why not? I like the sound of that! Nice one, Richie,' Shaun bellowed, nodding at the embarrassed doorman as the table mumbled its agreement.

Sweeping his gaze around the room, all humour evaporated from their godfather as he stood his ground.

'You have all read the histories! Anything with the name "Dark" in it will be deemed as being involved in some way with the legend himself,' he stressed, shaking his head in disbelief.

'Yeah, well, isn't he just a myth or something? He sounded like a badass, man, and it'll make them other factions think twice before gunning for us, won't it?' asked a thin-faced vampire seated at the far end of the table.

Closing his eyes, Cristian could almost feel the hand of fate pressing down upon him like a mountain of iron.

'He wasn't a damn myth!' he whispered, annoyed by the question, 'Dark existed! He was real and was fear itself to all who crossed him. He had a grievance against the Bloods and killed them almost to the point of extinction. It was they who gave him the name *Blaidd Tywyll*, "Dark Wolf".'

'Why did they call him that?' Richie asked, leaning forward in hope of a story.

Seeing that the doorman was not alone in his rapt expression, Cristian sighed and shook his head.

'Dark didn't hunt alone as the books would have you believe. He had extremely loyal "friends" who fought alongside him, though even without them, nothing could stand against his might in those days, for the land itself came alive at his bidding,' he continued almost dreamily, his eyes staring off to some distant time. 'Everyone feared him back then, and there are still those living today that refuse to speak his name. If they thought for one second...' he explained, but his words trailed off at the thought of what this might instil in all other factions.

With a slow smile spreading across his face, he began to warm to the idea before finally nodding his head.

'The Dark Brotherhood!' he announced, spreading his arms again to the room's thunderous applause.

\*\*\*

It was early evening when he eventually arrived, the sunset at his back casting orange and copper hues to everything it touched.

Tall, lean and handsome, his dark eyes shone with intellect as he looked upon the imposing structure before him.

'At last,' he sighed, believing he would need all his attributes to seduce the ones inside.

A light breeze ruffled his curly dark brown hair, but he seemed not to notice, frozen as he was in the act of looking unperturbed.

Leaning against a tree with arms folded and legs crossed, he looked as casual as could be, even downright unconcerned, except, however… that was a lie.

The object of his fixation looked to be a mere house upon first glance, standing tall and somewhat intimidating against the oak forest. The uppermost windows reflected the golden light of the waning sun that was setting behind him and would have looked welcoming but for the aggression he felt emanating from it.

Arriving in the back of the delivery van, he had kept himself hidden and unaware, keeping his awareness to himself for fear of triggering the protection that had been placed around the area.

After guessing correctly that he had failed to get here because of a magickal web of some kind, he understood that it must have been created by a master like his father.

He had smiled during the long journey, thinking about his secret new faction, his mafia-influenced, legend-associated Dark Brotherhood, and had shaken his head in amusement, feeling excitement for the first time in a very long time, until that was, he had seen this house.

The structure seemed to sit there on the edge of the forest as though placed there to guard it.

'*Or those inside,*' he thought, fearing what would happen if he were to cross the border and enter the dwelling.

Having tried to approach the house through the forest several months earlier, he had found himself walking out again several hours later.

Greatly impressed by the power employed to achieve such a feat, he knew for certain that he was dealing with an ancient, though someone far more powerful in the art of magick than himself.

*'But which one?'* he mused, having believed that all were accounted for within either the Egni faction or that of the Bloods.

On casting out his awareness, he had seen the magnitude of what was bound within the forest and the magickal web itself, woven with intricacies that he could not follow.

Only one that he could think of could achieve such a thing. Only one with the power and imagination to come even close to this masterpiece, but he would recognise his father's work and knew this to be crafted by another.

*'But whom?'* he pondered, puzzling over the problem.

Having decided to test himself against the web, he had sent his arcing silver lightning into it but had found himself walking out of the forest with no memory of what had occurred afterwards.

Looking up at the intimidating structure again, he shivered despite himself, for the house was looking right back at him, waiting, even daring him to come a little closer.

The house had turned to him almost immediately after stepping from the van, and its hostility had grown in time with his approach. On finally reaching the gate to the property, he had decided against entering and had moved back to stand by a tree opposite it to decide his next course of action.

In an attempt to keep his composure, he took a deep, shaky breath in and exhaled slowly.

'Christ compels you,' he whispered, laughing nervously, not having tasted fear like this before.

Taking another deep breath, he ran his fingers through his hair and chuckled anxiously.

'Be cool, House,' he whispered, walking tentatively back towards the gate before stopping again as every fibre of his being warned him to run.

Muffled sounds of movement suddenly caught his attention, and when he lowered his eyes from the intimidating building, he was surprised to see the front door crack open a little.

Rising his eyebrows in interest, he smiled when a young girl peered out at him and then a boy's face popped out horizontally at her waist level.

Chuckling at the comical scene, he felt his heart warm towards them on meeting their eyes but had to force the protective feeling aside until he knew its cause.

Taking in their appearance, he saw that the girl's curly blonde hair was tied back in a low ponytail, while the boy had a typical boy's cut of short brown hair.

Staring at them intently, he committed their faces to memory but still felt moved by something familiar in their eyes.

'Who are you, and what do you want?' Francesca demanded, speaking in a well-spoken and very 'Welsh' accent. 'You've been staring at our house for ages now, and as it's getting dark...' she said, looking at the twilight sky, '... I think it's past time to see what you want!' she said, frowning down at him from her elevated position.

'I think that I'm here to see you,' he replied, looking from one child to the other before giving them a smile of reassurance. 'I wish to invite you to join the Egni faction, now that you have made yourselves aware,' he stopped, looking from Francesca's stern expression to Lucian's broad, joyous one. 'I am here to...' he stopped again, hearing heavy footsteps thumping from behind the children like a herd of elephants.

The door was flung open wide, and he saw what could only be their mother barge her way past like an enraged bear protecting her cubs.

'Get *in* the house!!' Kristina stormed, more to the girl than to the boy, with heavy emphasis and a pointed finger.

'We are *in* the house,' the child retorted, looking pointedly at her feet which were just inside the doorway.

At that, Francesca was unceremoniously shoved back from the doorway as her mother took her place.

Closing the door on them, Kristina stared hard at the newcomer with hands bunched into fists at her side.

'Yes?' she demanded, all colour draining from her face.

Holding up his hands peacefully, Cristian took a step back to show that he meant them no harm.

'I am not your enemy, lady,' he replied, taking another step back so that he now stood on the road. 'My name is Cristian, and I have come to invite...'

'What faction?' she demanded, cutting him off rudely, but the fear in her voice betrayed her show of anger.

Taken aback, Cristian stared at her mutely for a moment before she continued yet again.

'Well?' she snapped, her face twitching with nervous emotion. 'What faction are you from, *Cristian?*' she asked, speaking with a heavy emphasis on his name. 'Please don't try to play games with me,' she barked, visibly shaking now. 'How did you get here?' she demanded, glaring at him with impatience.

Looking at her impassively, he understood her reaction and decided to wait it out rather than argue with her.

'I come at the bequest of my faction to invite you, or them...' he corrected, gesturing to the closed door, '... to join us. I represent the Egni,' he finally answered, arching an eye for her response.

Breathing out slowly, relief flooded through her at which kind of vampire he was.

Smiling at her reaction, he opened his mouth to speak again, but a raised hand silenced him once more.

'You should be able to sense that we already belong to a faction, so you are wasting my time and yours,' she announced, placing her hands upon her hips. 'My children are clearly too young anyway, no matter what they have achieved,' she continued, babbling now in defiance.

Irritated by her manner, the Egni Lord pursed his lips and held up his hand in the way she had before she could say any more.

'You should know that it doesn't work that way, lady,' he growled, his mild manner slipping into annoyance. 'The choice is for them to make... not you!' he added, unable to hide his irritation.

'They have already joined me in my coven!' she retorted, challenging him with her eyes.

Again, he shook his head, his carefree attitude dissolving into something darker.

'None may interfere in the choosing. It is for them to decide, and not you. I'm not sure if this "Amityville house" has the power it appears to, but you should know that all the factions will come, and all will have their say before this is resolved,' he replied, shaking his head at her stupidity. 'This is how peace was made! You must know this! Everyone knows this! You have broken the law!' he accused, pointing at her judgementally as her anger dissolved along with her pretence at confidence.

Sighing heavily, the vampire calmed himself and looked to the sky for help.

'Let's start again,' he sighed, breathing out tiredly. 'I am Cristian of the Egni, which means *Power*,' he began, letting his annoyance go.

Looking at him while wiping away her tears, she seemed to shrink after his reprimand had cooled much of her bluster.

'I know what it means,' she mumbled, looking down to the ground.

Continuing as though she had not spoken, he decided to lighten the mood a little.

'I'm rather intimidated by your house, lady,' he admitted, looking up at the daunting structure with a nervous chuckle.

An awkward silence followed until she finally smiled to break the tension.

'You have no idea,' she replied, nodding her head sadly. 'You can stop calling me "lady",' she added in resignation, depression hanging over her like a cloud. 'My name is Kristina,' she introduced, smiling tightly.

Nodding his head in acknowledgement, he returned the smile more warmly.

'Pleased to meet you, Kristina,' he replied, bowing a little.

'Where does this leave us, Cristian?' she asked, worry creasing her features.

The vampire's expression softened as he shook his head with uncertainty.

'They should have been given the choice. It's the way it has always been... to keep the peace,' he added, not knowing what else to say.

'Where does this leave us?' she repeated, locking her eyes on his.

Seeing him purse his lips as he considered the problem, her eyes widened a little in response before she disguised her surprise by wiping at tears that were no longer there.

'They have been placed within a circle and were accepted. Do you know what that means?' she asked, his expression unnerving her to the point where she tried to change it.

'Why on earth would you do such a stupid thing?' he asked, believing he already knew the answer. The children were too young, it was that simple, and he held up a hand again before she could answer.

'You silly girl,' he admonished quietly, trying to think of a solution that would not end in her death. 'You could have requested time for them to grow or simply kept them hidden as you have done, but to take their choice away completely?' he shook his head, holding her stare, 'Suicide,' he answered, regrettably adding to her fears.

She just stared at him, not knowing how to respond to his promise of retribution.

'Before I set out to come here, our seers sensed two new and untainted powers in this region. Those same seers will now sense what you have done and report the knowledge back. You have broken the law, and some will want to see you dead for it. If the witches' faction backs your circle, which they will, it means war! Don't you see that?' he asked, placing his hands behind his head and interlacing his fingers.

There was a long silence before she spoke again, in a tone full of regret and more than a little fear.

'I must try to find their father,' she sobbed but felt that she was dreaming the impossible after believing him dead for so long. *But what if he isn't?*' she quailed, fearing his wrathful response to what she had done.

Shaking his head in frustration, he threw up his arms at what she expected one man to do against the might of so many.

'Don't you see that there's no escaping this? The Bloods will come, and I'm surprised they haven't broken through your web already, to be honest,' he stressed, feeling suddenly invested in her situation.

Closing her eyes as the tears began to fall, she stayed like that for only a moment.

'This place is well protected,' she replied, trying to control the dread that threatened to overwhelm her.

Nodding, he unconsciously looked up at the house again and wondered at the true extent of its power.

'This place is the last defence, but there are others that will kill you before you reach here,' she said, looking past him to the fields of green that led down to the valley below.

Taking a defensive step back, Cristian eyed her warily before she spread her hands peacefully.

'That wasn't a threat, just a fact. I am truly sorry for what I've done, but not for the reasons you might think,' she said, looking back down the valley. 'I don't want a war. I just want my children safe. Can't you see that?' she asked, staring off sadly.

'That's plain to see, but you've put me in an impossible position and left yourself open to attack from all sides. My faction will more than likely be more tolerant if I have anything to do with it, but the wizards will be outraged simply because it's the witches who have done it,' he replied, scowling at the thought of the pompous faction.

He sighed then, knowing that his next words would scare her the most.

'But it is the Bloods that will come to kill you,' he continued, running his fingers through his hair before looking up to the heavens. 'They will attack, that is for sure, and no one will stop them. You've given them free rein to do whatever they want, the laws are only there to try and control them!' he stressed, shaking his head again.

'They'll definitely attack?' she asked, turning to look into his eyes.

'Absolutely,' he answered, speaking the word with utmost finality. 'The question is, will the other covens stand with you? Did you get their blessings beforehand?' he asked, raising his eyebrows in hope.

Shaking her head, she shrugged with a look of desperation.

'I don't know. A friend of mine introduced me to them,' she answered, sounding so vulnerable in that moment.

Closing his eyes, he threw back his head in resignation for what good it would have done in any case.

'It doesn't matter anyway. The Bloods will destroy you even with them behind you. They are too strong and too many. You may very well have doomed your religion, Kristina. Why didn't you just let this house defend you and keep the children free? I think even the blood drinkers would think twice before entering it,' he said, involuntarily looking up at the building again. 'How did you create such a thing, anyway?' he asked, unable to keep the note of wonder from his voice.

Tilting her head to one side, she weighed his words before responding.

'Free?' she asked, thinking of Daire's use of the word before shrugging it off. 'This is...' she began but paused before shrugging again. 'This house belongs to Dark, and those are his children,' she confided, narrowing her eyes to study his reaction.

Looking at her blankly, the revelation stunned him to the core.

'Cristian, listen to me. I know that you are not here to cause us harm. I know this, so I will speak to you plainly. Dark would not let his children choose, not ever. I did what I did because he is... gone... and I felt the need to act,' she continued, frowning at his reaction.

Barely hearing her, he was unable to accept what she had told him and looked at her in a daze of stunned confusion.

'Dark?' he asked, his composure lost completely.

Nodding slowly, the silence between them grew as each regarded the other in the darkness.

'Dark is dead,' Cristian stated flatly, his tone now cold and emotionless.

Seeing that all colour had drained from his face, she shrugged as his dark eyes searched her own for a lie.

'Maybe,' she agreed, placing her face in her hands to hide her emotion.

Only a week ago, he had created a faction using the legend's name, intending to inspire the much-needed fear required for the other factions to pause before acting, but on hearing the name now as though he still lived...

*Just can't be!'* he thought, unable or unwilling to believe what she was saying. 'What does he look like?' he barked, trying to catch her off guard.

Placing her hands on her hips, she felt annoyed at the accusatory line of questioning.

'Cristian, it's him! A little shorter than you with the same dark hair. Quick-tempered, annoyingly intelligent, laughs at his own jokes. Look at this place. You think witches could do this?' she asked, waving her arms around expressively. 'I didn't know the truth until just before he left. I only knew him as...'

Blanching at the description, his dark eyes looked at her wildly for a moment.

'Daire,' he finished, emotion flushing into his face. 'His name was Daire,' he whispered, swallowing at the lump in his throat.

The silence between them lengthened as the vampire's face became ashen once more.

'You have no idea, Cristian,' she whispered quietly, looking up at the house and gesturing around them. 'You sense this place, right? You feel its eyes on you?' she asked, knowing that he could.

Giving a curt nod, he stiffened as she smiled knowingly.

'That is what you are allowed to see, what he intended to be seen, but it goes far deeper than that. Why do you think you are the only one to get this close? You have been watched for a very long time and must have shown...' she paused, thinking of the right words, '... something of yourself that allowed you through. Most don't find this place, and those that do...' she continued, looking at him suggestively, 'Well, let's just say I don't get to meet them. Now, look with your eyes open!' she commanded, waving her hand grandly to the valley below.

'*Gwelwch,'* she crowed, sounding totally out of character as she pointed at his back.

Goosebumps spread across his flesh, and he knew instinctively that she had done something to him.

Rounding on her, he glared at her in anger but saw no mischief in her eyes and felt no different than he had, other than a growing sense of the protection she had spoken of. He felt other forces at work now, in the earth beneath his feet and in the very air he breathed.

'Would you like to use our toilet?' Lucian sniggered, peeking through a crack in the door.

'Shut up, Lucian!' his sister scolded, afraid of yet another backlash from their mother.

'Tempting... but I'll hold it in, thank you,' he replied before giving their mother his full attention.

She had the look of a school ma'am about her, he thought, noting her crossed arms and tapping foot that reminded him of one of those old cartoons he had seen in the past, though he suspected she did it more from nervousness than from true irritation.

His colour began to return after the boy's interjection, and in an attempt to calm himself further, he breathed in deeply before letting it out in a slow, controlled burst.

'Do not use your magick on me again!' he warned, looking her dead in the eye. 'Ever!' he growled, and she found that she did not want to find out what his response would be if she did.

'I'm... sorry,' she stammered, looking a little confused and more than a little scared by the threat in his tone.

Breathing out slowly again, he nodded his head in the knowledge that she had not used her power to cause him harm.

'Are you serious about them being his?' he asked, glancing at the door.

Nodding her response, she narrowed her eyes at him and wondered at the history between the two ancient men.

'I like you, Cristian. I feel that you're not here to cause us harm, so maybe it's for the best that their father is not here, for your sake,' she replied, smiling at him tightly.

Surprising her, she saw him smile confidently with a disagreeable shake of his head.

'We shall see,' he whispered, and she could see that he was holding something back.

Looking at him sternly, she placed her hands back at her hips, believing him to be dismissive of her warning.

'If you have come here for his children, he will kill you... no matter how powerful you believe yourself to be!' she warned, widening her eyes in annoyance. But he seemed not to be listening to her now, for his eyes had a faraway look to them as though he was reliving some distant encounter with the legendary Dark Wolf.

'They are his children,' she repeated, bringing him out of his reverie.

Stepping back, he looked up at the sky and saw the stars twinkling above them.

'I must leave you now, for a time at least, for I need to consult with my elder on the matter,' he announced, bowing his head a little as he took his leave.

Nodding, she felt drained by the meeting and watched him depart in silence.

*'He moves like him,'* she thought, shivering at the comparison. *'Like he's trying to slow himself down for my sake,'* she realised, remembering Daire after his night with the elements. *'Though less like he doesn't belong,'* she thought, thinking that at least Cristian still looked human, where Daire had definitely not.

Opening the vampire's heart and mind to see the elements had been a mistake, she knew, and she began to wonder why she had done it. Shaking her head, she had no explanation, for the desire had been spontaneous and not a conscious act at all.

*'How on earth did I know how to show him?'* she mused, trying to recall the rapidly fading moment. *'What was that word I used?'* she wondered, trying desperately to remember.

Finally shrugging the problem away, she shook her head and rolled her eyes.

'Stupid woman!' she chided, wondering how she could forget such a thing, before telling herself that she must have read it in one of the many books in the house.

Looking up at the starlit sky, she whispered into the cool night breeze.

'Forgive me my foolishness and deliver us from this evil,' she prayed, little knowing that her plea was heard and would be answered.

*** 

Laying down on the hotel bed, Cristian sighed as he stared at the cracked and flaking paintwork on the ceiling.

It had taken him an hour to reach the nearest town, walking down the country lanes with widened eyes of disbelief.

It was as though he saw the world in a new light, and maybe he did. For no longer did the world appear as it had... now it had power and a presence that almost took him to his knees.

'*Keep walking,*' he told himself, feeling like an ant upon the paw of a lion and knowing that it was aware of him, even now in this room.

Having believed that this new awakening would fade after time, he now realised that was not going to be the way of it. What had been done was not only permanent but appeared to be getting stronger. New thoughts entered his mind, or maybe old ones from before he had become a vampire, leaving his emotions to run wild as a consequence, and filling his eyes with tears for the first time since his corruption.

On the road back to the hotel, he had begun to sense the energy of the land vibrating beneath him as once it had, except he now felt that the earth was not only sentient but very much aware of him.

'I am not an enemy,' he whispered, staring up into the starlit sky with a feeling that it, too, was somehow aware of him.

Not expecting an answer, he was chilled to the bone when a gentle breeze whispered into his ear.

'We know this,' it breathed, causing him to spin with his arms raised in defence, but he was alone on the road, seeing it stretch back into the darkness which even his eyes could not penetrate.

Sending out his senses, he could find nothing around him, so turned back to the road.

'You're his ally?' he asked, trying desperately to control the shake in his voice.

The light breeze picked up again, blowing at him from behind as it had at first.

'Aren't you?' the wind countered, causing him to turn again on instinct.

'I am a vampire and serve my faction,' he answered, believing that the truth was the best course of action.

'Which one?' the element mocked, blowing at him now from all sides.

Feeling his face heat, he could only wait in the hope of learning something more from this gigantic presence.

'What do you mean?' he finally asked, but the wind had settled and could no longer be felt.

At last, he came upon the town of Port Talbot, a large settlement in the south of the country. High-reaching chimney stacks dominated the skyline, rising from the steelworks that overshadowed the buildings around it.

A huge bout of flame erupted from the largest stack to light the sky in an endless expenditure of gas, looking for all the world like a flaming eye.

'*Wales,*' he thought, one of the only places left of the original Britons before the fall of Camelot. 'The land of the mighty,' he whispered, smiling sadly.

Springing from the bed, he landed lightly on his toes before crossing the room. A natural series of moves, but altogether too fast for a human to achieve. Not a blur as one might expect from the countless movies regarding his kind, but fast enough to be there in a second and for the drawn curtains to be lifted by the movement of air.

Standing before the full-length mirror inlaid within the wardrobe door, he stared at his lean frame and shook his head. He had looked so much older before his vampirism, and though happy to be youthful, he wished to undo what had been done to him.

Closing his eyes, he remembered his first sensations of being a vampire. Feeling awed by his new strength and unstoppable vitality, he had thought it a gift, but as it is with most things, it was also a curse, for there was also a feeling of separation, of being cut off from the world of the living. Feeling as though he had been ripped from the natural order of things, he had become aware early on of the loneliness that accompanied it.

Though retaining most of his magick, he had found that he could no longer feel the magick of the earth and had cried pitifully at the loss of such a thing. All his desperate attempts to reconnect with the element had left him feeling lost and dreadfully unclean, as though he were now unworthy of its touch.

'*This is not what was promised,*' he thought miserably, resenting the so-called gift.

Shaking his head, he failed to comprehend how Kristina could have returned it to him, knowing absolutely that the kind of magick needed was beyond her capabilities.

Just a few hours ago, he had felt confident enough to handle any situation and, in delusion, had thought himself a god within this world of men. A Lord of the Egni perfected into a vampire without the need for blood, or so he had thought.

He laughed then, a nervous chuckle that caught him by surprise.

'*Am I still damned?*' he wondered before quashing the emotion for the task ahead.

Clearing his mind, he stood still and statue-like as he began to hum deeply from his chest. The air seemed to vibrate around him, and as he took the octave lower, the mirror itself began to rattle until it smashed along with the room, which fell away in the same instance, leaving him in a void of total darkness.

Focusing his mind, a light appeared like a star in the distance, and he felt himself moving towards it until it took the form of another mirror with a silhouette of someone within, though blurred as if by space and time itself.

Focusing on the one he sought on the other side, he approached from behind and saw the other lift his head as though sensing his presence. As the man turned, the blurriness around him broke away in fragments like those of the mirror, leaving the two ancients to regard one another in silence.

Though not as tall as Cristian, the man was more powerfully built and had a confidence that seemed to literally glow from behind his brooding dark eyes.

Being the first and most powerful of all within the Egni order, Colin ruled his faction with a will of iron that allowed none to contest him.

Looking again at the long black hair, Cristian saw that it was tied back from a face that seemed almost white in comparison. Seeing the deep scowl over dark piercing eyes made Cristian think of the legend again.

In the Dark Ages, during a siege upon one of the many wizard strongholds, Colin had wielded lighting that had never been seen again, for his gift of channelling the magick was believed unparalleled among the surviving ancients.

'Cristian! I was wondering when you would make an appearance,' the Egni Master greeted, his dark eyes locking in and cementing the bond between them.

Cristian simply stared for a moment, organising his thoughts before answering.

'*It all changes now,*' he thought nervously before finally giving voice to his response.

'I have just now returned,' he replied, sighing out the words in resignation.

Arching an eyebrow, Colin indicated with an impatient gesture that he should continue and that he was in no mood for small talk.

'They are children, very young children. Too young for the choosing,' Cristian sighed, seeking an angle to manipulate the man before him.

Glaring at him, Colin's deep brow frowned with ill-disguised anger.

'That is not for you to decide!' he growled, stepping in a little closer.

Used to such outbursts from his elder, Cristian ignored the aggression and continued.

'The mother is a witch and has sealed a circle using them, foolishly thinking to protect them. The children are now unattainable,' he replied mechanically, waiting for what he knew would come.

'What?' Colin snarled, white light flashing in his eyes. '*What?*' he spat again, curling his lips back from his white, fanged teeth.

Unfazed by the reaction, Cristian shrugged and sighed audibly.

'I believe it was done in panic rather than malice, for as I have already said, they are very young,' he answered, holding his father's glare without expression.

Wrath exploded from the master vampire, his dark eyes glowing brighter still as he vented his displeasure.

'Too young? Unattainable? They will be only too "attainable" when her coven lies in ruin!' he snarled, still speaking through his clenched teeth.

'There's more,' Cristian added, taking a calming breath before continuing.

'The children are protected by more than just magick, for I sensed the elements at work, not one as before, but all of them,' he informed, arching an eyebrow as he awaited the response.

At this, Colin stepped in closer still, a look of concern masking his features as he looked into the other's eyes.

'Tell me everything,' he ordered, and so was told of all that had happened at the house.

Colin listened intently until Cristian paused in the telling, feeling apprehensive about speaking of the legend's return.

Considering the tale told, Colin pursed his lips and stared down in thought.

'This kind of power was lost with... *him,*' he whispered, refusing to speak the name 'Daire' aloud. 'Do you think these children awakened them somehow?' he asked, looking back into Cristian's eyes.

Slowly shaking his head, Cristian felt unable for the moment to verbalise his response.

'Or the mother?' Colin prompted, raising his eyebrows inquiringly.

Again, the shake of his head, for Cristian wished only for his elder to say the name that was dancing on the tip of his tongue, but then realised that it was but a dream that would never come to pass.

'She said that the children are...' he took a deep breath, steadying himself, '... she said they are... *his* children,' he finally enlightened, his eyes never leaving those of the other.

Colour instantly drained from Colin's face, and he stood regarding Cristian in silence for a time. Finally recovering from the initial shock, he pursed his lips again.

'This, Kristina... she said that only you got through the protection?' he asked, chewing on the inside of his cheek as his mind worked out the problem.

Cristian merely nodded, and the silence grew again for a time.

'That makes sense if what you say is true,' Colin remarked, looking into his eyes again, clearly trying to read him. 'Do you think that she could have lied to you?' he asked, but looked as though he already knew the answer.

Cristian shook his head anyway, leaving little room for doubt.

'She called him by name,' he answered, then sighed when his elder closed his eyes.

'Did she say where he was?' Colin asked, keeping his eyes hidden for the moment as though they would betray him somehow.

'I had the feeling that he had been gone for quite some time and that there was great fear in her, but whether it was fear *for* him or fear *of* him, I am not entirely sure,' he answered, stating the facts as he saw them.

Colin opened his eyes at that, the emotion within hidden and unreachable.

'You know as well as I that it was he who awakened the land,' he replied, continuing to chew his cheek before shaking his head in depression.

'He survived,' he breathed, showing just a hint of emotion, but whether he was happy or not, Cristian could not tell.

'They look like you,' Cristian replied, trying to provoke a reaction. 'They have the scowl,' he added, looking for a sign, anything, that would spark any emotion other than anger.

Closing his eyes again, Colin felt unwilling to let his thoughts be seen in that moment, but when he opened them again, there was nothing but cold stone within their depths.

'Come home,' he ordered, all traces of the bond between them lost. 'It's unlikely that anyone else will get through if what you say is to be believed.'

*'Again, with the suggestion that I'm lying,'* Cristian thought, seeing the ongoing attempt to read him. *'What does he suspect?'* he wondered, thinking then of his secret faction.

'I do want the area watched, however, to tackle any wizardly involvement. I want all the factions to feel our presence there in force. I will consult with Azazel directly before we finally go to war,' Colin said, already planning a strategy with the Bloods in mind.

Widening his eyes with an unnatural light like that of the other, Cristian stared back as the glow emanated from their depths.

'War?' he gasped, causing his elder's frown to deepen.

'There's no avoiding it now. *His* witch has doomed herself and her faction, whether they get involved or not. The wizards are of no concern either. It's the re-emergence of *him* that complicates matters,' he replied, still unwilling to use the legend's given name. 'The Bloods reported that he had returned but have said such things before, such is their continued fear of him. They will not be happy to have it confirmed this time, not one bit,' he continued, pursing his lips again in thought.

Shaking his head, Cristian denied his elder for the very first time.

'I will wait to see if he returns,' he stated, unwilling to become a mere sheep in this matter.

The master of all the Egni studied him again, trying to read what lay within whilst trying to control his anger at this clear sign of insubordination.

'We have a pact with the Bloods and are vampires ourselves, whether you like it or not! Would you have me break my oath?' Colin growled, curling his lips back from his teeth. 'An oath that dates back to the treaty!' he raged, spitting the words through his clenched teeth.

Cristian's blood ran cold, and his eyes flashed again.

'Some things are more important than even your word, High Wizard!' he growled, unwilling to bend the knee at this time.

Colin's face softened at that, and Cristian saw regret for the first time in his eyes.

'Those days are gone, Cris,' he whispered, fighting to lower his tone, 'and we owe nothing to a memory,' he continued, his eyes suddenly steeling again. 'The witches have doomed themselves, and a new war was always in the offing. Dark was our enemy then, as he will be again. Nothing has changed!' he stressed, his eyes beginning to blaze.

'He will not be my enemy again,' Cristian spat defiantly, standing his ground against the wrath before him. 'We wronged him, and you know it! If I can see the truth of it, then so can you!' he replied in a low, dangerous tone.

Growing ever fiercer, Colin's body became more animated as he threw his arms out wide.

'Enough, Cristian! Who you look for in him is dead! He took a different path to us and drew first blood from your brothers!' he roared, trying to justify his reasoning.

Waving off the statement, Cristian shook his head and refused to give ground.

'Paul sought out the confrontation, and you know it! His ego would allow for no other course of action. That, mixed with Daire's reactive nature, and something was bound to happen. Paul had the problem, not him, and you did nothing to prevent it from escalating!' Cristian accused, then sighed at the blind rage in his father's eyes. 'You only remember what you want so that you can justify yourself!' he continued, shaking his head sadly.

Maddened beyond reason, every word was spat from Colin's snarling mouth, spraying spittle into the void as the words came forth.

'He stood against us!' he replied, stabbing his finger into his own chest with force. 'He chose to move against us and attacked your brothers! Did you forget that? Your brothers are lucky to be alive!' he raged, looking ready to strike.

Shaking his head, Cristian felt unwilling to support what was being proposed and would stand and fight against the injustice intended upon the mother and her children.

'Carl told me the real story of that ages ago, and...' he began, but the closing of the other's eyes and the growl of frustration stopped him mid-sentence.

'He's dead! Do you hear me?' Colin's voice was cold and the whites of his eyes colder still. 'He is dead, and what you cling to is a dream, a memory that you cannot relive. Do you think that he is the same man he was? The power corrupted him as it has many others! What do you think he's been doing all this time to stay alive? He's probably more a monster than Azazel and his Bloods!' he stressed, running his fingers through his hair in a tell-tale sign of annoyance.

Seeing the stubborn expression on his son's face, Colin almost attacked him.

'I don't expect you to see it,' he spat, stabbing a finger in Cristian's direction. 'But *I* see it! He was resentful of Paul's fame and sought him out,' he seethed, glaring madly as though he had finally lost control. 'It's why I stopped him then and why...' he began, stabbing himself in the chest this time, 'I will stop him again,' he promised, speaking with a cold note of finality.

'Stop him from doing what? He's hidden himself, man! What

would you stop him from doing? It's we who must be stopped!' Cristian shouted, rising immediately to the threat.

Regarding him coldly, Colin could see that they would never agree on this issue.

'He hunts vampires, and he hunts us! So, it falls to me to finish it, once and for all,' he replied emotionlessly, steeling himself for the task ahead.

'You would kill him?' Cristian asked incredulously, blood flushing into his face. '*You* would *end* his existence? Think about what you are saying!' he continued, holding the other's enraged expression.

'We must look to ourselves, our faction,' Colin sighed tiredly, ignoring the question as he set his iron mind to what lay ahead.

Staring back with eyes now the match of the Egni Master, Cristian felt something snap inside and tensed himself for action.

'You think to challenge me, Cris?' Colin asked aggressively, stepping forward with an inviting spread of his arms.

And so it was that Cristian, second only to Colin, master of the Egni vampire faction, said only one word in reply.

'Begone.'

The image of his elder exploded, the darkness around him shattering into a thousand pieces, causing the previously expelled light to come flooding in around him.

Cristian found himself staring into the mirror again and wearily walked back to the bed. He thought of the war to come, of the part that he was to play in it, and then of his brother, Paul, the Blade Master, before shaking his head sadly.

'Your ego has undone us all, brother,' he whispered, remembering how his jealousy of Daire had destroyed all that had been.

Paul had sought to challenge Daire at every turn, whether it be verbal, physical or magickal, and though his own fighting skills were well-renowned, he felt a need to test himself further, jumping at every opportunity to show off his skills to the waiting crowd.

Also an accomplished magicker, Paul would send unseen mind attacks at the future legend, trying to provoke a seemingly unwarranted response in his need to outdo him.

Seemingly amused by their constant clashing at first, Colin had allowed it to continue in the belief that their competitiveness would grow his son's power, but that had changed when blood had been spilt.

Never known to be crowd-pleasers themselves, Cristian had been by far the closest to Daire, the bond between them as unbreakable as anything could be.

*'Until I changed that!'* Cristian thought drearily, feeling a lump in his throat as he remembered what had happened between them.

It had been Daire's anger that had set him apart. *'That and his razor-sharp tongue,'* he thought, remembering the roguish man in a time when he had been almost worshipped by the populace, having legendary status even then after facing down the unbeatable Gilgamesh.

'Gilgamesh,' he whispered, calling the image of the godlike ancient to his mind.

Seeing again the flaming hair and black eyes, he remembered suddenly the unbeatable power that had radiated from the man.

*'Maybe you should have fought Daire then and possibly lived instead of what he did to you later,'* he thought, seeing again what the Blood Sword could do.

Shivering at the memory, Cristian saw again the destruction that had been wrought upon this most feared of all ancients, of how he had been dissected by the red sword and how his magick had been thwarted with such dreadful grace.

Even Colin had been wary of Gilgamesh, for he seemed to have inherited the most powerful of both the physical and magickal enhancements that had changed them all.

What Paul did not know, however, was that after the initial confrontation, Daire's might was compared not to his at all, but to that of the one he had confronted.

Cristian had wondered many times if Paul had ever known that the initial standoff between Daire and Gilgamesh had been over the Blade Master himself.

*'He would never have sought him out so vigorously if he had known,'* Cristian believed, shaking his head in frustration. *'Or maybe he had known and felt the need to prove himself,'* he mused, seeing the

corresponding duel in his mind and the blur of red upon black on the golden sand.

'You should have stopped it!' Cristian choked, remembering Colin as he once was.

Picturing Daire in his mind, he wondered if he still looked the same or whether he was now the demon he was portrayed to be. The image in his mind had faded over the ages, blending now into that of Colin, for so close had the resemblance been between them.

'You have been wronged for the last time, *Brawd Bach,*' he whispered, feeling shame at the look of betrayal he had received on more than one occasion.

The old legends of the Dark Wolf had been told and retold again, gradually being exaggerated in the telling to make him sound more like a demon than the man he had been. Cristian knew the truth of it, however, and for the first time in centuries, he felt an overwhelming sense of remorse over it.

Remembering that fateful day when the two warriors had agreed to duel, he recalled that it had been greatly anticipated, for both had never known the sting of defeat, and it had been rumoured that Gilgamesh himself was to attend the spectacle, though he did not, when the time came.

*'Did you fear what you sensed in him?'* he wondered, remembering again when Gilgamesh had backed down from the legend's wrath. *'Then you should not have fought him when he hunted you,'* he thought, returning his mind to the duel.

Colin had decreed that magick was to be forbidden in the contest and that they were to rely on their swordsmanship alone. He had enchanted the Swords of Power himself so that for this fight alone, they would be merely weapons without the magick that defined them.

Even then, Cristian suspected that Colin had known the power within Daire and had wanted to give Paul every chance to win.

Both fighters seemed equally skilled with the blade, though had completely different styles. Paul, 'The Blade Master', was a pleasure to behold and, without doubt, the better fighter upon first glance.

Daire, for the name Dark was given to him much later, was

like a thunderstorm that emanated power compared only to that of Gilgamesh. His movements were lightning-fast but without the wasted twirls of his opponent's blade.

Closing his eyes, he saw Paul attack with perfect catlike grace, only for his blade to be blocked by small, blindingly fast parries that sent him stumbling back. When Daire attacked, it was lightning, the speed and power of the strikes causing Paul to almost fall in his desperation to get away.

The crowd had clapped for the Blade Master at first, clearly appreciating his swordsmanship. It had appeared that the fight would end quickly, but as the duel wore on, that opinion had slowly changed.

Though breathing heavily, Daire showed none of the fatigue of the other, and as they clashed again, it became clear who was going to win the contest. The contact between the two swords had been so powerful that it had caused Cristian to wince when the blades clashed, for there was no holding back by either party. They were fighting to win, and to the death, it seemed.

They had looked like gods down there on that sandy arena floor, and Cristian had marvelled at each man in turn, but even he had not truly known the extent of their dislike for one another.

Suddenly, Paul was disarmed and viciously punched from his feet, only to have his sword kicked back to him time and time again. Finally, the Black Sword flew from Paul's hand when, at the last, the sheer force of his brother's defence had sent it flinging into the dirt.

Backhanding him to the sand yet again, Daire had stood over the defeated warrior and had looked about to kill him when the Blood Sword flared into life as it was lowered to the throat.

It had been Colin who had stopped him, appearing like Zeus himself, who sent down an arc of light that struck the victor square between the shoulders to send him sliding several paces beyond that of the fallen blade of his brother.

'Coward!' bellowed the ancient High Wizard, standing up from his seat with a maddened look of disgust. 'How dare you!' he thundered, seemingly enraged by the glowing of the sword. 'You have used your power to defeat your better!' he spat judgementally, glaring down at Daire with a look of loathing.

Cristian, too, had felt anger at the villainous act, glowering down from his seated position beside the High Wizard.

'You are vile indeed to use your power so secretively,' Colin growled, shaking his grey-bearded head in anger before the crowd shouted its disagreement, having seen that the sword only glowed after the fight was over.

Struggling back to his feet with his hood having fallen over his head, Daire looked every bit the villain he was now portrayed to be. An evil, despised thing that had no honour and no place amongst them.

He had stood there, crippled from the attack, and Cristian had seen the hooded head turn in his direction.

What had passed between them in that moment had stayed with him throughout these long years, and he felt great shame for the look that had been on Daire's face.

Still smouldering from the unseen attack, Daire slowly staggered to his feet.

A deathly hush fell upon the arena, the many disputes of who was in the wrong silenced as they waited for what came next.

Painfully wounded, Daire glared up at his attacker, who still stood like an imposing god within the royal box of the uppermost tier of the arena.

Locked in an unseen battle of the mind, the seconds slipped by until Colin stiffened with eyes wide in disbelief.

Nodding sinisterly, the hooded figure turned to leave before his defeated opponent regained his feet.

'You will answer for your crime!' Paul raged, looking from him to his father and back again.

Nodding to the guards who stood at the entrance, they nervously put their hands to their hilts as the crippled fighter turned back once again.

Like a judge contemplating a condemned man's fate, the High Wizard gestured to the guards before something passed between the two again. Staggering back into his seat, Colin clutched at Cristian for support, clearly shaken by what had passed between them. When he had finally recovered, Daire was gone, leaving two dead guards in his wake.

Closing his eyes, Cristian wiped the tears away, but more came unbidden to his eyes. He cried for his part in allowing the tragedy to come to pass and cursed himself for what had happened after. His judgement over the perceived betrayal had been too swift, and the guilt he felt after the legend had finally been put down had lingered with him all these long years.

After so much time of contemplation, he now believed that after defeating Paul in combat, the flaring of the Blood Sword had merely been done to show that he had also defeated Colin by unbinding his enchantment upon it, and it had been that act alone that had unhinged the High Wizard.

'Why didn't I see it immediately?' Cristian wept, shaking his head in regret as a cold determination took root within him.

'I will not be on the wrong side again,' he swore, speaking his oath into the silence of the night.

# CHAPTER TWELVE

What was known as the 'Great Hall' appeared very much like the House of Commons in its design and architecture. A place that looked lost in time and was often the subject of debate as to which had ultimately influenced the other.

The dark-stained benches were filled now to capacity, taken up by the many different magickal disciplines that discussed, or rather yelled at each other, over what had occurred in regard to the children.

What might have been politicians squabbling incoherently at each other from across the chamber were actually wizards, witches and the other slightly smaller disciplines of druids and the like.

Normally less than half-full, the great chamber was now filled to the rafters, and the roar of their dispute could be heard reverberating off the high wooden ceiling.

They had come today to discuss just one issue, the unlawful creation of a witches' circle and the corresponding retaliation that it would provoke. The law had been broken, which had never happened before, and due to the severity of the consequences, the magickal world was now in an uproar.

The verbal onslaught had been brought about by the wizards' faction accusing the witches of wilful law-breaking in an attempt to monopolise the situation of those newly ascended.

'Why weren't they afforded the opportunity to choose?' an elderly wizard asked, his rasping tone full of accusation.

At this, the yelling recommenced, and both factions began to clash again more fiercely.

Seated on the front bench opposite the wizards, a voluptuous witch with flowing blonde hair stood up slowly, lifting her chin defiantly against her opposition. Waiting for silence, she answered the question, speaking with an air of authority for her faction.

'We know not of whom you are referring or why this has been done,' she replied coldly, narrowing her bright blue eyes scornfully. 'Furthermore, I would like to convey to all here present that we of the witches' faction denounce this despicable act,' she finished, slowly taking her seat again.

The chamber erupted again as accusations were hurled at the now-seated woman.

'You expect us to believe that?' a shout was heard amid the chaos, causing the woman to puff out her cheeks as she exhaled with a look of boredom.

The only faction to remain in their seats at this time were the druids, who continued to sit in silence as they watched the commotion from their deeply hooded robes.

Slowly, the High Wizard, Kreig, rose to his feet, and the chamber immediately fell into silence. Bowing to the High Priestess, who had spoken just moments before, he glowered around the room with a look of impatience.

'This is not so much about blame as it is about consequences,' his deep voice boomed, sounding almost bored as it echoed around the chamber. 'Blame is irrelevant at this point, for we all know that a circle was made, and that is the fact of the matter,' he continued, letting the seriousness of the situation sink in.

The hall remained silent, hanging onto his every word as he led the proceedings.

'We are here now to discuss what we can do about it, not the reasoning behind it. I have sent word to both vampire factions relaying our ignorance on the matter and to negotiate with them on a satisfactory outcome,' he relayed, pausing again for effect.

A born politician, Kreig was now in his element, and with great subtlety, he pressed his attack.

'Chloe?' he called, turning to the shapely blonde High Priestess. 'Do you know whom it was that performed this heinous crime?' he asked, knowing that she had previously stated her ignorance on the matter.

Paling at being addressed so informally, Chloe rose gracefully to her feet with a dangerous glint in her eyes.

'As I have previously stated, I have no direct knowledge of what has occurred,' she answered stiffly, eyeing the wizard with distaste. 'Though I have investigated the matter and summoned the priestess involved to discuss it further, and will discipline as needed,' she added, rubbing her fingers against her thumbs like a gunfighter before a shootout.

As both were the leaders of their disciplines, the mood in the hall turned dangerously low as the two opposing factions began to fidget nervously.

'I am to meet with her immediately after we convene,' she added, remaining on her feet as she glared at the wizard, clearly sensing the trap he was weaving about her.

Looking around the great chamber, the powerfully built High Wizard spread his arms dramatically.

'I think it best that we *all* meet with this woman,' he advised, smiling at her in victory as the chamber began baying for blood.

Waiting patiently for the calamity to die down, Chloe ran her hand absently through her long golden hair as though unbothered by their fierce reaction.

'None may break a circle that has been blessed by a goddess. None!' she warned, and as if to enforce her statement, her entire faction leant forward as one.

Smiling back at the wizard, the High Priestess warned him with her wide blue eyes not to continue this dangerous game.

'Be assured that there will be a reckoning for her crime and a punishment enacted, but the circle will ultimately stand,' she stated, before shaking her head imperceptibly. 'Do not test me on this,' she hissed sinisterly, her smile evaporating as the air began to crackle with static.

A silence fell on the chamber, like the calm before a storm, as wizard and witch faced off against each other.

It was at that point that the Arch Druid stood and softly intervened before the battle of wills spiralled out of control.

'There is, we druids believe, more to this than meets the eye,' he announced, stifling the rising aggression for a moment as all eyes turned to him.

A slow, wolfish grin spread across his face at the ease with which he had ended their political struggle.

'Why is it that the elements have a will of their own, and why are they stopping us all from reaching these new powers?' he asked, sweeping his dark eyes across the chamber before pausing briefly to indicate the druids who sat with him. 'We, too, have been barred from the area, we who have dedicated our lives to the very forces we thought to have controlled,' he continued, spreading his arms wide as the High Wizard had done, imitating him with mocking accuracy. 'What has changed? Or more to the point… *why* has it changed? We have not seen magick like this since the fall of the Dark Wolf,' he announced, looking at Kreig with a knowing smile.

Everyone in the room took a collective gasp at what he was suggesting, clearly not expecting the talk of legends to disrupt their proceedings.

'Dark,' Kreig announced, silencing the mass misgivings in an instant. 'These new powers are his children,' he informed in his deep tone.

The Arch Druid lowered his head in thought, taken aback by the wizard's openness. With his gift, he had gleaned the legendary name from those closest to the wizard, hearing the name as though in the back of his mind, but he had not for one second expected this revelation.

'Dark,' the name was repeated over and over as the chamber erupted at the news.

'He's just a fairytale!'

'What proof is there to support this?'

'The wolf is dead!' came the frantic replies, panic and disbelief mingling into one.

'Enough!' Kreig bellowed, silencing the chaos. 'My reaction was the same at first, but I have been given the information from a reliable source, and so believe me when I say that not only was Dark real… he lives!' he growled, glowering at them all.

'Then we must leave his children be,' the Arch Druid replied, sweeping his gaze around the great hall, 'lest we wake a sleeping giant! Dark is an enemy we can ill-afford at the best of times, a foe best left forgotten. If he has chosen to remain silent all these long ages, then I say we let him,' he advised sagely, deciding to let sleeping dogs lie.

The hall erupted in agreement, for none wanted their dreadful history to repeat itself.

'That option is sadly unavailable to us,' Kreig replied, looking back slowly towards the High Priestess, 'because they have been taken into a coven and bound within a circle,' he continued, looking venomously at the witch.

Chloe raised her chin again, but the witches around her looked fearfully unaware and glanced at her with questioning eyes.

'How long have you known this?' she asked smoothly but was interrupted by the sound of a door opening to the side.

Entering the chamber, a small, slender-looking wizard with thick-lensed glasses crossed quickly to the High Wizard to whisper in his ear.

'Are you sure about this, Richard?' he asked before slumping back to stare vacantly ahead, draped in what looked like despair.

The chamber waited with bated breath until Chloe grew impatient and began snapping her fingers irritably in his direction.

'What?' she demanded haughtily, believing this to be yet another ploy to control the situation.

'The Bloods have killed my envoys and have declared war upon us all,' he mumbled as the resulting panic rippled through the crowd.

'Why?' came the question from many places at once as pandemonium began to break out.

Jumping to her feet, Chloe's face was a mask of rage.

'Not because of a rogue witch who created a circle with unchosen children, that's for damn sure!' she shouted, speaking in a tone that could have cut through glass.

Nodding his head in agreement with all political gain irrelevant to him in that moment, Kreig's bluster seemed to have blown out of him as he sat there deflated until she snapped her fingers at him again.

'Because an army of Bloods have been killed in pursuit of his children,' he informed, swallowing hard at the lump in his throat.

Shocked outbursts came from all sides, and even the druids seemed to have lost their composure.

'The Wolf hunts again,' an old wizard wailed, a wild glint of madness shining in his eyes.

'Goddess, I beseech thee, deliver us from his evil,' cried an older witch, who stood shakily up from a back bench.

'The elements must answer to him,' a druid cried aloud, shouting the words in an unaccustomed shrill.

'An army of Bloods!' Chloe echoed, unable to comprehend how much power it would take to achieve such a feat.

Regaining his composure, an idea sparked to life in Kreig's mind, and he rose to his feet with raised hands.

'The only way we can possibly survive this is to unite the factions as once they were,' his voice rang out, silencing the room once again. 'We must form a council of leaders!' he announced, looking around the chamber. 'We three!' he decided, looking from Chloe to the Arch Druid with a question in his eyes, 'And we must do it now, without hesitation. What say you, John?' he asked desperately, looking from one to the other.

The Arch Druid lowered his hood and slowly nodded his agreement, causing his long silvery-brown hair to shimmer in the firelight.

Nodding her assent also, the High Priestess, too, saw no other choice before them.

'We three,' she intoned, looking about the room. 'What say you?' she asked as all the factions of mankind stood and became one once again, cheering fanatically.

A deafening boom of what sounded like cannon fire echoed around the chamber, quickly followed by another and more that caused dust to fall from the ceiling.

'Strengthen the shields!' Kreig roared, raising his hands high into the air.

Glancing at John, he nodded his approval at seeing him already acting before instruction had been given.

The booming became louder and more insistent until it sounded as though there was but one continuous peal of thunder. The walls began to shake under the bombardment, causing cracks to spread along them and then up to the arched ceiling above. Finally, with a tremendous explosion of sound, their shield cracked and then shattered completely, sending fading hand-sized pieces of energy floating to the floor like the dying leaves of autumn.

A bright ball of dazzling white light like that of the moon burst through the roof an instant later, sending chunks of wood and other debris to fall upon the cowering inhabitants. It hung there for a moment, suspended in the air before slowly dimming to allow the stern face scowling from within to be seen.

Framed in darkness, eyes glinting with malice surveyed the chamber with a cold disdain.

'Colin!' cried the High Wizard in dismay, recognition causing his deep voice to tremble. 'Why do you attack us? We are not your enemy and would have peace with the Egni,' he pleaded, sinking to his knees.

The glowing eyes snapped to the wizard and narrowed angrily.

'Peace!' Colin spat, sounding as though the very word was poison to his tongue. 'There can be no peace now that blood has been spilt,' he continued, as his image expanded to dominate the room.

'It was not us that killed them, please believe me, for I have knowledge on the matter,' Kreig begged, clasping his hands before him as though in prayer.

Arching an eyebrow at him with a sneer curling his upper lip, the Egni Master shook his head in disgust.

'Do you think for one second that I put the feat of killing so many at your door, Wizard?' he asked mockingly, chuckling in dark disbelief.

'You speak of the legend's return, I presume? Did you think that you would know before me?' he asked, sneering down at the petrified man.

A cold, sick feeling filled the wizard's abdomen, and his shoulders slumped lower in defeat.

'Can we do nothing?' he asked, speaking in a tone that was barely more than a whisper. 'Can we not step back and allow you free reign to seek your retribution on those who deserve it?' he asked, flicking his eyes briefly towards the High Priestess.

Looking down at him coldly, Colin clearly disliked his show of weakness.

'You fail to see what these conniving witches have done for

us,' he replied, smiling viciously then at the High Priestess.

Puzzled by the statement, Kreig looked at the witch again and saw that she was as clueless as he was. Locking his eyes back on the vampire's visage, he saw Colin smile more wickedly.

'They have given us an excuse,' the ancient hissed as the sphere of light began to expand even further. 'Welcome to the beginning and end of the second great war of the races. The final war,' he added before seeing movement out of the corner of his eye.

Standing with his druids behind him, John raised his arms to unleash a crackling power of his own. The lightning struck the vampire in the eyes, causing him to flinch and turn away in pain.

Seeing his chance, John gestured to the marble floor directly below the vampire and with a sound like cracking glass, it split.

Recovering quickly, Colin's eyes flashed with power as he bared his teeth in anger.

'Time to die!' he hissed, his sphere of light beginning to crackle more dangerously.

John, however, the epitome of serenity, raised his arms before him, hands clenched with one finger protruding. As he did so, the ground beneath the marble rose up violently in time with his obscene gesture.

On contact with the orb, Colin let out a howl as his power was instantly drawn down into the earth, his might absorbed completely.

With a growl of rage and then a wail of agony, Colin's sphere was sucked into the earth, casting the room into almost complete darkness.

Remaining where he was, John pivoted on his heels in the direction of the High Wizard, who had remained on his knees throughout the attack.

'Let's not give the game away just yet, shall we?' he asked sarcastically, slowly lowering his fingers to the deafening sound of applause.

# CHAPTER THIRTEEN

Sitting on her sofa, Kristina stared dreamily into the fire, watching the flames eat hungrily into the dried-out wood. Smiling in satisfaction, she had lit the wood with a mere wave of her hand, no longer having to rely on the use of speech.

Every morning she would rise, and after setting the logs in the grate the night before, she would practise lighting them with her unspoken will. It had been slow going at first, with only small pieces of wood smouldering at her command, but after strenuous visualisation exercises and a strengthening willpower of her own, she was now able to light the fire without much effort at all.

The logs had been cut by Jack, her newly appointed gardener and friend, who seemed always to be out in the shed, sawing away.

'Cut only from the fallen branches, mind you,' he had said, holding her eyes so that he knew she was listening. 'Dead wood! Never cut from the living,' he warned, waving a calloused finger at her.

Smiling at the memory, she thought warmly of the old man and considered him a true friend after she had gotten to know him.

'They don't make them like him anymore,' she thought again, smiling as she imagined him sawing up the wood.

Always dressed in the same clothes, she pictured him in his hobnailed boots and white shirt with the sleeves rolled up. Remembering his tweed waistcoat when she had first set eyes upon him and loving that old style on men, she realised she never actually saw him wearing it when working on her garden. His black trousers looked battered but seemed to suit his worn-out appearance, and she found herself smiling at the thought of him.

Cocking her head to the side suddenly, she could hear him sawing up the wood.

'*Even now!*' she thought, rolling her eyes with a shake of her head and a chuckle in her throat.

Heaving herself up from the sofa, she pulled out the books for today's lessons. She loved home-schooling her children, and though hard on them at first, they were now happy with the routine.

Sighing happily, she was overjoyed that her daughter had stopped asking after her father, and the three of them now appeared inseparable.

'*It all worked out in the end,*' she thought, wondering why she had fretted at all.

Walking into the kitchen, she filled the kettle and randomly thought of when the house had caused the water to drench her for casting the circle. It had all ended when Francesca had forgiven her, and she had realised afterwards that the house had carried out the punishment only while her daughter had been angry with her.

Shaking her head at the memory, she placed the kettle on its stand and flicked down the switch. No longer worrying about the factions' retribution or even the dreaded Bloods for that matter, she felt safe now, for there had been no sign of them in all this time.

Her mind wandered back to Cristian, having liked him despite the fact that he was a creature of the night. She assumed that he must have been true to his word and had somehow gotten them all to back off.

After making herself a cup of tea, she stared out at the forest from the kitchen window and wondered again what had happened to their father. She felt sure that he was in the forest, for she still sensed him there, or what was left of him after all this time, and pictured his rotting remains for a moment. She felt a need to know what had happened to him and ultimately lay what was left to rest.

A knock on the door caused her mind to return to the present, and she smiled at hearing a key being inserted into the lock mechanism. Waiting for the expected struggle, she knew that the house would still refuse her friend entry, and no amount of coaxing would change that, even when it was her daughter who asked.

Stifling a laugh, Kristina rolled her eyes before calling out.

'Hey, Jan!' she greeted, then lowered her tone to say something else, 'Are you ever going to let her come in?' she asked, readying to open it herself.

The door opened suddenly and then slammed closed by the force of her friend's vented anger.

'Bloody door!' Janet complained, flushing with annoyance before taking a calming breath. 'Hi, Kiki. It's absolutely gorgeous outside! Fancy a picnic or something?' she asked, smiling hopefully.

Shaking her head, Kristina pointed at the schoolwork laid out on the kitchen table.

'It's a school day,' she replied musically, shrugging in apology.

Thumping footsteps came tearing down the stairs, causing Kristina to groan at her friend's loudly asked question.

Sliding to a stop on the tiled kitchen floor, Francesca's hair was a mass of unruly curls.

'A picnic?' she asked, her blue eyes wide with excitement.

'No, Cesca! We have to…' she began but was cut off before she could finish.

'Lucian, we're going on a picnic!' Francesca called, causing Janet to put her hand to her mouth to hide her amusement.

Kristina closed her eyes as Lucian thumped across the landing, shouting a muffled, 'Yay!' which brought an unbidden twitch to her mouth.

'Cesca, you really are too intelligent for your own good,' Janet laughed, rolling her eyes at her friend and spreading her arms apologetically.

'Can we go into the forest, please, Mammy?' Francesca asked innocently, opening the bread tin to make some toast.

Glancing back at Janet, a thrill of exhilaration caused Kristina's skin to prickle.

*'We are more than capable of protecting them, especially now that Janet has magick from the circle,'* she thought, shrugging her shoulders at her friend, *'and it's been so long without any sign of danger. What's the worst that can happen?'* she asked herself, feeling a flush of nervousness.

Seeing her friend willing her to agree, she began to warm to the idea.

'*Bugger it!*' she thought daringly and put her hands to her waist. 'Okay, into the forest we go!' she answered, her wide eyes dancing with the thrill of excitement.

\*\*\*

Lathered in sweat, Jack stepped out from the shed and wiped himself down with a dirty cloth that looked as old as he was.

Rippling in sinuous, well-worked muscle, he had the build of a gymnast that he was careful to hide from most people. Sighing contentedly after cutting twenty new logs, he pulled on his shirt and dressed swiftly before wiping at his balding head with the already damp cloth.

Not yet completely bald, he sported an inch-thick band of short white hair that ran around the back of his head, literally from one ear to the other, before ending in longer than normal sideburns that stopped just above the jawline.

Though considered a small man at five-and-a-half feet tall, he emanated a quiet strength that belied his age and gave those who would cross him a moment of pause.

Sitting himself down on a squat, thick-legged stool, he unwrapped his homemade sandwiches and took a hungry bite before sighing in appreciation.

'Good stuff,' he mumbled, speaking around the mouthful of food.

On hearing the door to the house open, he looked up to see the little girl, Francesca, running his way.

'Jack!' she called, stopping before him to pant from the exertion. 'We're going on a picnic,' she gasped, smiling at his grumpy expression.

'You shouldn't be out of breath from running across that small stretch of grass,' he admonished, shaking his head in disapproval. 'When I was your age, I could run up and down the mountainside and still not be as out of breath as you are right now,' he grumbled, waving a heavily calloused finger at her. 'Here, have a sandwich,' he ordered, thrusting the food into her hands.

Taking the sandwich, she peered at it dubiously before raising it to eye level to better see its contents.

'Eat!' he growled menacingly, causing her to giggle and step away.

'What's in it?' she asked stubbornly, inspecting the contents with one of her thumbs.

'Strength,' he growled, pushing her hands up to her mouth. 'Now, eat!' he commanded, unwilling to take no for an answer.

Giving him a sideways glance, she tentatively took a bite before lifting her eyebrows approvingly.

'I like strength,' she remarked, speaking with her mouth full whilst attempting to smile at the same time.

'Give one to the boy,' he grumbled, thrusting another into her hand before glancing towards the house. 'You never know when you might need strength,' he whispered, shaking his head in annoyance.

*** 

Walking through the forest, Kristina kept her children close and her senses alert as Janet maintained a shield around them.

'I'm tired,' Lucian moaned, dragging his feet dramatically over the moss-covered route they were taking.

'Not long now,' she replied automatically, feeling a flutter of excitement building in the pit of her stomach. *'He is so close,'* she thought, sensing his essence just up ahead and slightly to the right. 'So close!' she whispered, unwilling to turn back at this point.

Glancing at her daughter, Kristina saw that she, too, looked in that same direction, and the realisation hit her like a punch to the stomach.

*'She knows!'* she quailed, feeling the need to take her child in her arms and hug her close. 'Which way?' she tested quietly before growing pale when her daughter pointed in the same direction.

'Just through there,' Francesca answered, turning back with a nervous smile.

Closing her eyes, Kristina felt a pang of sympathy for the child and cursed herself for bringing them. Francesca had never once forgotten about her father, not for a second, and her mother finally understood that she never would.

Nodding silently, she decided it was now too late to turn back, so gestured for her child to lead the way.

'Stop!' Kristina screamed suddenly, seeing Francesca break away and run full tilt into a large meadow with her brother close behind. 'No!' she cried, not wishing either of them to see what no child should. 'Come back!' she screamed; all thoughts of stealth forgotten in her alarm.

Finally catching up, Kristina saw that the children were sitting on a massive stone block that looked odd as it lay upon the ground, as if placed atop the grass by some giant hand.

Sighing in relief, she saw Lucian laying on his back, enjoying the sun's warmth, and Francesca sitting next to him cross-legged with her eyes fixed upon a point a little distance away.

'What's that?' she asked quietly, causing Lucian to sit up straight and look at everything other than where he was being directed.

'Wait here!' Kristina commanded, looking at her daughter sternly to see if she would listen, but Francesca had not moved and merely stared at something half-hidden in the long grass with a look of fear bright in her eyes.

'*Oh, my baby girl!*' Kristina silently cried, seeing that her child was too scared to take the final step.

Taking a deep breath, she walked towards the black blot amidst the green before looking over her shoulder at her friend with a look of warning.

Nodding in response, Janet summoned up more of the earth's magick into her shield before nodding again.

There was not much left of the thing, Kristina realised, approaching whatever it was with a nervous disposition. Charred black, it lay motionless within the lush tones of the grass and would have been easily missed if not for the familiar feel it gave her.

A cold shiver of apprehension rippled through her body as she cautiously moved a little closer, before stopping down to part the grass with her hand.

'Oh,' she murmured, squatting over the dried-out husk of something long dead.

Wishing again that they had never come, she now believed in that sickening moment that some things were better off not known.

'Too late now,' she sighed, peering a little closer.

Steeling herself, she ran her eyes over what looked to be the burnt remains of some forest animal and gasped in relief.

About to turn away, something bright reflected the sunlight and caught her eye. Leaning in once again, she brushed at it with a crispy leaf before opening her mouth in a silent scream of horror.

'Oh my god,' she gasped, finally recognising what it was. *'It's his ring!'* she realised, turning away to retch. *'That's his ring!'* her mind reeled, fighting down more of the bile that rose into her mouth.

For as long as she had known him, Daire had worn a ring on each little finger, and one of them was this one. She could never be mistaken in this regard, for the snowflake design was so unusual and beautifully crafted that she would know it anywhere, and to the best of her knowledge, he had never once taken it off.

'Oh my god!' she cried, staring down at the snowflake design.

Swallowing hard, she reached down to pinch it free before gagging again when the decimated mass moved along with it. Snatching her hand away, she found that she could not tear her eyes away from the intricate design that seemed to beg for its release, but something was holding the ring in place, as though it was a prize to be earned or won from the decimated mass that laid claim to it.

Steeling herself further, she pulled on it a little harder, and with a delayed, sickening understanding, she vomited as the ring finally came free.

*'It's still on his finger!'* she quailed, retching again onto the grass, unable to stop until there was nothing left to give.

'What is it?' Francesca called in frustration, standing now to better see what her mother was up to.

'Stay there!' she gasped, trying to get her breathing under control.

With tears on her cheeks, Kristina scrambled back from the blackened corpse before running back to her children.

'What's wrong?' Francesca demanded; her little fists clenched tightly at her sides.

'It's nothing,' Kristina lied quickly, intent on saving her from the terrible truth. 'Just a dead animal,' she continued, sharing a fearful look with her friend before secretly showing her the ring.

Lifting her hand to her mouth, Janet's face drained of colour as she looked back at the black blot in the grass.

'I don't want to stay here anymore,' Kristina announced, expecting some resistance from at least one of her children, but they seemed not to have heard, rapt as they were upon something in the shadow of the trees.

Following their line of sight, Kristina froze at what she saw looking back at them.

Three figures stood just inside the clearing, their dark silhouettes still as statues, and though she could not see their eyes, she could feel their hunger as though it was her own.

A cold sweat crept up her back, and she knew in her blood what these creatures were.

'*Vampires!*' her instinct screamed, but the worst and most lethal of them, and in a panic, she voiced what they were. 'Bloods!' she gasped, hating herself in that moment.

She had been warned not to come, threatened even, and yet she had ignored him as she always had.

'You stupid bloody fool!' she cursed, knowing that she had done it simply to prove that she was her own woman, but after seeing his corpse, she now realised how foolish and petty she had been.

'Jan?' she sobbed, but her friend had seen them also and drew up all the magick she could to feed their defence.

'I see them,' Jan whimpered, fear causing her whole body to shake.

'Is your shield up?' Kristina asked, and as though in answer, the three figures blurred across the clearing to hit the shield so hard that white fractures appeared in the now very visible barrier.

A tremendous impact from behind brought them spinning around to see yet another trio of vampires hitting them from that side.

'Put up your shields, both of you!' Kristina barked but saw that her children were rooted to the spot and unresponsive to her order.

Screaming as a third trinity of vampires hit the shield from yet another side, Kristina attempted to aid her friend by pouring her might into the shield that had now whitened on all sides.

Reaching for Francesca, she took her by the chin and forced her to look away from the vampire who had her under some kind of spell.

'This is your father's ring,' she stressed, holding it up before her vacantly staring eyes. 'Put it on!' she demanded, hoping that any ring of the legendary Dark Wolf would be more than just decoration.

Slowly picking up the ring, Francesca placed it dreamily on her index finger before clenching her little fist around it.

'They can make you stop moving!' she gasped, looking around wildly.

Instinctively taking hold of her brother's hand, she felt the flush of power ripple down into her hand before he, too, was freed from the vampire-induced trance.

'Raise your shields!' Kristina instructed before nodding nervously after sensing them comply.

With her own already joined to that of Janet's, she took them by the hand and stared at the nightmares around them.

The nine vampires looked to be human upon first glance, except for the unnatural glint in their eyes and the sickly fear they inspired.

She had known in that first instance that they were like nothing she had ever encountered before, not even Cristian, who was apparently kin to these loathsome creatures, for they felt like death to her... death incarnate.

'*As he had felt,*' she recalled, suddenly reminded of when Daire had stood in the darkness of the doorway. 'We need to get home,' she whimpered, taking a step back towards the trees.

'I think not!' a vampire with long, dark hair replied, stepping to the side to bar their way.

Letting out a scream of alarm, Kristina backed up with her arms held protectively over her children.

'What do you want?' she shrieked, fear bright in her eyes.

Ever so slowly, the vampire raised his arm and pointed two

long-nailed fingers at her daughter and then, slower still, split the index finger away to point at her son.

'Them!' he hissed, striking out against the shield with his free hand.

Feeling the children's shields harden on reflex, she felt more than a little relieved that they had chosen to include her within them.

Feeling petrified of these nasty-looking people, Francesca looked down at her father's ring and silently pleaded for his protection.

'Daddy!' she cried, bringing it to her lips on instinct.

The familiar feeling of calm flowed over her like it had after first putting it on, but it was enhanced now, casting her fears aside to fade on the wind that suddenly blew around them.

Stepping out from her mother's skirt, she looked up at the man and smiled with an expression that did not belong to a little girl.

The vampire looked down at her with an odd expression, clearly taken aback by the look in her eye.

'Feeling brave, little one?' he mocked, running a long nail down the edge of the shield and causing a white line to trail behind it.

Glancing down, Kristina saw a wild, untameable magick dancing in her daughter's eyes and an expression she did not recognise on her child's face, a look of emotionless detachment with a will of steel behind it.

Raising her hand, Francesca lifted the vampire from his feet, causing him to thrash in the air as he fought for release. With a flick of her wrist, he was then thrown back hard against a tree in the distance, but it was up and at her again almost immediately, ripping and tearing its way through to her.

The vampires on all sides joined in on the assault, causing the barrier to glow dangerously around those it protected.

'Fire!' a voice shouted in Francesca's mind, causing her to remember what her father had taught her, but she did not want to kill these frightful men, even though she knew what they were.

Indecision creased her features, and without knowing why, she looked to her brother for support.

As though sensing her reluctance, the power that was in her seeped into him, and she saw the wild magick come alive in his dark eyes.

'*Llosgi,*' Lucian screamed, immediately unleashing the borrowed power with a word he had not known.

Flames instantly engulfed the vampires, enveloping them in white-hot fire that turned most of them to ash.

Feeling drained from the expense of so much magick, the boy faltered and clutched at his mother for support.

'Mammy,' he cried, staggering momentarily before being swept up into her arms. White-faced, he whispered at her weakly. 'I feel sick,' he moaned, feeling totally exhausted by the ordeal.

Tearing her hand free to break the connection, Francesca tried to summon the magick anew, but her father's will had withdrawn from the ring, and all that was left was its unguided might.

'We are never going to make it!' Janet wailed, looking about frantically for a way to escape.

Feeling a flush of anger after witnessing the pain on her son's face, Kristina cast her magick about them. Visualising first the movement of her attack, she spoke the name that her son had called to unleash it.

'*Llosgi,*' she snarled, sending out a wall of fire from her shield to rise around them.

The remaining vampires screamed as the fire washed over and into them, driving them back from the badly damaged shield. Sectioning off her mind, she kept the searing sea swirling around them whilst drawing upon the power of the earth to replenish the expenditure from her body. Next, she sent the earth's energy into the shield, causing it to become a little brighter.

'Run!' she screamed, grabbing at her daughter's hand as they made for the trees.

\*\*\*

The woods were dark and gloomy after the brightness of the glade, causing them to pause for a moment to pant in the darkness until their eyes could adjust.

'Kiki, that was incredible,' Janet blurted, the fear she felt making her giggle hysterically. 'What the hell was that?' she asked in amazement, having never even read of anything like it before.

Turning to her friend, Kristina smiled weakly and shook her head with a shrug.

'*His* magick. I've been reading more of his books,' she replied, her eyes suddenly brimming with tears. 'Come on, there might be more of them,' she warned, trying to force the emotion down.

Making their way back, Kristina had to stop many times to recover her strength, the added weight of her son taking its toll on her reserves.

'Mammy!' Francesca shouted, pointing through the trees towards a lone figure who waited ahead of them in silence.

Squinting her eyes in the shadowed undergrowth, Kristina widened them again in sudden recognition.

'Jack!' she called, waving at the old man before rushing towards him.

'I didn't expect you to travel this far from the house,' he grumbled, speaking with a note of chastisement. 'No matter, we had better head back now,' he added, scanning the trees around them.

Looking at Francesca, he smiled wearily and patted her head fondly.

'I wonder, do you have one of those sandwiches left?' he asked, looking more tired than she had ever seen him before.

Reluctantly opening her bag, she pulled out the food he had given her for her brother.

'I was going to eat it later,' she admitted, glancing at her brother guiltily.

Laughing at the mischievous little girl, he accepted the food from her graciously.

'I'm glad you kept it, little one. I'll make you a load more tomorrow,' he replied, winking at her in amusement.

Making small work of the sandwich, he stood back and sighed in relief.

'That's better,' he stated, stretching his arms and looking as strong as ever.

Frowning at him in concern, Kristina dreaded that he was going to be more of a hindrance than a help on the way back.

'Why are you all the way out here?' she asked, looking at him suspiciously, but continued before he could reply. 'We need to be getting back to the house. There are *unsavoury men* in the forest,' she continued, choosing her words carefully.

Nodding knowingly, Jack arched an eyebrow in response.

'I will come with you, I think. I feel as tired as you look, and there is always strength in numbers, after all,' he replied, with a dangerous glint in his eyes that she had not seen before. 'This old body lets me down sometimes, especially over such long distances,' he grumbled, turning to lead them back home.

The journey was slow and filled with threatened perils, the sounds of distant hissing forcing them to stop often. Sometimes, Jack would stop them for no apparent reason, until Kristina realised that it was whenever the forest had become silent around them, and would only continue when the birds had begun to sing again.

As the trees began to thin, the birds silenced yet again, causing Jack to turn to wave them back as black shadows detached themselves ahead of them.

'Shields!' he growled, turning to face the oncoming threat.

Raising his hands in defence, a blinding flash of light came from behind, causing him to turn at the sounds of heavy hooves thundering from all around and an accompanying white glow that lit up the darkness.

'Run!' Jack barked, gesturing them away from the battle taking place behind them.

'What's happening?' Kristina cried, struggling with the effort of dragging her children with her.

Not looking at all where they were going, both children had eyes only for the battle. Widened in outright disbelief, they could not tear them from the single-horned horses and the silver-clad riders who sat atop them.

'Move!' Kristina screamed, dragging on their wrists and snapping them out of their shock.

'Mammy! Can you see them? They're...' Francesca gasped,

still trying to get a clear look.

'I don't care! *Move!*' she stormed, cutting her daughter off before she could finish.

Running headlong through the remaining trees, they stopped again to scan the carnage before them.

'What on earth?' Kristina gasped, taking in the burned and decapitated remains of many more vampires.

'What indeed,' Jack answered, crouching down beside the closest corpse and poking it to ash with an outstretched finger. 'Let's get to the house,' he advised, rising to his feet again without waiting for them to agree.

All agreed in any case, save Janet, who just stood there staring vacantly ahead, seeming not to have heard the instruction.

'Jan?' Kristina called softly, looking at her friend worriedly.

'What? Oh, yes! Let's get the hell out of here!' she babbled, nodding her head manically.

Careful not to step on anything, the five picked their way through the battle's aftermath whilst looking for signs of those who had fought it.

'Nothing,' Jack informed after scouting a little way ahead. 'Not even a hoof print,' he added, shaking his head in disbelief.

'Were they truly... unicorns?' Kristina asked, still not believing what she had seen.

'You mean those giant horses with horns on their head?' he asked sarcastically, giving her a ridiculous expression. 'I was more focused on the elves that rode them,' he continued dryly, amusement shining in his greying eyes. 'Come! We are not safe yet!'

Taking the lead again, he guided them towards the house, followed by Kristina and the children, each of them held tightly by the wrist. Janet took up the rear, silently holding her dread in check as her head twitched nervously from left to right.

Raising his right fist, Jack signalled for them to stop again, reminding Kristina of a war film she had once seen, which caused her to wonder about his past before making a mental note to ask him afterwards.

Cocking his head to one side, the old man listened to something up ahead, clearly spooked by something as yet unseen.

Closing her eyes, Kristina did the same and heard a faint noise, but it took her a second to identify the sound.

Turning back to Janet, she mouthed what she had heard up ahead.

'Bloods!' she mimed before silently stalking closer to the sounds of vampires hissing their hatred.

Creeping forward, Jack saw many more dried-up husks of the undead, some with their heads completely removed, as well as other random limbs spread about the area.

'Oh, thank god!' Kristina cried, seeing the house looming up out of the greenery, but then moaned at the acre of land that stood between them and their front door.

Vampires massed in the garden, fast and deadly as they attacked a solitary figure in shining silver armour. Believing at first that it was another elf, it was only when one of the fabled swords of power was raised into the air that none, but one knew who the fighter was. Slashing through the air in a blur of motion, the glowing silver sword caused the Bloods to fall back either in flames or in pieces. Dozens of them lay dead at the warrior's feet, their black blood darkening the ground beneath him, causing him to sidestep often to keep a sure footing.

Watching in horror as a vampire launched itself at the man's back, Kristina almost clapped when it was repelled by a suddenly visible shield at the last. The creature stood dazed after the attempt before a flash of silver removed its head from its shoulders.

As the small group watched in fascination, several of the vampires got too close to the house and were ripped from their feet by its terrifying might. Hanging by their necks, they struggled futilely before dissolving into thick grey ash.

A dark form, far larger than the others, burst through the throng to enter the field of battle, and with a defiant roar of hatred, it smashed at the warrior with a ground-shuddering force. The impact of the strike was felt under Kristina's feet, and she cried in terror at the power of the thing.

Screaming in horror, Francesca watched as the warrior was sent to his knees by the mighty blow, his shield exploding like the shattering of glass that faded almost instantly in the dazzling sunlight.

Flinching as blue lightning arced past her head, Kristina saw it strike the creature and drive it back from the fallen man. Arcing from one vampire to the next, the crackling blue light created a circle of death around him, protecting him in his hour of need.

Following the source of the blue energy, Kristina found herself gaping at Jack and at his outstretched hands that the lightning was issuing from.

'Move!' he growled, on catching her eye, before running ahead to clear a path before them.

Passing the fallen hero, he hauled him to his feet before pulling him towards the sanctuary that the house provided.

The garden seemed to come alive in the old man's wake, the long-barbed hawthorn bushes uncoiling and wrapping themselves around their pursuers.

'Good god almighty!' Kristina cried, seeing the wicked-looking tendrils whip out all around her.

The double doors flew open invitingly, as though beckoning them on as they ran for its safety.

'We're not going to make it!' Jack shouted, seeing the largest vampire move to block their path, ripping off the barbs as he did so.

Raising his hands, Jack sent out his magick once again, slowing the monster but not stopping it.

The creature grimaced in pain but kept moving as the warrior leapt to meet it, his silver sword blurring in motion as it cleaved its way towards its head. But in the blink of an eye, the creature appeared several paces closer to the warrior and within the sweep of his deadly silver blade. Safe within the deadly arc, the Blood struck the bladesman in his solar plexus, launching him back with the sword spinning fatally from his grasp.

Blue lightning hit the creature again, but it was prepared this time and merely snarled in pain as it continued towards the fallen warrior.

After unconsciously kissing the ring, Francesca raised her hands and cast her magick in the man's defence. Fire instantly erupted over the huge vampire, causing it to stop momentarily and lock its eyes on her.

Screaming in terror, Kristina saw it finally change direction towards her daughter and turned to her gardener with a look of desperation.

'Your "Sith Fire" isn't bloody working, Jack!' she cried, jumping in front of her child with a new shield expanding out of her.

During the confusion, Janet saw a clear path towards the house and away from the madness, and on seeing her chance... she took it.

'Mammy!' Lucian screamed, standing in shock at being left all alone.

Not knowing which way to turn, he stood there frozen as more vampires swarmed towards him.

Seeing his plight, Kristina tried to draw power from the earth, but the panic within prevented her from doing so.

'No!' she screamed, seeing the vile creatures reach him. It was as though time stopped for her in that horrific moment, dragging out her worst nightmare in excruciating slowness.

She saw the huge vampire crack her shield with a thunderous hammer blow of his fist, but it was the sight of her little boy being swept away by a black tide of darkness that sent her to her knees.

Witnessing what had happened, Jack unleashed his lightning towards where the boy had been, decimating those unable to withstand his magick as the larger one had. Fury blazed in him, a manic determination that fed his power more than he knew.

'Die!' he howled, clenching his teeth in anger. 'I want you to die!' he raged, driving all his might into the attack.

With the familiar sound of shattering glass, Kristina's shield broke under the vampire's strike, and it bared its teeth in victory. The massive Blood reached for her with a large, black-nailed hand, but it was her daughter's scream that tore her from her grief and shocked her once more into action. Without a second thought, she turned and covered her daughter's body with her own, waiting dreadfully for what must surely be her end.

'I will die before they do,' she wept, remembering her promise before closing her eyes in grief.

A dazzling light hit the vampire in the face, causing it to

scream in agony for the very first time before issuing a lower hiss of anger as it clutched at itself protectively.

Flinching away from this raw, untamed power, Kristina saw it drive the creature back. Crackling deafeningly from somewhere beside her, the lightning caused the creature to cry out a second time as it backed away further.

Looking down, she saw a mask of hate etched into her daughter's face and felt stunned by the immense power she wielded. Briefly wondering how her child had known how to do such a thing, she wept in moanful understanding at the answer.

'*He taught her,*' she realised, knowing that her father would have given both children the knowledge of how to defend themselves.

Striding forward into the mix of battle, Jack unleashed his might like never before, releasing his anger into a cold, unyielding hate, and for the first time in his life, it ignited something new within him. The blue lightning burned more dangerously, turning the undead to ash even as it passed by. Continuing his assault, he threw all of his might against them before glimpsing the briefest flash of white.

Focusing upon that area, he hurled his hatred forth, causing ash to swirl high into the air from the vampires crumbling remains, the last vestiges of their unholy existence.

A vampire landed atop him, attempting to scratch its way through his protection, sparking a memory in his mind.

'*I wish I had his shield!*' he thought, thinking of the legend before turning his attack up.

He had once seen his friend's shield incinerate those who came against it and thought it more of a weapon against insurmountable odds than any bolt of lightning. Having tried to duplicate the feat many times thereafter, he had never quite known how it was done and wished now that he had badgered his friend into telling him.

'*Imagination and advanced sense!*' Daire had answered after being asked how it was done. '*You'll not figure it out with common sense. You must use the more advanced kind, as I do,*' he had teased, winking at his friend secretively.

All Jack's shield did was grow white when under attack and grow steadily weaker as all others did.

'Gilga's balls!' he cursed, seeing several Bloods turn to him at once.

Throwing his magick out into a sweeping arc, he hurled his will against them, his only goal now to avenge the boy or die trying, for the time of hope had passed, and all he wanted now was revenge. He cut them down with wide sweeps of his arms, his magick turning them into hissing clouds of dust as he forcibly removed the life from them.

Crying silently in the aftermath, he sent out his magick in the futile hope of once again seeing that elusive flash of white.

Clenching her teeth in determination, Francesca fought to keep the energy of the earth flowing through her, but somewhere at the back of her mind, she knew that it was the ring that kept her focused.

The creature's eyes fixed upon her, and she felt the immediate pull of its will, but the talisman blocked the attempt and protected her from its mind-numbing control. Not knowing how the ring did what it did, she understood instinctively that it was designed for exactly this purpose but guessed that it could do so much more.

Snarling in rage, the huge Blood stepped in close, intent on finishing her off with its bare hands.

Gasping at seeing the creature's intention, Kristina made to step forward again, but her daughter's shield was securely in place and began to pulse before the monster's fist smashed through it.

Crying out again, the vampire was brought crashing to its knees as the child's shield turned suddenly hostile.

Turning the creature's skin to a scorched and crispy black, the shield turned silver as it locked the vampire's grasping hand in place before continuing to defend her.

*'I am with you,'* her father's voice echoed in her mind, causing her to feel safe as the shield struck out from all across its surface.

Widening her eyes, she saw the silver sword cut through flesh, severing the hand that clutched for her. Looking down at it dispassionately, she thought dreamily that it resembled a giant spider as it twitched upon the ground. Feeling her father's presence begin to recede, she felt the return of her panic like a slap to the face.

Looking up desperately into the eyes of the warrior, Kristina's mouth fell open in shocked recognition as the monster fell back in agony.

'Cristian!' she gasped, seeing the Egni vampire who had made it through to her house.

Ignoring her, he continued the motion of the blade to open up the creature's neck with a manoeuvre that took the Blood by surprise.

Backing up desperately in its attempt to survive, the vampire could do nothing as the silver blade opened a wound over its eyes, causing inky black blood to obscure its vision.

Fawning a stagger, the creature suddenly hit out with its remaining hand, batting the sword of power from the warrior's grasp to spear itself into a nearby tree.

Backing away, Cristian raised his hands, and a blast of silver light ripped into the creature, causing it to buckle under the force of it.

'Cristian,' it hissed, speaking the name in a grotesque kind of gurgle. 'Oath-breaker! I will dine on your blood before this day is done,' the creature promised, crouching down low against the continuous attack.

The Egni Lord glared back, breathing heavily from the expense of so much energy.

'All things die, Bael,' he replied, holding his arms out in a sacrificial manner.

'No!' Kristina screamed, seeing the massive vampire step forward with its long-nailed hand reaching for his throat.

Summoning the image of fire to her mind, she opened her mouth for its release when a glowing shaft of light swept across the creature's throat for a second time, causing its severed head to bounce before rocking slightly in the freshly cut grass.

The headless body stumbled back several paces with its arms thrust out as though searching in the dark, causing a familiar laugh to freeze Kristina with inaction for a moment.

On finally turning, she let out a wail, not daring not believe what her eyes were showing her, and so turned to the only one who could reassure her.

Looking back grimly, Jack nodded at her slowly, the slick sweat upon his bald head running down the side of his face.

Staring at him in shock, she felt unable to acknowledge his deed as her emotions swept through her, for under his protective arm was her beloved son, Lucian, and with a cry of relief, she rushed forward to take her child in her arms.

'Oh, my boy!' she cried, hugging him tightly before kissing him all over his face.

Tears of joy coursed down her cheeks as she looked up, shaking her head in disbelief at the wily old man.

'How... Thank you!' she sobbed, choking on the words.

Standing alone with her shoulders jerking rhythmically, Francesca cried silently now that the fight was finally over. Looking up, she caught sight of Cristian's awed expression as he knelt before her.

'You are truly a goddess in the making,' he whispered, raising her hand to his lips. 'I am your champion from this day forth, little one,' he swore, looking at his niece in open admiration.

Shaking her head in disbelief, Kristina stared at each of the brave souls who had defied an army to see her children safe. Feeling exhausted from the battle of her life, she took her children by the hand before gesturing for the others to follow her into the house without waiting for them to do so.

Next to enter was a weary-looking Jack, who almost stumbled through the double doors due to his utter exhaustion.

Looking up at the house rather nervously, Cristian could sense it looking right back at him as it had before, causing him to feel uneasy about entering uninvited.

As though sensing his concerns, the house opened the doors a little wider before he felt its attention shift from him to another.

Nodding curtly, he felt grateful for the acceptance but still held his breath before stepping through the doorway.

A glow of white light expanded from the house, spreading out immediately after the doors had closed behind him. Having expected them to close gently due to their overall size and girth, he started in surprise when they slammed with a thunderous bang, sounding more like a castle gate than the delicate-looking glass doors they appeared to be.

No one spoke as they entered the living area, each feeling too drained and lost within their own thoughts in the aftermath. Wary beyond belief, they stood in silence before beginning to smile at one another after surviving against all probability.

Looking from face to face and not knowing where to start, Kristina simply stood there with nothing to say.

Francesca looked up tiredly with eyes that had seen far too much for one so young and began to sob.

'I can still see him,' she whispered, fresh tears rolling down her cheeks.

'I know, baby. I know, but he's dead now,' Kristina soothed, lowering herself to the child's eye level before taking her in her arms.

'Shhh, baby, it's over now. We're safe. See?' she consoled, pointing out the Egni Lord. 'See, there's Cristian, remember him? He killed the horrible man,' she soothed, causing the child's eyes to flit over to the warrior as he nodded back reassuringly.

'Dead as a dodo,' he confirmed, winking at her warmly.

'Chopped his head right off!' Lucian added, imitating the motion of the killing blow with comical accuracy, accompanied by a 'light sabre' sound effect.

Flowing seamlessly from victor to foe, he raised his arms to stumble about like the Frankenstein monster.

The antics of the boy dissolved the shocked silence into hysterics, causing everyone to explode with spontaneous laughter, and even Francesca began to chuckle as she wiped away her tears.

'My beautiful, brave children,' Kristina whispered, feeling as though she was about to cry herself before she saw a look of rage enter the old man's eyes.

Paling at the reaction, she turned to see her friend's slim form shuffling into view.

Hugging herself tightly, Janet had clearly been crying as she entered the room from the kitchen with her head lowered in shame before looking beseechingly at her friend.

'You left him!' Kristina shrilled, moving forward aggressively.

Flinching back, Janet's eyes widened in alarm before she began to cry again.

'I'm so sorry, Kiki. I don't know why I did it. I just saw the doors and ran. I didn't think!' she wept, desperately looking to her for support.

'Get out of my house,' Kristina shrieked, screaming the words at her lifelong friend, 'and take your damned coven with you!' she roared, a murderous glint shining in her eyes.

'Kiki, please! There's no going back. Please? I'm so sorry,' she pleaded, backing away from her friend's righteous anger.

Shaking her head, Kristina looked back in disgust before finally placing her hands at her hips.

'House?' she called in a loud voice, causing her friend to shake her head in horror. 'Would you be so kind as to remove this coward from the... from *you*, please?' she asked, waiting expectantly with raised eyebrows.

The temperature was the first to change, plummeting rapidly before they heard a deep growl that steadily grew louder.

Pulling her children close, Kristina hid their faces from what she expected to happen.

The latch on the front door clicked delicately before they heard it creak slowly open in readiness for what would come next.

'Goodbye, Jan,' Kristina whispered, her disgust etched upon her face.

Lifted into the air as though by a hangman's noose, Janet began choking as something unseen crushed her throat. Slamming against the far wall, what breath remained in the woman was forced from her lungs.

Hell-bent on causing as much pain as possible before carrying out the deed, the house launched her into the hallway whilst hitting her against every conceivable object before bouncing her off both walls on her way out.

On finally reaching the front door, it slammed on her before battering her repeatedly until Kristina called out in a panic.

'Simply *out* would suffice,' she yelled, closing her eyes with a wince.

Pausing but for a moment, the door hit her lifelong friend a further three times before finally launching her out into the street, then closing rather delicately with a soft click of the latch.

Speechless at the ejection method the house had used, Cristian shared a look with the old man and was forced to take a deep breath in an attempt to calm himself.

'Well, it's definitely his house!' Jack chuckled before smiling wickedly at the vampire's reaction.

'I didn't know it would do that!' Kristina defended, shrugging her shoulders rather sheepishly.

'Please don't ever ask me to leave, Kris!' Cristian whispered, looking at her seriously. 'Simply give me the nod, and I will happily depart under my own steam, so to speak,' he added, his features looking strained.

'That was awesome,' Jack blurted, throwing back his head as he laughed in amusement.

Closing her eyes, Kristina felt saddened by what had happened but reminded herself that her son had been left to die and that his father's response would have been so much worse and far more permanent.

At the thought of their father, she pictured his decimated remains and began to cry, realising at long last that he had died so that they could live.

\*\*\*

Keeping herself busy, Kristina bathed the children before packing them off to bed. Deciding to let them both sleep in her bed for the night, she tucked them in with a kiss goodnight.

'Don't be afraid of the house, it was defending you when it hurt Janet. You're not afraid, are you?' she asked, looking down at them both.

Smiling reassuringly, Francesca shook her head slowly before pushing against the dead weight of her brother, who had already drifted off to sleep.

'The house did what Daddy would have done,' she replied, sounding thoughtful as she worked it out in her mind. 'I think it is him in a way. It feels like him, anyway,' she added, shrugging her shoulders under the duvet.

Feeling a cold shiver run up her back, Kristina felt a flush of goosebumps rise on her flesh.

'*Even in death, you haunt me,*' she thought, kissing Francesca goodnight before closing the door.

On entering the living room, she was surprised to see both wizard and vampire sitting there in silence, smiling at one another politely.

'Well, this isn't awkward at all,' she remarked before walking into the kitchen to open a bottle of wine. 'I thought it best to wait,' Jack replied, patting the seat beside him.

Shrugging, she seated herself with glass in hand before sighing tiredly.

'Okay,' she began, taking a deep swig. 'Where do we start?' she asked, taking another sip before raising her eyebrows expectantly.

Glancing from one to the other, she rolled her eyes before resting her head back.

'You both know my story, so who wants to go first?' she pressed, beginning to feel annoyed. 'Cristian, why are you fighting your own kind?' she asked, not bothering to sugar-coat anything at this point.

Sitting deeper into the opposite sofa, the vampire's deep scowl showed her his reluctance to go first.

'I made a choice,' he replied flippantly, shrugging the telling away.

Stubbornly raising both eyebrows questioningly, she stayed like that for several seconds whilst waiting for him to elaborate.

'I wronged him in the past and want to make amends,' he confessed sadly, speaking the words in a clipped tone of voice that frustrated her even further.

'He turned his back on him when he needed him the most!' Jack growled; his tone full of resentment.

Colour instantly drained from the vampire's face, and a cold few seconds passed before he narrowed his eyes in suspicion.

'He judged him and then went to war against him,' Jack continued, clearly not intimidated in the slightest, 'and I am most glad that you have finally seen the error of your ways,' he added, smiling slyly.

Leaning forward in his seat, Cristian studied the old man before tilting his head to one side.

'Blue?' he asked as a slow, quizzical half-smile spreading across his face. 'I thought you long dead!' he confessed, wondering how the old man had survived all these years without resorting to vampirism.

Rising to his feet, Jack bowed as though to congratulate himself on his masterful performance.

'At your pleasure,' he replied, winking back mischievously.

'What the... who?' Kristina stammered, causing both to glance her way.

Seating himself again, Jack patted her knee affectionately before smiling a little guiltily.

'Oh, I am sorry for my deceit, my dear,' he whispered, looking at her tenderly. 'I mean that. But I had to make sure they were protected,' he explained, pointing up at the ceiling.

'Why?' she sobbed, feeling totally betrayed after all this time.

'He came to see me, maybe a year or so ago,' he began, weighing his words carefully, 'and he was changed,' he continued, knowing that she would understand what he meant. 'I would go as far as to say, "otherworldly",' he added, glancing at the vampire.

Leaning forward, Cristian perched at the very edge of his seat, shaking his head doubtfully.

'Otherworldly. What exactly does that mean?' he asked, frowning at the old man.

'Not... of... this... world,' Jack replied, pronouncing each word slowly. 'He was changed physically, mentally, and dare I say, felt far darker than he ever had,' he explained, struggling to find the right descriptive words.

'He was named Dark by the Bloods because he was *dark*, even to those wretched things!' he said, cutting the old man off.

Waving off the comment with impatience, Jack glared back at being interrupted.

'Yes, yes! Anyway, as I was saying, Daire had changed... *massively!*' he stressed, overemphasising the last word. 'I barely recognised him even after he told me who he was,' he explained, closing his eyes in remembrance. 'He came to me for help, to find a way to control or undo what had been done to him,' he whispered, shaking his head again with a look of regret. 'I could do nothing, however, for he was no longer human and beyond anything I've ever seen,' he confessed, locking eyes with the vampire again to make his point clear.

'Beyond anything we've seen?' Cristian asked incredulously, remembering all they had seen through the ages. 'Describe him,' he whispered, though found himself dreading the answer.

Shaking his head, Jack was unwilling to recount the demonic countenance of his friend, especially the reflective white eyes that had seemed to stare right through him.

'Take a wild guess?' he grumbled, waving his hand in irritation.

Leaning back into his seat, the Egni Lord rested his head on the high-backed sofa and closed his eyes with a slow intake of breath.

'Black as pitch, white eyes, huge and unstoppable,' Cristian breathed, the descriptive words causing Jack's eyes to flare at the uncanny accuracy. 'At least that is what the survivor said, if the Bloods are to be believed,' the vampire added, shrugging in such a way as to suggest that this would not be out of character for them.

'Survivor?' Kristina asked, looking from the vampire to the old man, who shrugged his ignorance on the matter.

'An army of Bloods marched on this place and had very nearly made it through when they were stopped. Something of that description wiped them out, leaving just one alive to tell the tale,' he informed, turning to look at Kristina. 'The creature gave its name as Dark,' he continued, giving her a tight-lipped smile.

'That must have been after he left me,' Jack reasoned, looking directly at the vampire. 'But before he left, he swore something that frightened the life out of me, and it's for that reason alone that I am here now and why I shall not leave until this business is dealt with,' he continued, frowning sagely at them both.

'Well? What did he say, for Christ's sake?' Kristina snapped, spreading her hands wide before huffing loudly.

Irritated by her manner, the old wizard's eyes grew fierce as he pointed at the ceiling in warning.

'He said that if *they* were to die, he would destroy this world and everyone in it,' he announced, glaring at her resentfully for spoiling the mood he was trying to create.

'His bark was always worse than his bite,' she scoffed, shaking her head tiredly at his over-sensitivity. 'He threatened many things in the past but always calmed down before carrying out the deed. Yes, he tended to overreact but was only truly dangerous in the moment. He always simmered down given the time,' she enlightened, fresh tears beginning to gleam in her eyes.

Scowling, Jack rebuffed her opinion with a wave of his hand.

'I not only believe what he said, I believe he now has the power to do it,' he replied, angered by her conceited tone. 'He got through my home security easily enough,' he mumbled, folding his arms crossly.

'What happened after the death of the Bloods?' she asked, turning to her heroic vampire.

'War is upon us and has been for quite some time,' he answered, nodding at her after their first conversation. 'Colin is the master of my faction and has sworn to uphold the Blood Pact, which is the agreement made after the share of knowledge,' he explained, speaking of when the Egni were created.

Closing his eyes, Jack looked pained by the news and was clearly concerned about the loss of life this would incur.

'He attacked the wizards while they were in council, thinking to deliver a crippling blow with one mighty strike, but it didn't go quite to plan,' Cristian continued, smiling at the wizard.

Leaning back, Jack sucked in his cheeks as though he was sucking on a straw for a moment before finally exhaling with a satisfied sigh up towards the ceiling.

'The druids defeated him using elemental magick,' Cristian finished, causing the old man to smile, picturing the ballsy High Druid in his mind.

'Will they come back here again?' Kristina cut in, far more concerned with their current predicament.

Looking from one to the other, her face paled when they both nodded their certainty.

'The Bloods will always come back, of that you can be assured,' Jack answered, blowing air out slowly through his nose. 'Only next time there will be more than one lord with them,' he assured, realising that this must be hard for her to hear.

Shivering at the memory of the large Blood, Bael, she quailed at the thought of more like him marching on the house.

Nodding in acknowledgement of her reaction, Jack smiled at her sadly before glancing at the vampire lord.

'That big brute our friend here took care of was a "Blood Lord," and a very old one at that,' he explained, smiling appreciatively at the warrior.

'How many vampire lords are there, and how are they made?' she asked, dreading the thought of more of them.

'They are many,' Cristian answered, holding her eyes. 'They were wizards once but chose another path to stay alive, sacrificing their magick for something far darker. They have an ability to withstand almost anything you can throw at them, and add that to their phenomenal strength and speed, and there are few who can oppose them,' he continued, seemingly happy to discuss the topic.

'Then I am doubly glad you chose our side,' she whispered, causing Jack to laugh in amusement.

'He's one of them!' he hooted, shaking his head in amusement. 'A vampire lord from the old world, and happy I am to have him with us,' he added, noticing the warrior grow sullen after being 'outed' in such a way.

'You've gone against your race to help us, Cristian.' Kristina stated, looking at him seriously. 'Why would you do that? To redeem yourself to a friend you knew in another life?' she asked, knowing she was missing something important.

Looking from her to the floor, Cristian pursed his lips as he considered whether or not to tell her the truth.

'He was not just my friend,' he finally confessed, almost choking on the words. 'We are brothers, he and I,' he whispered, tears suddenly welling in his eyes.

Dumbfounded by the confession, she pieced together all the stories she had read in a new light.

'Of course!' she gasped, smacking her head with the palm of her hand. 'The battle of the brothers. I should have guessed from the swords!' she admonished herself, thumping her head again.

Standing up, she moved to sit by him and tenderly placed her hand in his.

'There is a clearing not far away, deep within the forest at the foot of the mountain,' she whispered, almost sobbing out the words. 'That's where he is, Cris. I found his body today,' she whispered, unable to say anymore.

'No!' he growled, flinching away as though burned by her words. 'That can't be,' he hissed, refusing to accept what she was saying.

Shaking her head in apology, she lowered her face into her hands and wept uncontrollably.

'Speak, Wizard!' he growled, his eyes flashing dangerously as he turned to the old man.

'That is where his body is, his old one anyway. I believe that is where the change in him took place, for it was not the same flesh he wore when last I saw him,' Jack replied, looking at Cristian fiercely to drive the truth home. 'Dark lives, even if Daire does not!'

\*\*\*

The morning air was fresher than Kristina had anticipated, and she chided herself for not turning the heating up the night before.

Huffing in annoyance, she saw her breath fog from her mouth before a wall of warmth hit her upon reaching the door to her living room. Immediately picking up her pace, she paused only to flip the dial to twenty degrees before entering.

Sitting in front of the fire, Jack stared into the flames as though searching for something within and only broke contact after hearing her approach. His grey eyes were glazed and out of focus when he looked up and only cleared after he blinked them rapidly to dispel the trancelike state.

'Good morning,' he greeted, gesturing to the fresh cup of tea that sat steaming on the coffee table.

'It's rare to find someone who rises earlier than me,' she remarked, seating herself opposite him before reaching for the beverage.

'Can I ask you a question?' she asked, looking at him from over the rim of her mug.

'You're going to ask anyway, so ask,' he growled, but his grey eyes were twinkling with mischief.

Smiling with her eyes, she sipped at the hot tea before finally asking her question.

'Why didn't the elements protect us?' she asked, causing Jack to cough mid-swig.

'My girl!' he replied in a fatherly tone, 'I have been trying to think of something that I missed, and that's it!' he shrilled excitedly before looking at her seriously. 'After his sacrifice, I would have thought they would have held to his wishes. They presented themselves when your circle was cast, didn't they?' he continued, frowning in concern.

Jumping up from the sofa, Jack rushed outside as a startled Kristina followed at his heels. Stepping barefoot onto the lawn, he began wiggling his toes in the moist grass before holding a finger up for silence.

'Shhh,' he whispered, causing her to scowl at his back.

Letting his eyes go unfocused, he looked up, shaking his head at the thin web of electrical currents spreading from one horizon to the other.

Probing it with his mind, he instantly felt a hard slap to his face that caused him to wake up groggily. Looking bemused with a muddy circle imprinted on his forehead from his impact with the earth, he rubbed at his cheek, which still stung from whatever had awakened him.

'What the hell?' he howled, looking up at her accusingly. 'What are you doing to me, woman?' he grumbled, tenderly probing at the reddening skin.

'Waking you up, you grumpy old git!' she stormed, placing a hand on her hip.

'What am I doing out here?' he asked, still holding his hand at his cheek. 'I was thinking of something...' he mused, pressing tentatively at his muddied forehead with his index finger.

Squatting down beside him, she glared at him in frustration.

'You were looking for the reason the elements didn't help us?' she prompted, scowling at his dopey expression. 'Wake up, you silly bugger!' she barked, flushing in anger as he began to drift off again.

'It's not his fault,' came a soft voice from behind, causing her to pivot in alarm as Cristian walked forward to place a hand upon the old man's brow.

*'Chwalu,'* he whispered, causing the wizard's eyes to clear instantly.

'What an elegant piece of weaving!' Jack gasped, looking at the vampire in appreciation before shaking his head in an attempt to clear it.

Watching as Cristian rose smoothly to his feet, Kristina was reminded again of how Daire had moved after his transformation.

*'Definitely a vampire!'* she thought, believing that this was what he had turned himself into.

'There's a web of magick over us!' Jack announced, speaking in a high-pitched, excited tone of voice. 'It's an awesome bit of crafting, to be sure,' he admitted, shaking his head again. 'Very impressive...'

'Yes. Yes, I'm sure it is!' Kristina snapped, glaring down at him in annoyance. 'It's beyond you, I get it. So what does it do?' she asked, widening her eyes in irritation.

Ignoring her tone, Jack got slowly to his feet and began brushing himself down far slower than he could have managed.

'It's a web that basically knocks you out – very subtly though. It confuses you and...' Jack's eyes popped open. 'It put the elements to sleep!' he shrieked, speaking in so high a tone that it could have been a woman's.

'The elements have been put to sleep,' he declared, speaking far deeper than he had a moment before, as though having disliked the sound of his womanly outburst.

Looking up at the sky and seeing nothing of note, Kristina looked back at the wizard.

'If it's so far beyond you, how can we break it?' she asked sourly, shaking her head in disappointment.

Finally biting at her condescending tone, Jack glared at her venomously.

'I may not be able to create something as grand as this,' he grumbled, his tone thick with haughtiness, 'but the thing about webs is...' he continued, smiling smugly, '... the more intricate they appear, the easier they are to break!'

# CHAPTER FOURTEEN

Leaning back in his chair, John smiled wolfishly at the priestess before placing his hands behind his head. The small office was littered with official documents and large metallic filing cabinets, giving the room a governmental vibe.

Looking around critically, Chloe wrinkled her nose at the bland shades of grey that dominated the room, inviting depression and eventual madness, she thought, quirking her mouth in distaste.

'Why on earth are you in this dingy, disgusting cesspit of a room?' she asked, seating herself opposite the druid with lips pouted in disapproval.

Ignoring her question, John placed his feet up on the desk and sighed contentedly.

'What's the story with your renegade coven?' he countered, smiling slyly as he changed the topic.

Tall, dark and rangy, the druid's long limbs gave him something of a treelike quality, hinting at the strength he tried to conceal within. His easy smile, which seemed always to be worn, hid a fierce intellect and a craftiness that few knew to have existed at all.

The victory over the Egni Master, however, had seen an end to that self-made illusion for, now, everyone hailed him as the hero of the hour, even after all this time. His abilities and quick thinking had elevated him to that of celebrity within the magickal world, and a shift in power within the wizards' faction had set the druid order, or rather, John specifically, at the head of the newly unified factions, now called, 'Mankind's Magickal Defence Department', or MD, for short.

War had been upon them for over a year, and, up to now, there proved to be none better to lead them in this second war of the races.

'You know very well what the situation is, Johnny,' Chloe replied, a mischievous smile playing at the corners of her mouth.

The druid smiled wolfishly again, enjoying their little game of cat and mouse.

'So, you are still going to ignore their transgressions and move on?' he asked, watching her reaction intently.

'For the time being, I fail to see the benefit of dealing with the situation,' she answered, pouting her lips again.

'It's been over a year! How long will you take, I wonder?' he pushed, knowing this to be a touchy subject.

Holding his eyes, she crossed her legs before shifting her weight and was not surprised when his eyes flickered to her hips before travelling down the length of her legs. Closing her eyes, she stretched languidly like a waking feline, knowing all along that his eyes would never leave her. Meeting his gaze once again, she smiled enticingly, causing him to do likewise.

'And the fact that the children are Dark's and probably have more power than ten of your covens has absolutely nothing to do with it, I suppose?' he asked intuitively, shaking his head.

Raising her eyebrows in surprise, Chloe smiled at the druid's perception.

'It is a delicate situation, Johnny boy! If played correctly, we might gain a valuable ally in him. The circle can't be broken without killing all thirteen witches, and so, in this, he is impudent. What other option does he have?' she asked, crossing her legs again before smiling at the desired result. Holding his gaze, she leant in a little.

'I must confess, it is my desire that he will, in the end, decide to join us,' she continued, leaning forward further to look him deep in the eye.

Unwilling to be distracted by her wily ways, John leant in closer himself.

'You think that he has no other choice? If history has taught us anything, High Priestess, it is that Dark does not play by the same rules as the rest of us. I fear for that little coven of yours, maybe even for your entire faction,' he continued, looking at her with concern.

Chewing at her lip thoughtfully, she appeared to weigh his words before shrugging the problem away.

'Time will tell,' she replied, dismissing the warning with a smile.

The door to the office opened, and in walked the newly-elected High Wizard, an aura of control seeming to emanate from his very pores.

'Hi,' he greeted in a friendly manner, his ebony skin gleaming dully in the artificial light and his short black hair showing little signs of age.

Eyeing him approvingly, Chloe nodded her head slightly as she teasingly patted the seat beside her.

Charlie had replaced the High Wizard after what had happened at the Great Hall, and, though fighting the calls for his removal, Kreig had finally been replaced for his show of weakness against the Egni Master.

Though Charlie was not present during the attack and was seldom seen in political circles, he was nevertheless voted in by his peers for his experience in offensive magick.

Walking to the offered chair, the new High Wizard sat down smoothly before sensing a tension in the air and a vision in his mind.

'Guard your thoughts, John,' Charlie teased, chuckling at the druid's immediate embarrassment. 'Okay,' he continued offhandedly, the smile slipping abruptly from his face. 'Enough banter! We need to discuss our response to the attacks in the south and the whereabouts of our missing legend,' he began, clasping his hands together on the desk.

Studying the man, John found a grudging respect forming for his no-nonsense approach.

'Where have you been hiding, Charlie?' he asked, keeping his features controlled.

Staring back emotionlessly, Charlie wondered briefly whether or not the druid was sincere.

'Strictly speaking, I'm not a wizard, though my little faction does lie within the wizard community,' he began, smiling at the frowning faces before him. 'I'm a *mage* and the head of my order. This role has been thrust upon me, for believe me when I say I am the best man for the job,' he continued, again with his no-nonsense approach. 'I'm not one for politics, but this is war,' he added, as though this explanation was enough for them for now. 'I propose that we take the fight to the Bloods and try to draw them out into the open, or these small battles across the south *will* get worse,' he suggested, talking of the many skirmishes that had been fought since the declaration of war.

Looking at him as though he were mad, Chloe grimaced unattractively as she shook her head in disbelief.

'No one can defeat the Bloods in open warfare,' she stated matter-of-factly before looking at the druid for support.

'You need to open your mind to all assets at our disposal,' he replied, smiling wider at her disbelieving stare. 'The Bloods are not our main concern, anyway,' he stated, gaining himself even more scowls of disagreement. 'Our biggest problem lies with the Egni, and though there has been no open conflict thus far, Colin is an ancient who has had literally ages to perfect his art. Add to that the other ancients he has under his command, and we are in for one hell of a ride,' he replied, looking from the witch to the druid fiercely. 'You have shown them all that he can be beaten, John, and for that, I give you thanks,' he said, nodding at the druid in acknowledgement of his deed. 'Colin is not the only one with great power,' he added, 'but he showed us his weakness by attacking alone,' he continued, raising his eyebrows for the answer.

'Overconfidence?' John asked, feeling like a child in a classroom.

Looking at Chloe, the mage raised his eyebrows at her with a little impatience.

'Um, rashness?' she guessed, shrugging her shoulders doubtfully with a flush of embarrassment.

Slamming his hand down hard upon the desktop, Charlie glared at them both as the priestess flinched in her seat.

'Ego!' he corrected, looking at them sternly. 'He believed himself capable of destroying us all and that he alone would get the job done. Even after his defeat, he will put it down to blind luck that he did not destroy you. Such is his ego!' he finished, breathing out passionately.

Beginning to raise a hand questioningly, Chloe quickly turned the action into a stretch which caused John to smile despite himself.

'Colin very nearly *did* destroy us all,' she responded, looking rather uncomfortable at the igniting fire in the mage's eyes.

'Because of your inability to act!' he barked, slamming his hand down hard again. 'Because you all just sat there, like lambs for the slaughter! If that same situation were to happen again, would you react the same way?' he asked, glaring at her now.

Shaking her head vigorously in answer, a lock of blonde hair fell into her eyes before she could verbalise her response.

'No. I have thought of many things since,' she answered awkwardly, having berated herself often for doing nothing and handing the druid the limelight.

'Don't think!' Charlie growled, looking at her fiercely, 'That is what it is to take action. You react! There is no time to deliberate or to plan. Act and react!' he instructed, looking back at the druid. 'As he did!' he acknowledged, leaning back once more.

Staring at the mage, the druid found himself thankful that this man had been Kreig's successor and not some puppet of the establishment.

'He was nothing more than a politician, though I believe he was treated unfairly in the way he was removed from office,' Charlie sighed, seeing the image in the other's mind. 'I would have succeeded him anyway, however – even without him handing me the reigns so eloquently. For once the horns of war had sounded, it was only a matter of time before they would call on me and my faction,' he stated, supremely confident in his faction's standing within the wizard community.

The druid's smile widened, impressed beyond reason by the confident mage.

'What is your expertise, Charlie?' he asked, though he believed that he already knew the answer.

Regarding him with a wide, knowing smile, Charlie could see that the druid had already gleaned the truth for himself.

'This war was always going to come,' he answered, holding the druid's gaze. 'If you knew something was coming and that it was unavoidable, what would you do, John?' he asked, avoiding the question with one of his own.

Sitting back, the druid spread his arms wide, resembling an old tree that draped across the small office.

'I would prepare for it,' he answered sagely, smiling his wolfish grin.

Looking from one to the other, Chloe frowned and was clearly lost within the conversation.

Giving her a reassuring wink, John knew she would know nothing of what this High Wizard truly was.

'Our new friend here is a Battle Mage,' he announced, feeling like he should get a gold star or something similar.

'I thought them merely a myth!' she confessed, looking a little unsettled by the grand announcement.

'As Dark was a legend?' John asked, shaking his head and feeling pleased that he could show her his historical prowess. 'Battle Mages were an ancient class of wizard, sometimes called War Wizards,' he informed, glancing over at the mage.

'They were something else entirely,' Charlie corrected before waving the druid on after seeing his eyes widen with interest.

'Their primary focus was, or is, the study of war, training themselves in all forms of attack. They had, or have, an arsenal of offensive and defensive magick at their disposal, spells you won't find in any book, I'd wager. Strategists to a one, Battle Mages were feared by the vampires almost as much as Dark himself,' John finished, clapping his hands together in delight.

'They feared none more than him,' Charlie corrected again, lowering his gaze to the desktop for a moment.

'Are you the real deal?' the druid asked, holding up his hands in case he had caused offence. 'Forgive me for asking, but have you simply followed in their footsteps, or are you an original?' he asked, smiling apologetically.

Rocking back in his chair, Charlie placed his hands together before interlacing his fingers.

'I was there when Dark fell,' he answered, his voice low and respectful. 'My order is the very same that existed in those ancient times. Formed by Colin himself before he lost his… humanity,' he continued bitterly, grimacing as he spoke the last word.

'So you're one of the immortals?' Chloe asked excitedly, her blue eyes shining wantonly.

'I tell you that I was there at the legend's fall, and that's the question you come back with?' Charlie asked, shaking his head in disappointment. 'I have found a way to forestall death, but I am not immortal. And before you ask, none but those in my order get to know the secret,' he added, reading the desire in her eyes.

Staring hard at the mage, John's pretence at being the affable rogue slipped for a moment.

'You saw him?' he asked reverently, a different kind of need shining in his eyes.

Saying nothing, the mage nodded once in response.

'You actually saw Dark?' John pressed, causing the other to frown.

'Yes!' Charlie snapped, irritated at having to confirm his response verbally. 'I knew him,' he whispered, resting his head back.

Closing his eyes, he remembered the battle that until recently had been believed a fantasy.

'There is no other like him that I have ever had the displeasure of fighting, and not one I would wish to face again. His power was something else, like that of his father's but more lethal somehow, more creative,' he said, opening his eyes and looking up.

'When I was young, I used to seek out all I could about him… him and his brothers. Dark was not always the creature you have read about, not the killer you have been led to believe. In my youth, he was a hero loved by the people,' he continued, smiling sadly at their shocked expressions. 'The people loved him, for it was always Dark and his brothers that would fight to keep them safe. Always Dark in the thick of it, though he was known by another name in those days. But it is the name, Dark, that history remembers,' he sighed, lost in another age. 'The stories told in those early days were of his glory, not as they are now. After he was cast out, he was believed to have died many times before new stories would arise of his exploits… darker tales that chilled the blood,' he said, staring at them seriously.

Waving the memories away, he took a deep breath before sighing it out tiredly.

'Do you know why the Bloods named him The Dark Wolf?' he asked, raising his eyebrows.

'Didn't he kill wizards, too?' Chloe asked, ignoring the question and snapping the wizard out of his reverie.

'A great many of them,' he answered, sighing again at her question. 'Little did we know at the time, though, that he was actually killing the wizards sent to parlay with the vampires,' he confessed, finally sharing the truth of what had really happened. 'I have carried regret in my heart for my involvement in his downfall, and a part of me is glad that he has actually survived,' he conceded, turning to face the druid, who looked agitated.

Gripping the desk as he leant forward, John was clearly incensed by his choice of words.

'A part of you?' he asked, unable to hide his annoyance. 'It seems clear to me that he was one of the good guys!' he blurted, throwing his arms wide in exasperation.

'One of the good guys?' Charlie echoed, laughing out loud. 'Dark was, if nothing else, wild and unpredictable. Quick to anger and quicker still to kill. He was feared by almost everyone a long, long time before the war had even begun,' he stressed, giving the druid a sideways glance. 'Why the passionate defence, John?' he asked, seeing heat in the druid's cheeks.

Shrugging awkwardly, John tried desperately to look nonplussed, but his emotions would allow for no such deception.

'I've studied the histories and read between the lines. I think that his reputation of killing without regard was intentional on his part, and, to be honest, anyone who can raise the elements as he has can't be the wild thing that you would have me believe. I've always thought him kind of… cool,' he confessed, colour deepening his cheeks.

Grimacing with a look of pain, Charlie placed his face back into his hands again.

'Oh, my gods,' he mumbled, speaking through his palms. 'A fan!' he moaned, shaking his head in woeful disbelief.

'Will you at least tell me why he was called The Dark Wolf?' John asked sheepishly, swallowing his pride.

\*\*\*

It was late evening when the taxi pulled to the curb, its indicator blinking to light the wet pavement periodically with a rhythmic glow. After several seconds, the rear door opened, and a fragile form eased its way out delicately from within. Moving slowly as though in pain, the slender form shuffled through the drizzling rain towards the light from a house up ahead.

On reaching the front door, a thin, badly bruised hand reached out to knock tenderly upon the wood until it swung open to reveal an angry-looking woman.

'Janet,' the woman greeted, staring at her visitor with little warmth. 'You had better come in,' she continued, gesturing the battered woman inside with a wave of her hand.

The living room was lavishly decorated, though the gold furnishings would seem more at home in an Egyptian tomb than in any house she had ever seen.

'Sit,' ordered the priestess, motioning her to a high-backed Chesterfield chair.

Lowering herself delicately into it, Janet winced as the pain caught her by surprise even though she was prepared for the movement.

'I see that you weren't exaggerating,' Jacky observed, noting her injuries.

In simple terms, Janet looked beaten, her face still clearly bruised from her ordeal with the house, and Jacky noted by the way she positioned her arms that her body had fared no better. Seating herself on the opposite chair, Jacky spread her arms out questioningly.

'You say the "house" did this to you?' she asked, looking at the woman cynically.

Nodding tentatively in reply, Janet winced again at the movement.

'Yes,' she whispered, speaking the words through clenched teeth.

Sitting back in her seat, Jacky looked for a lie in the younger woman's eyes before nodding her satisfaction.

'On Kristina's bequest?' she prompted, forcing Janet to answer again.

'Yes,' she answered simply, keeping her head still this time.

'That seems greatly out of character for one so timid. One has to wonder what you did to elicit such a response,' Jacky mused, a cold smile playing across her lips. 'Why, pray, did she order such a terrible thing?' she asked, leaning forward with eyes full of contempt. 'You must have been very naughty,' she added in a mocking tone, peering at the broken woman savagely.

Shrinking back in her chair, Janet whispered in a pitifully low tone of voice.

'I left her son to save myself when the vampire lord turned up,' she answered, lowering her head to hide her tears. 'I am ashamed of what I did. I didn't plan it. I just saw my chance and took it,' she finished, her voice breaking.

Relaxing back into her chair again, only her knuckles betrayed the priestess, whitening as she gripped the armrests tightly.

'It is called fight or flight,' she sighed offhandedly, as though she were discussing the weather. 'It's caused by the quick release of adrenaline into the bloodstream and always triggered by fear. If you had chosen to fight, then you would have fought more vigorously than you had ever fought before,' she informed before leaning forward a little to accentuate her next words. 'You, however, chose to run!' she spat, with a sudden look of hate contorting her features.

Janet flinched, lulled as she had been into a false sense of security.

'I bet you ran very fast, though,' Jacky cackled, revelling in the woman's distress. 'Oh, don't feel too badly, dear. You're not the first and certainly won't be the last to perform such a cowardly act. I am, however, glad to know which of the two you prefer should a fight come to *my* door,' she continued, shaking her head with a scowl.

Staring at Janet coldly, she seemed to realise that she was gripping the chair and consciously relaxed her hold upon it.

'Tell me again of what she said regarding our beloved coven?' she asked, with a growing edge to her tone.

Swallowing hard, Janet cleared her throat before speaking.

'She told me to get out and to take my coven with me,' she answered, happy at last to move on from her cowardice.

Shifting her weight in her seat, she winced again with the effort.

'I tried to explain that she couldn't just leave us, and that is when she turned the house on me, leaving me to die out in the street!' she continued, weeping sadly at the state she was in.

'Did you know that a coven can lose witches and still function?' she asked but continued before the other could respond. 'Oh, yes, it's true. Once a circle is cast, all thirteen witches must die before the link can be severed completely,' she informed, nodding her head assuredly.

Looking scared, like a rabbit in the headlights, Janet began to cry at what was being asked of her.

'How do you fancy redeeming yourself, Janet?' the priestess asked kindly, forgiveness showing at last in her eyes. 'Kristina has chosen her path and is lost to us now,' she continued, narrowing her eyes. 'Though you have no discernible power of your own, you are one of us, and valued, dare I say,' she soothed, causing the injured woman to cry all the more.

Intimidated and feeling alone without her best friend, Janet closed her eyes, unwilling to meet those of the priestess.

'Where else can you go?' Jacky asked scathingly, her false kinship fading as quickly as it had come. 'You have no right to magick yourself and so leach it from us like the vampires that scare you. I knew that when I first saw you, seeing not what you could add to our coven but whom you could bring into it,' she rasped, failing to keep the sneer from her tone.

Janet moaned, knowing absolutely what was being asked of her.

'Look at me!' Jacky shrilled, enraged at being ignored by one so insignificant. 'Without us, you are nothing! Your magick comes from us! You use our magick and give nothing back!' she shouted, shaking in her fury. 'Do this, and you will remain, do it not, and as I have said, a coven can survive the loss of one useless witch.'

\*\*\*

The wizard leant back in frustration, looking at the vampire who merely shrugged and spread his hands unhelpfully.

'You are less than useless,' Jack stated miserably, puffing on his unseen cigarette.

'This is Colin's magick,' Cristian stated, as though the comment explained everything he needed to say. 'It's a little more complicated than hiding your filthy little habit,' he added, wrinkling his nose in distaste.

Ignoring the chastising words, Jack puffed again at nothing before blowing it out towards the vampire.

'This should be easy!' he grumbled, stomping off to the shed to saw some wood.

Standing in the garden, Cristian stared at the outbuilding and shook his head in amusement.

'She has enough wood!' he called, baiting the old man further.

'It helps me think!' the old man growled grumpily, raising his voice above the sawing of the wood.

A trace of a smile touched the corners of the vampire's mouth as his reply came to mind.

'Then I suggest that you saw faster,' he replied sarcastically, smirking to himself at his witty remark.

Snapping his head up, Jack glared at the young-looking man through the window before slumping his shoulders.

'I wish it were that easy,' he replied, finally smiling.

Slumping down into his chair, the wizard massaged his shoulder tenderly, kneading the muscle in a circular motion with his thumb before closing his eyes.

Watching intently as a healthy colour returned to the old man's complexion, Cristian nodded his head at finally witnessing what he had been waiting for.

Opening his eyes, Jack breathed a sigh of relief before looking up innocently.

'That's better,' he mumbled to himself, slapping his palms down on his knees.

'How did you do that?' Cristian asked, shocking the wizard after having entered the shed undetected.

'Do what?' Jack asked guardedly, attempting to look innocent.

Holding the wizard's stare, all humour faded from the vampire's face.

'I knew that if I waited long enough, you'd slip up and show me how you survived all these long years. You just took several years off yourself in a matter of moments, and I want to know how!' he demanded, his manner as cold now as the first touch of frost.

Looking long and hard at the vampire, Jack arched an eyebrow at the other's tone before steeling his expression.

'You have your way, vampire, and I have mine!' he replied, intent on keeping the secret intact.

'You can't even break my father's web, and you mean to imply that *you* found a way to conquer death? I think not!' Cristian replied, intent on annoying the old man further.

'I could have!' Jack retorted, scowling up at the towering vampire.

'You could have,' Cristian agreed, nodding slowly, 'but you didn't!' he stated, daring the wizard to lie with the widening of his eyes.

Staring at each other stubbornly, it was clear that neither one would back down from their battle of wills until the vampire began to smile.

'*He* showed you,' Cristian guessed, knowing that he was right.

Clearly annoyed by the insightful vampire, Jack could not help but resent the implied lack of wisdom.

Pursing his lips in thought, Cristian read the truth in his eyes and no longer needed the old man's confession.

'He always liked you, Blue,' Cristian sighed, looking at him sadly. 'You'd be dead now if he hadn't,' he added, turning his back to leave.

'The name is Jack!' the wizard roared, his lined face draining of colour. 'Jack!' he snapped, looking ready to explode with fury. 'Not Blue, not David, but Jack!' he growled, his voice quivering with emotion.

'What does it matter when you are all three of them!' Cristian retorted, growing angrier himself. 'You wear your aliases like a woman wears a skirt, never knowing which one to wear,' he added, smiling at the analogy.

Widening his eyes at the comment, Jack looked about ready to attack in that moment.

'He isn't here to save you this time, Blue. Be warned, if you turn on me now, you *will* regret it!' Cristian promised, speaking in a deadly whisper.

'I don't need him to kick your rancid arse!' the wizard replied, slowly rising to his feet. 'Gilga's balls, I'll not go down without a fight!' he raged, feeling the might beneath his feet flowing up into him.

The two faced off like two gunslingers in a spaghetti western, each waiting for the other to make the first move, but after only a few seconds, Cristian realised that a strike was not forthcoming and released his breath slowly.

'Would you like to tell me why you nearly attacked me, Jack?' he asked, addressing the wizard by his preferred name.

Unable to believe what he was hearing, the wizard grimaced with incredulity as colour flushed into his face.

'You threatened me!' he shrieked, the red flush replacing the white face of action.

'When?' Cristian demanded, spreading his hands in flabbergasted confusion.

The old man's face began to boil again, but the vampire knew the danger had passed.

'You said that I would be dead if not for Daire!' he shrilled, clenching his fists at his sides.

Throwing his head back in exasperation, Cristian looked up at the heavens and shook his head tiredly.

'Not by me, you donkey!' he groaned, finally understanding the wizard's reaction.

Blinking back owlishly, Jack made to reply many times before he finally answered.

'Then by whom?' he demanded, feeling his anger fade into embarrassment.

'I was talking of the past!' Cristian sighed, shaking his head in disappointment. 'You tit!' he grumbled, turning back to the doorway.

'Wait!' Jack squeaked, causing the vampire to throw his head back with a groan.

'What?' he asked, not bothering to turn back.

'What were you talking about, then?' the old man asked, looking totally bemused.

'Gilgamesh!' he hissed, rounding on him angrily, and was not disappointed when the wizard paled at hearing the ancient name.

'What of... him?' Jack stammered, unable to keep the shake from his voice.

Arching an eyebrow, Cristian saw that the wizard was oblivious to what had happened so long ago.

'What indeed?' he countered, staring down at the shorter man.

Widening his eyes a little, Jack shook his head in denial.

'No way!' he gasped, stepping back, but the vampire followed to see the truth home.

'Yes, way!' he replied, stalking the old man until the tale was told. 'What did you think killed him, the pox?' he asked sarcastically, shaking his head in answer. 'Gilgamesh wanted you dead, probably because you're a dick,' he added, scowling down at the bewildered little wizard.

Blinking up at him, Jack's eyes looked round and wide as he shook his head in misery.

'All I knew was that he died,' he sobbed, shocked to the core by the enlightenment.

'That he did,' Cristian confirmed, nodding at the memory. 'With a red blade through his guts!' he informed, poking the wizard in the belly before he could be stopped.

Looking flabbergasted, Jack flinched back from the touch as though hurt by the contact.

'He beat Gilgamesh in a sword fight?' he asked, puffing out the words in disbelief.

'How else do you get a red sword in the guts?' Cristian growled, irritated by the wizard's slow comprehension.

'I didn't realise,' Jack whispered, his previously high pitch returning to normal. 'He was desperate to become younger, as were we all, I suppose,' he sighed, staring off into the trees. 'I had become young again, and that swine demanded the secret from me,' he explained, looking back with a faraway glaze to his eyes.

Sighing sadly, he watched a fox rear its head up from the undergrowth, only to disappear again a moment later.

'But the secret was not mine to give,' he whispered, looking up at the tall warrior before nodding in resignation. 'He wanted to torture it from me and hunted me for a long, long time,' he stammered, feeling the terror anew before looking down guiltily.

Nodding his understanding, Cristian smiled knowingly.

'So you told Daire,' he replied. It was not a question.

'So I told Daire,' Jack confirmed, closing his eyes. 'Gilgamesh frightened me like no one else. I still dream about him sometimes,' he confessed, shivering at the memory.

Seeing the old man's pain, Cristian felt pity for him and reached out to squeeze his shoulder.

'Well, he's long dead now,' he assured before narrowing his eyes suspiciously. 'Why was it such a shock when I told you who killed him?' he asked, putting his fists to his waist.

Laughing through his tears, Jack shook his head as another memory resurfaced.

'Daire was there when I was told of his death,' he answered, tearing up at the memory.

'Good performance?' Cristian asked, laughing quietly.

'Worthy of an Oscar,' the wizard confirmed, feeling a flush of anguish for his lost friend.

Feeling it, too, tears glistened in the vampire's eyes, causing Jack to smile sadly.

'Do you know that you have the same mannerisms as him?' he asked, nodding his head. 'You both do that thing with your mouth,' he observed, slapping the vampire affectionately on the arm. 'You remind me so much of him, of how he used to be,' he said, seeing the brimming tears threaten to spill. 'You are correct, of course,' he continued, eager to move on from the morbid conversation. 'It was Daire who unlocked the secret of eternal life,' he admitted and then frowned suddenly, looking up with a question. 'How was it that you saw Gilgamesh fall?' he asked, knowing this was many years after the family feud.

Closing his eyes, Cristian felt unable to voice his reply as a solitary tear rolled down his cheek.

'Come on,' Jack sighed, letting the vampire keep his secret. 'Let's go and tell her that we failed to break this poxy web.'

***

Sitting in the kitchen, Kristina was in full conversation when the two walked in and flushed slightly when they saw who she was with.

Hissing through his teeth, Cristian reacted instinctively to the danger and crouched a little on instinct.

Turning to him, Jack raised an eyebrow critically before quirking his mouth down.

'Did you really just do that?' he asked, shaking his head with a scowl.

Looking a little embarrassed, the vampire ran his fingers through his hair self-consciously before smiling awkwardly.

'Sorry,' he apologised, shrugging his shoulders lamely. 'Just surprised to see her here,' he mumbled under his breath, glancing again at the women.

'So, you hiss?' Jack asked, milking the moment so that he could process what was happening.

'Be quiet!' Cristian whispered, causing the wizard to smile. 'Sorry,' he added in apology, nodding at Kristina before standing back silently.

Studying their guest, Jack noticed that she still looked to be healing from her 'departure' several days before.

Smiling at their banter, Kristina took note of the friendship growing between them.

'I've decided to forgive Jan for what she did and ask that you do the same,' she announced, placing her hand on top of Jan's reassuringly.

Seeing the gesture, Jack nodded slowly but felt his blood run cold in his veins.

'You've got some balls, I'll give you that,' he remarked, looking at Janet coldly. 'Coming back here after what this place did to you,' he added, glaring at her judgementally. 'It's a shame you showed no such compulsion to save the boy,' he growled, looking down his nose at the injured woman. 'You're seriously allowing her back in?' he asked, glaring at Kristina as he threw his arms into the air.

'It's in the past,' she replied, smiling tightly. 'I have forgiven her and ask you to do the same,' she continued, staring back with wide eyes.

Folding his arms stubbornly, Cristian said nothing but made his position clear on the matter.

'Once bitten, twice shy,' Jack warned, his face settling into a stern expression. 'Fool me once, shame on you. Fool me twice…'

'Yes, yes, but that is for me to decide!' she cut in, wondering how many phrases he would have come out with.

Seeing the unwavering determination on Kristina's face, Jack sighed loudly and huffed in exasperation.

'As long as she isn't left in a position of trust in regard to the children,' he conceded tiredly, looking her dead in the eye.

'They are *my* children, Jack,' she replied firmly, leaving little room for negotiation on the matter, 'and only I decide what is best for them,' she continued, daring him to challenge her by widening her eyes.

Sharing a look with the vampire, Jack shook his head in disagreement.

'We are here to ensure their safety. The repercussions, if they were to fall, are simply too great. They must survive, and that, *there*, is a risk!' he replied, pointing a long, calloused finger at her friend. '*There* is the potential for disaster!' he warned, glaring again at Janet. 'No offence, but you have proven your worth when it comes to a fight,' he added, sensing the vampire nod beside him.

Rising angrily to her feet, Kristina put her hands to her hips in her trademark show of displeasure.

'They are *my* children, and this is *my* house!' she stormed, the muscles in her face twitching with restrained emotion. 'If you can't accept my decision, then it is you who will have to leave,' she stormed, looking pointedly at Cristian.

At the implication of what that might mean, what little colour was there drained from the vampire's face, causing Jack to put a steadying hand upon his shoulder.

'Fear not, my friend,' he whispered confidently, looking again at the woman.

'That was a low blow, and to one who has bled for you already!' he stormed furiously, disgusted by the threat. 'I dare you!' he challenged, raising his chin defiantly.

'Now, wait a minute. If she wants me to leave, I will leave,' Cristian interjected, backing towards the door.

Continuing his glare, Jack opened his arms invitingly for her to carry out the threat.

'Make my day?' he dared, goading her into action, 'I dare you!'

he taunted, incensed by Janet's hidden smile.

Trembling with fury, Kristina's wrath boiled up into her eyes before issuing from her mouth.

'House?' she called, keeping her eyes fixed upon his.

Sucking in air, Cristian turned for the open door, only for it to slam abruptly in his face. Jumping back in fright, he turned to face the smiling wizard with nothing but questions in his dark, brooding eyes.

Staring in open-mouthed shock, Kristina saw her friend shrink back into her seat while the wizard smiled his knowing little smile.

'You have no idea, do you?' he asked contemptuously, disgusted that she had actually called upon the house. 'This isn't *your* house, it's *his*, in the truest sense of the word, and it obeys only *him*,' he informed, smiling again. 'This house *is* him, for all intents and purposes,' he continued, letting the statement sink in. 'Daire has somehow managed to imprint himself within these walls. Don't ask me how, but this house *is* him, on some base level,' he explained, waving his arms expressively in the air.

Standing like a statue, Cristian held out his arms as though attempting to keep his balance as the showdown reached its conclusion.

Smiling at the vampire, Jack winked to let him know that all was well.

'He did it first and foremost to protect his children, and it knows that *we* are here to protect them also,' the old man continued, indicating the vampire and himself. 'So, I'm guessing that it will not want us to leave just yet,' he said, smiling broadly after reasoning it out correctly. 'I'm also betting that this "Dark House" will not take orders from just anybody,' he said, his face dropping the humorous expression. 'So, guess what? We are staying,' he announced, folding his arms in triumph. 'Your move, you ungrateful witch!'

Kristina could feel the power of the house coiling around them like a snake readying itself to strike and looked at her friend with the same fearful expression that was mirrored back at her as they both realised the same thing… the house wanted Janet out.

'This has escalated out of control,' Kristina cried, seating herself back at the table. 'Please sit, and let's discuss it in a civilised manner,' she continued, gesturing for them to take a seat.

Standing where they were, an awkward silence ensued as they all stared at each other in turn.

'How can you be called Cristian?' Janet asked randomly, breaking the stalemate with nonsensical babble. 'Don't you predate Christianity?' she asked, forcing a smile.

Unwilling to do likewise, the vampire stared hard at her, unable to keep the dislike from his face.

'History has a way of repeating itself,' he sighed, dismissing the idea of making small talk.

Jack, however, jumped at the chance to keep the conversation going.

'There has been more than one attempt at creating that religion, and I honestly haven't a clue how it keeps surviving,' he said, shaking his head a little. 'Daire used to say that it was created to keep mankind down and from growing into one mind. Stopping them from uniting under one belief system. He believed that religion was the killer of peace, keeping mankind in chains and at odds with one another,' he explained, feeling exhausted suddenly after the morning's toil. 'I now think he might have been right, especially seeing how combative religion has become in this age. Or maybe there's a force driving it from the unseen corners of the world. Who knows?' he sighed, slipping back into silence.

'Can we get past this, please? She is my friend, my best friend, and I know what she did was terrible, but it was in the heat of the moment. Please, for me?' Kristina pleaded, looking from wizard to vampire and back again.

'Just as long as she's not given a position of trust. She has a long way to go before I let her abandon them again,' Jack replied, holding her stare.

Rolling her eyes at the obvious statement, Kristina smiled in relief as she squeezed her friend's hand.

'It'll be fine,' she assured, waving off his concerns before turning to the vampire.

Cristian, however, said nothing.

# EPILOGUE

The living room looked more enchanting in the firelight, the flickering flames casting shadows that seemed to dance upon the ceiling as though telling a story that few could understand. Every now and then, the logs would crackle and hiss before a cracking loudly when the wood split.

Gazing into the fire, Francesca began to see the flames dance elegantly along the uppermost edge of the logs and willed her intention with all her might.

'Find him,' she pleaded, clasping her hands together as though in prayer before another loud crack spat many glowing embers high into the air.

'Find him, please?' she begged, her bottom lip beginning to tremble.

Glowing more brightly at her words, one of the embers drifted a little closer to dance before her eyes.

'Please?' it echoed, causing goosebumps to rise upon her flesh.

Growing in stature, the ember suddenly became a fairy no bigger than her hand before smiling up at her.

'*A fairy!*' she thought, unable to tear her eyes from the almost transparent butterfly-like wings.

'Not heard a "please" or "thank you" in such a long time,' it cooed, pouting its lips dramatically. 'Can you not seek him for yourself?' it teased, fluttering its eyelashes with a sad expression.

Shaking her head, tears came to her eyes as more fairies floated closer, each as beautiful as the first.

'We shall help you, we will,' said one, winking at her conspiringly.

'If,' said the first, waving a delicate finger of warning, 'you promise to call upon us again,' it bargained, holding out its hand as though to shake on it.

Before she could answer, however, all three rose to fly around the room, making her head turn this way and that as they began to sing.

*'Promise us this, and you will see,*
*fairy-friend say, and you will be.'*

The softly sung rhyme caused her eyes to droop and her body to sway to the motion of the flying fairies, but something inside her rose up in defence of what they were doing, snapping her back with a touch of fear prickling her skin.

'Why?' she gasped, the cold sensation of panic now spreading up her back.

'So we can play with you, of course!' they chorused, clapping their hands in excitement.

Looking about nervously, Francesca felt that they were not as friendly as she had first thought and began to shiver despite the heat of the fire.

The first stopped its dizzying flight to hover before her again.

'Would you be a fairy friend, then?' it asked, tilting its head sweetly to one side.

'You really are fairies?' Francesca asked, looking at it in wonder.

'That we are, and more besides, for we would have you be a friend to us,' the fairy replied, curtsying a little before her.

Nodding in agreement, Francesca clapped her hands together excitedly with a rush of relief.

*'Fairies are good and never bad,'* she thought, thinking of all the stories she had read. 'Yes, I would love to be your friend,' she decided, clasping her hands over her heart.

Crying out in triumph, the fairies closed in, causing her to step back with a renewed swell of fear, for the once beautiful faces had lost all of their warmth.

'Whom do you seek?' the first asked, eager now to complete the transaction.

*'Speak the name, and we shall tend, in exchange for a fairy-friend,'* the fairy rhymed, to the delight of the others who waited in the wings.

With the smile faltering on her face, Francesca sensed the fairy's manipulation but could think of no other option before her.

'I seek…' she began but then paused, wondering what name to use. 'I seek… Dark,' she finally answered, wringing her hands together nervously.

Stopping dead at her request, all fairy eyes opened in alarm before they glanced at one another nervously.

*'Family or friend are you to he? Speak now to the Sidhi,'* the fairy asked, its features now an unreadable mask.

'Family,' the girl answered, not really knowing whether it was a good answer or not, but felt that it held some sort of weight with these creatures of myth.

Huddling together, the fairies whispered furiously to each other in hoarse, rasping tones. Now and then, they would glance over their shoulders at her with sly, calculating expressions before resuming their debate.

Silently stepping forward, she tried to listen to what was being said but could only make out the odd word during the heated exchange. The word 'friendly' was repeated more than once and a word that sounded like 'kin'.

The squabbling continued for some time until the first let out an exasperated moan of displeasure. Glaring for a moment, the fairy's expression turned resentful as it crossed its arms like a spoiled little child.

'What you ask is forbidden, and to call on such a one might indeed summon another,' the fairy warned, speaking the words with childish overemphasis.

*'Call his name, and another may come. All your world will be undone,'* a fairy sang from behind the first, turning its back on her.

Before she could respond, another loud crack sounded from the fire, causing her to flinch and glance back in fright.

Crying out in alarm, the fairies became embers again and disappeared within the flames in an instant.

*'Too late now for he has heard, to speak his name was totally absurd,'* the fairies sang, their musical tones fading into the crackling of the fire.

'But I would like to be your friend!' Francesca called, causing their cries of woe to grow ever louder.

At their departure, the fire died low, casting the room into almost total darkness. The shadows seemed to take on a life of their own, making her jump from left to right. Feeling that she was being watched from somewhere as yet unseen, she cast a shield about herself.

Hearing a low rumbling, not unlike thunder, she put her hands over her face in dread, only to peep through her fingers, compelled to look on.

The low flames took on the semblance of a face, causing her to cry in terror as two ferocious-looking eyes began searching the room.

The fire appeared to darken further, turning into a smouldering ash that rose up before her to frame the most frightening visage she had ever seen. Power emanated from those terrifying eyes, the force of them hitting her like heat from an opened oven door.

Closing her fingers so as not to see, she decided that this time, she would not open them again despite the fact that the thunderous grumblings were getting louder. She knew instinctively that whatever this thing was, it was coming for her and would take her without much effort.

Parting her fingers against all better judgement, she looked to see what was happening just as the creature stepped from the fire, and then she did what any child would do when living out a nightmare… she screamed

Here ends Book One of Magick – The Dark Wolf.

Don't miss…

Book Two of Magick – The God King's Fall.
Book Three of Magick – Midnight's Hour.
Book Four of Magick – Shadow of War.
Book Five of Magick – The Gift.

Printed in Great Britain
by Amazon

30575119R00148